Set In Stone:
The Life & Death of Medusa

R.C. Berry

Set In Stone: The Life & Death Of Medusa

Cover design by Hi-Rise Visions

Published by Touché Publishing
P.O. Box 173
Goshen, NY 10924
www.touchepublishers.com

Printed in the United States of America
1st Edition

ISBN 10: 0-9844532-8-8
ISBN 13: 978-0-9844532-8-3

ACKNOWLEDGEMENTS

Matt

Thank you for your undying love, and unending support.
Thank you for knowing I can do anything
and for making me believe it too.

May

Thank you for being the hand at my back
the ear for my mouth, the shoulder for my head
and the fire under my...

Family, Friends, and Fans

Thank you for this opportunity to connect with you.
I do hope you enjoy.

AUTHOR'S NOTE

I've always been fascinated by Greek Mythology and, especially, by Medusa. It has always bothered me that there's not been more information about her background. So, I decided to take matters into my own hand.

In this book, I take several parts of Mythology to make up this story. I understand Greek Mythology is not just a collection of stories; it is part of history and a rich culture. I intend no offense in any part of this story, and do not cite anything here as absolute fact. This story is purely for entertainment purposes.

I hope you all enjoy!

PROLOGUE

Present Day
On the coast of Dia, Greece

This was not how Jonathan wanted to spend his day. He hated hiking. His feet hurt and he would much rather be in his nice, air-conditioned museum. But, he really loved his job so; maybe today it would love him back.

Jonathan rounded the last curve and then he saw Bella. *Thank God,* he thought to himself, *I've finally made it.* He took a long look at Bella. She looked as though she was intoxicated. Her eyes, normally chestnut, shone a deep cocoa and sparkled almost as bright as her childlike smile. That look nearly made him forget his discomfort. It was hard to believe she would soon be thirty. She always looked so young, and her youthful enthusiasm didn't help much in that regard.

"Oh Professor, it's wonderful. I can hardly believe it!" Bella squealed.

Jonathan raised his eyebrow at her customary nickname for him. He had no idea why she insisted on calling him that, but she always had. He couldn't imagine what had her so flustered this time and, even less, what she had found that actually required him to leave the museum…but, leave he did. There were suspected to be countless artifacts hidden all over Greece. Bella had even discovered a few herself.

Granted, Bella was, essentially, an amateur explorer at best, if one could call her an explorer at all. She had never unearthed anything of too much value. Personally, Jonathan thought she more enjoyed the thrill of *possibly* finding something. Undoubtedly, she enjoyed the thrill of being where she shouldn't--the more dangerous the better.

"I'm very happy for your discovery, Bella. Now, why don't we see what you've uncovered this time," he chuckled.

She giggled and bounced off, leaving him to follow her. Jonathan shook his head as he trailed behind. He felt very much like Humphrey Bogart in Casablanca-- *Out of all the museums in all of Greece, why did she keep coming into his?*

Bella was always barging into his office to show him some broken item, usually encrusted with dirt, sometimes wet, other times, sticky for no apparent reason. Jonathan wrinkled his nose as he thought of some of the things she had plopped on his desk, always with a smile of triumph.

"Professor, I've found something," always ***"Professor, I've found something!"***

She often reminded him of a puppy who had mutilated some garden animal and decided to share it with the family. How many times had she stood before him, breathless, her cheeks flushed, waiting for her praise? Now, here she was once again, still breathless, still flushed, but this time, thanks to his brisk walk, so was he.

Finally, in the middle of his thought process, she stopped walking. Jonathan said a silent prayer of appreciation, and then looked at her expectantly. Kneeling, Bella indicated an opening in the rock and clasped her hands over her mouth. Giggling, she looked up at him. Jonathan's mood went from confused to angry very quickly.

"Congratulations, Bella. You've found a hole in a mountain," he said bitterly.

Wounded, Bella frowned. When she spoke, her voice trembled. "It's not a hole. It's a tunnel," she said quietly.

"A tunnel? Are you sure?" he asked, bending to take a closer look.

Nodding, she showed him a large bruise on her shoulder. "I've been through to the end."

Jonathan closed his eyes and sighed. This is why he worked *inside* the museum. This was why he never went out and explored anything. He hated small spaces. Especially small, dark spaces. Not to mention, small, dark spaces, leading to somewhere unknown.

"How long is this tunnel?" he asked.

"About fifty yards," she thought out loud. "Did you bring the flashlight?"

Was she being this frustrating on purpose?! Jonathan tilted his head and gave her his most serious look. "Yes I did, ...and what is at the end of the tunnel?"

"... a cave," she replied calmly.

Bella was still stinging from his disparaging remark. She would not make this easy on him. Out of everyone in all of Greece, she decided to share her discoveries with him. She didn't expect him to be grateful, but he didn't have to be rude. Lying flat on her belly, she started to crawl her way through the tunnel.

Exasperated, Jonathan knelt down and stared at her retreating derriere. With a groan of frustration, he crawled in after her.

"And what's in the cave?" he shouted.

The only response he heard was a patronizing chuckle.

"...Professor... I've found something," she whispered.

Just as he thought his claustrophobia would overtake him, the tight, suffocating, darkness became open, suffocating, darkness. Finally, Bella switched on her small flashlight. Jonathan pretended to look around as he calmed himself. Once he had his cool, educated mask back in place, he flipped the switch on his own flashlight.

"Oh that's much better! I really need to get better supplies. I could hardly see anything in here before," Bella exclaimed.

Jonathan smiled at her. It was hard not to admire her vitality. "This is great Bella. There's no way anyone would have guessed there would be caves here. You've made a pretty good find today," he said warmly.

"Oh, ***this*** isn't my find," she clucked.

Bella took his hand and led him deeper into the cave. The antechamber opened into an even larger space. Stopping, she gave his hand a little squeeze and pointed her flashlight.

There, in the cavern, were sculptures, nearly 50 in all. They were all men, warriors from what he could tell... heroes. Many of them were from different lands, different armies. They also seemed to be very ancient.

This is impossible! What is the likelihood of this hidden cache of sculptures, inside a mountain, on an island thought to be un-inhabited? With the differing armor, they must've been created by different artists. But they all looked so similar in composition. Jonathan reached out and lightly touched one of them. Suddenly, confusion marred his brow. None of this made any sense.

Bella watched him with a deep sense of satisfaction. She had finally done it. He was always so cool, always so self-assured. Jonathan was confident, so he never lacked for something to say. Seeing him like this, so in awe, almost in love, made all the past failures worth it. She loved what she did, but today, **he** loved what she did too. And, that meant more than he would ever know. More than she would ever tell him.

"This is impossible," he whispered.

"What do you mean impossible?! I swear I found them just like this," Bella whined.

Jonathan grabbed her hand and pulled her to him. Standing behind her, he placed her hand on the sculpture.

"Do you feel that?" he asked.

"Feel what? His nose?" she puzzled.

"No. The stone… it's granite," he said. At her blank expression, he continued, "Most Greek sculptures are made using marble. Marble is softer, much easier to work with. Look at the amount of detail on the armor, the clothing. I mean, they're nearly perfect. There's no telling how old this is but, at first glance, I'd say centuries… how in the world could someone have done **this** with granite?!"

It was Bella's turn to be speechless. She was sure whatever Jonathan was saying about granite was very interesting, but she wasn't really listening. While he was talking, his flashlight was pointing towards, what she'd thought earlier, was a wall.

"Jon Jon, there's another room…," Bella whispered.

Jonathan raised his eyebrow at her endearment. He would have laughed if he wasn't so shocked. Shaking himself out of his trance, he looked to where her attention was. They walked together to the entryway and they both gasped. There was a small alcove that had previously been cast in the shadows.

Jonathan was enthralled. A few feet in front of them was a sculpture.

Probably the most beautiful sculpture he had ever seen: a woman, completely nude, and amazingly formed. Slowly Jonathan approached it. There was no head on the sculpture, probably to protect the woman's identity. With a body like that, her reputation, as well as her personal safety, would be at risk. He reached out and caressed her arm tenderly. One thing was certain, whoever made this, had certainly loved this woman.

"My God, She's beautiful isn't she?" Bella sighed. "I wonder who she was."

GODS AT PLAY

Mount Olympus

You are looking lovely as ever, Hera. If I wasn't positive my brother would have my head, I'd ravish you here and now."

Poseidon slid past his sister-in-law, placing a kiss on her cheek. He noticed she was smiling today. Zeus must be on his best behavior lately. One never knew with those two. Looking around, he whispered, "Speaking of which, where is he?"

"Right behind you, brother," Zeus chuckled.

Even when it was mirthful, Poseidon could never quite get used to his brother's thunderous voice. Every time, it took all of his strength not to leap out of his skin. Thankfully, when he's home, the fathoms of ocean between them drowns it out.

The two brothers laughed good-naturedly. With a sultry glance for her husband, Hera excused herself.

"So, all is well once again on Mount Olympus, I see," Poseidon prompted. "I take it your latest indiscretion has been forgiven?" he asked.

Zeus rolled his eyes. "Eurynome… I suppose it has," he sighed. "Especially since I've ended it. Also, I promised Hera some time alone."

They chatted at some length about the many women they'd had, and the inevitable problems that followed. Both favored mortal women above all others. Mortal women were so full of life, because their own lives were so short. No one loved like a mortal woman.

And they should know… since they had loved many. Expectedly, that conversation led to the subject of the many women they had in common.

Zeus leaned towards Poseidon conspiratorially. "Brother, I need your assistance in a manner," he spoke in a hushed tone. "I need your watchful eye on the waters near Argos. The King Acrisius has exiled poor Danae, and with her, my son."

Poseidon allowed his shock to show. He had no prior knowledge of this Danae, or of a son. From the way Zeus was looking about and whispering, he reasoned that he was not the only one uninformed. He decided to test his theory.

"No trouble, brother. Would you like me to bring them to you?" he asked.

"No!" Zeus raised his voice more than he had meant to. He continued more calmly. "No, just see them safe and taken care of."

"I shall. Think no more on the matter." Poseidon paused, and smiled thoughtfully. "So brother, am I to understand that you are finished with Eurynome?" he asked. There was no reason he should get nothing for his kindness, not to mention, his silence.

Zeus simply raised his eyebrow at him then, chuckled. "I've had my fun, resulting in three beautiful daughters. Have at her, brother, with my blessing."

They automatically quieted when Hera sauntered in. She didn't think it was ever a good idea to leave those two alone together for long. Sitting on the arm of the dais, she placed a gentle hand on her husband's shoulder.

"And, what have you two been scheming in here?" she teased.

"My brother was trying to tempt me away from you, my love. Never fear though, I resisted him. In fact, I've even convinced him to take the girls home to their mother." Zeus gave his brother a knowing smile.

Poseidon smirked and nodded in concession. Zeus would always be one step ahead of him.

Hera kept her cool mask in place, but they both saw her eyes light up. "Well, I guess we'll be alone sooner than expected," she calmly replied.

Yes, and I'll be able to meet Eurynome, Poseidon thought.

BEAUTY BORN

Eurynome, you're being silly," Poseidon groaned. The one thing he would never find attractive about mortals was their incessant whining.

"I am not being silly, those… ***things*** frighten even me, and now you want me to expose my children to them," Eurynome cried.

Poseidon glared at her. This was the problem with consorting with human women. After you've shared passion with them, bestowed them with gifts, they seem to forget their place. Poseidon had more power than she could ever imagine. He was a god, and he would be obeyed.

Grabbing her arm in a viselike grip, Poseidon roared. "You will watch your tongue, Eurynome. Those ***"things"*** are direct descendants of the Earth and the Sea. If you ever speak out against them again, you and your children will endure horrors unlike any in your worst nightmares. Do you understand?!" He squeezed harder.

Crying out at the pain, she nodded tearfully.

"Good, now go and get the girls, and hurry." Pushing her away, Poseidon released her.

Eurynome winced at his tone. She knew there would be no arguing with him. Now that the passion was done, he felt he had to assert his unlimited power. That was the problem with consorting with Gods. She hadn't meant to speak out against the ancient Gods, but their appearance was so disturbing, and her daughters were so young.

"Darlings! It's time to go," she called out to her daughters.

Three beautiful young ladies floated in. The oldest, Thalia, had curly blonde hair, with sweet, silver eyes. She was short with a slight frame, and a ready smile.

Euphrosyne bounced in, having wispy, titian hair that reached her hips and laughing, green eyes. She was tall and slender with rosy cheeks and a musical giggle.

Aglaea was the last to glide in. Even though she was of average height, Aglaea was stunning. With wavy, raven hair and eyes like the Mediterranean Sea, she stopped everyone's heart with just a look. Her body was already soft and voluptuous, despite being only thirteen years old. She was quite easily one of the loveliest creatures in all of Greece, able to rival even Aphrodite.

Poseidon smiled at his nieces, the Charities, as they were known throughout the land - called such, because the Gods had obviously been kind to them. He couldn't help but laugh at that.

Taking each one of their faces into his hands, Poseidon breathed into them. He'd had them in his underwater lair many times, but the ancients abandoned humanity long ago, so they lived deep below, deeper than any human had ever survived on their own.

Once in his chariot, Poseidon began their descent. Before long, darkness started to close in around them.

Eurynome shut her eyes. She always hated this part. Even though she could breathe, the knowledge that she shouldn't be able to, made the darkness all the more suffocating. Just when she felt she would lose her senses, she opened her eyes to a faint glow in the distance.

They had finally arrived.

A deep rumble shook all around them, and a large figure filled the mouth of the cave. It had the look of a man, covered with red scales and spikes, with massive crab-like claws and legs. An expansive tail spread behind it, coming to an end at a sharp point.

Phorcys.

No matter how many times Eurynome saw him, she always experienced the same debilitating horror. Hearing the gasps of her daughters, she knew they felt the same fear. Poseidon approached the creature and began to speak to him in a language Eurynome had never understood.

Eurynome left the chariot and, making sure not to betray her fear, walked boldly towards the mouth of the cave. She knew what her first time meeting the ancients was like, and she was determined things would be better for her daughters. She stopped a few feet behind Poseidon and fell into a deep bow.

Following her example, her daughters fell in step beside her, all bowing low. Poseidon smiled proudly, and continued speaking. With barely a glance at Eurynome and her daughters, Phorcys stepped aside to let them enter.

Just inside the cave, lying on her side, was a breathtaking sea serpent. Her sinuous body was covered in golden scales. She had slender, feminine arms that ended in razor-sharp talons. A sweeping, graceful neck ascended to a dragon's head, where lie the palest of green eyes.

Ceto - Too beautiful to be a monster; Too monstrous to be beautiful.

Eurynome and her daughters dropped into another bow, this one more heartfelt. Ceto spoke to Poseidon in a melodic tone. Smiling, he spoke back. She rolled her large eyes and made a comment.

"She says our children are beautiful, Eurynome," he chuckled. "I told her they were the daughters of Zeus, not mine. Then, she called he and I… harlots."

Eurynome smiled. "Well, I thank her for the compliment to my daughters," she said.

Ceto spoke again, ending in a sigh.

Poseidon continued, "Ceto is about to give birth to another daughter. She thinks she would like a beautiful child this time, like you have."

The hideousness of her children was legendary. They populated the seas' most dangerous areas, and were a cautionary tale to all who favored the water.

Aglaea stepped forward and knelt. Keeping her eyes lowered, she spoke in a trembling voice, the language Poseidon had used to speak to the ancients. "If it would please, Great Ceto, I, and my sisters could bless your child with beauty." Nervously, she looked back at her sisters.

Thalia and Euphrosyne quickly went and knelt alongside her. Panting, Euphrosyne said "Yes, she would be quite lovely, and have a pleasing disposition…" Thalia cleared her throat and paused. Finally, she spoke in a frightened rush. "Of course, My Lady, she would be born mortal…"

Ceto smiled warmly at the three brave girls. They were obviously of Zeus' loins. As she stared at them, the girls nervously joined hands. Slowly, her mighty tail wound its way behind them and pulled them closer. Swirling and spinning, it wrapped around the three girls, until they disappeared from view.

Eurynome screamed, and started forward. Poseidon grabbed her and held her by his side. Crying, she struggled against him, but to no avail. She didn't know what was happening. All she knew was, that thing was taking her children. Distraught, she slid to her knees.

Faintly, she could hear her daughters' voices. They were chanting in a strange rhythm. She hadn't even known her daughters knew the language of the ancients. It sounded almost musical. Suddenly, the ground beneath them trembled slightly, and Ceto roared.

Slowly, her tail unraveled.

Eurynome sighed in relief. There were her daughters, safe and sound, standing in a huddle with their heads together. She was paralyzed by her happiness. The girls parted. There, Aglaea was holding a tiny baby. A silent baby.

"Uncle, she's dying," Thalia cried.

Smiling, Poseidon took the child from her and, holding her tiny head, touched his lips to hers and breathed. Then, after her chest began to rise and fall, Poseidon placed the child in Ceto's large claw.

Phorcys moved closer to his wife, as they looked upon their beautiful baby girl. They spoke to each other in low tones, then spoke to the child.

Euphrosyne went to stand by her mother. "They are pleased, and love her very much. But, she cannot stay here. This is no place for a mortal. She will have to live among the humans. They will never see her again," she said softly.

Eurynome felt a stab of sympathy for Ceto. She knew how she would feel, if she would never see her daughters again. Before she could think, the words tumbled out of her mouth.

"My lord, I will take her."

Everyone looked at her in surprise. They had almost forgotten she was there. Ceto looked at her for a long time. Then, after a few words to her husband, she spoke to Poseidon.

He took the baby from her, and he and the girls went to join

Eurynome. Placing the baby in her arms, he smiled.

"Her name is to be Medusa, for she will surely be a queen among women," he said.

BEAUTY REALIZED

Sixteen Years Later

Medusa! Are you up? They will be here any minute," Eurynome shouted.

Eurynome paced, nervously. Oh, to be young again. Being young made you feel like one of the Gods. Time has no meaning, and it seems that eternity stretches out endlessly before you. It's only as you get older, that every second counts.

Eurynome learned that, from not only being young, but also being in the presence of the Gods. Being with a God was liberating, yet it was imprisoning. She had never felt more alive, yet she had never been more aware of her mortality. She had never felt more important, and still, she had never felt more insignificant. Especially when they grew tired of you.

Poseidon had tired of her ten years ago. There had been no heartfelt speeches of apology. Nor had there been any thundering exits. For him, it wasn't an ending, or a beginning. It just was.

For her, it was heartbreaking.

She'd had no aspirations of being his wife. She'd even expected to be left at some point. But to be discarded, like a child's toy, as if she'd never meant anything-- it was reprehensible. The Gods admired mortals, even to the point of envy. Yet, they always seemed to end up not treating them like humans.

Zeus was no exception. He had ended their arrangement gently enough, certainly more gently than Poseidon had. But, she herself had still been passed off to Poseidon, when Zeus had tired of her, traded, like cattle.

The very day Poseidon took her as a lover, he left her bed to save yet another of Zeus' conquests, Danae, and her child. They were given over to the care of another and, so the cycle continued.

It hardly seemed that humans received all they should from the Gods. Then again, maybe it is their humanity that makes them expect more of the Gods.

Eurynome remembered a saying of the elder women:

Expect no say

Expect your day

A God at play

Will have his way

Looking out her window, she wondered how many of the elder women the Gods had had their way with, over the years.

"...Eurynome are you listening to me?"

Shaken out of her reverie, Eurynome noticed Medusa had been at her side, talking to her for some time. Smiling, she patted her cheek. "I'm sorry, my love. I was lost in thought," she mused.

"Do you see them yet?" Medusa asked, peeking over her shoulder. She was very excited. Today was her sixteenth birthday, and the Charities were on their way. It had been six years since she'd seen them. She wondered if they would notice how much she had changed.

Eurynome turned to her fully. What a beautiful child she was. Her skin was flawless, her body soft and plush. She possessed an ample bosom and welcoming arms. Her waist flared out to rounded hips, and long, firm legs. The body of a woman, with the face of a cherub.

She had full lips that were always stretched in a smile. Her button nose and plump cheeks lent innocence to her gaze. She would, indeed, look absolutely angelic, if not for her eyes, her mother's eyes. Their color, a bright, pale green, made them sparkle. Their shape, a tilted almond, seduced and hypnotized. And, of course, there was her hair.

Gods! Everyone knew that hair. Her long, bouncing ringlets were legendary. It was the color of golden honey, threaded with thin, ebony locks that made the loveliest pattern when it was braided. Medusa certainly stood out in a crowd.

Eurynome saw so much when she looked at Medusa. She was their creation. It was as if the Gods had taken the best of them all, and made the gift of her. It was sad when Eurynome thought about it. She belonged to all of them, yet she belonged to none of them.

With a sad smile, she whispered, "Beauty."

Medusa looked at her curiously. *Beauty* --Eurynome always called her that, but this time, she sounded so sad. Eurynome was awfully pensive today. Obviously, she had been missing her daughters. It couldn't be easy letting your children go. The Charities, young and explorative, were always on the go.

She couldn't imagine having children that she didn't see for years at a time. It made her think of how her mother might feel. Medusa wondered if she was missed, if her mother ever thought about her.

Coming back to the present, Medusa looked at herself. "Gods! I have to finish getting ready," she gasped. Running to her room, she adjusted her chiton. She decided to use the pins Eurynome had given her on her last birthday. She'd never worn them before.

They were coiled, golden serpents, with peridot eyes. Eurynome had said that, when she saw them, they reminded her of Medusa's mother. They were her most precious possession, so she would only wear them on special occasions. Today felt like a special day. She took a deep breath and, closing her eyes, she moved in front of the looking glass.

"Medusa… they're here!" Eurynome called.

Medusa gasped, and ran out the room, not bothering to look at herself. She chased after Euryneme, both of them giggling like children.

Eurynome ran into the courtyard and gathered her daughters to her. They were a symphony of giggles and tears. Medusa slowed as she arrived at the entrance. Leaning against the brick, she watched them for a few moments.

Sensing her presence, Aglaea turned. "Oh my… little cousin!" she cried.

Medusa ran to join the group.

The girls had taken to calling Medusa little cousin at a young age. She supposed that, had she ever called Eurynome her mother, they may have addressed her as their sister. But, from the beginning, Medusa knew she didn't quite belong with them. Still, they were somewhat of a family. For the last sixteen years, they were the only family she had.

The five women fluttered back into the house, chatting rapidly, trying to relive every event of their six-year separation.

"Medusa, I can't get over how you've grown," Thalia said.

Euphrosyne giggled. "Yes, she rivals even Aglaea. Finally, someone to knock you down a peg, sister."

They all burst into laughter. Lounging in the aule, they talked well into the evening, over food and wine. Eurynome and Medusa heard all about the girls' travels, the festivals they attended, and their times on Mount Olympus.

Medusa couldn't help but feel a deep yearning. She was born of the sea and, therefore, longed to flow, to be ever moving, ever changing. Hearing their adventures, she ached to have adventures of her own.

Eurynome caught the wistful look on Medusa's face, and sighed internally. This day had been a long time coming. She didn't know if she could delay it any longer, but she would surely try. Eurynome knew what the world could do to a young lady, especially a beautiful young lady.

BEAUTY RELEASED

Eurynome lie awake in her bed, shaking her head. *Had they even slept*, she wondered. They had been up for hours, giggling, bouncing, and whatever those other noises were. She smiled to herself, remembering how it was when she was young.

Her smile faded. Her daughters were not so young anymore. Her youngest was a woman now, and yet, the voices that carried down the corridor were reminiscent of years ago.

Her daughters had always been fascinated by Medusa. Eurynome was grateful for their interest in her, but she was also secretly worried. How many times had she had to correct them, when she caught them treating Medusa like some living doll? She saw so much of their father in them.

And now, laughter and the pitter-patter of pretty feet filled the house. She was sure there was quite a lovely stampede occurring this very moment. Sighing, she tossed her coverlet aside. She'd better get up before her home crumbled around her.

The foursome burst into the bathing chamber in a flurry of mirth. Medusa quickly stripped off her clothes and sank down into the warm water. She loved bathing. She would often spend hours in this room, splashing and floating. She always felt a certain freedom when she was in the water. Sometimes, she would close her eyes and just sink to the bottom. The warmth and safety she experienced under the water was indescribable.

Lounging in the water, she turned her attention to the threesome. As they helped each other pin their hair, Medusa couldn't help but admire their harmony. They were like beautiful doves in flight. Finally finished, the girls began to disrobe. Aglaea turned her attention to Medusa.

"You don't pin your hair before you bathe, Medusa?" she asked.

Medusa wrinkled her nose. "No, I don't like my hair restricted."

Stepping into the water, Euphrosyne giggled. "But it must take ages for your hair to dry."

Medusa shrugged. "It does." She leaned back into the water, and let her hair float around her. "But, a freedom like this is worth it," she sighed.

Thalia tapped her lips thoughtfully. "Medusa, I believe you are an absolute hedonist."

Medusa flicked water at her, and they all exploded into laughter.

As they bathed, Medusa peppered the threesome with questions about Mount Olympus, and the Gods. She absorbed every word with rapt attention, letting the glory of it all wash over her.

Again, she couldn't help but watch the Charities. As with everything else, they were perfectly in sync. They spoke in turns, or sometimes in unison, three voices of the same mind. They ebbed and flowed with each other, turning even the simplest of conversations into a dance. She had missed them so much.

Lost in thought, she stood slowly. Pulling her hair over her shoulder, she softly twisted it, squeezing the water out. She tossed it back over her shoulder and stepped out of the water. She was so oblivious, that she didn't notice that the Charities were mesmerized by her every movement.

She walked over to the nearby bench. Her hips swayed gracefully, and she bounced slightly as she walked on her toes, like a child sneaking into the kitchen. Water traversed over every curve, slowly, almost reluctant to leave her body. Bending slightly, she picked up a bath sheet and wrapped it around her shoulders, hugging it to her.

After a few careless pats here and there, she dropped it at her feet and sat, retrieving a bottle of oil from under the bench. She poured some into her hand and began to rub it into her skin. Her chest rose and fell deeply, as if each breath was a heavy sigh. She enjoyed the art of touching, and she enjoyed the art of being touched. Occasionally, her eyes would drift shut from pure bliss.

She was naked, and unabashed. She gained pleasure from the simple caress of her own hand. She let her hair float freely in the waves, and the water run wildly over her skin. She had the enthusiasm of a mortal, and the soul of a goddess.

As she finished, she finally focused on the threesome.

"Gods Medusa!" Thalia exclaimed.

Innocent confusion covered Medusa's face. "…What?" she asked.

"What?!… Medusa you're…" Euphrosyne began.

"…absolutely stunning!" Aglaea finished.

Medusa scoffed and rolled her eyes. "Well, of course I am… thanks to you three." She smiled indulgently.

Sitting up, Aglaea looked thoughtful. "Physically, yes. But there is so much more to beauty, Medusa. Those are the things that can never be given, they simply must...be," she said.

Nodding, Euphrosyne continued, "You have what not many can achieve... beauty in form and beauty in spirit. You are quite rare, Medusa."

Medusa suddenly felt oddly embarrassed. She had always been told she was beautiful, but generally discounted the compliments. Her beauty was a gift. She couldn't take credit for what was given to her. She never thought before that she had a hand in the beauty everyone saw. Thalia's chuckle brought her attention back to the present.

"Oh Medusa... Olympus would **love** you, when we go back, you should go with us," she mused.

Medusa laughed. "I can't go to Olympus!"

"Why not?!" the three asked in unison.

"Only the Gods are allowed on Olympus," she said, as though they were dense.

Aglaea waved dismissively. "Father brings humans all the time. They all do. Besides, your parents **were** Gods, of a sort."

Thalia chimed in. "And even if it weren't allowed, father would allow it...for us."

They sure did know how to build a case. Still, Medusa was not so sure.

"Oh please come Medusa! We're going for Panathenaia. It's always so much fun, and I know how much you would enjoy it," Euphrosyne said.

That sealed it. Panathenaia - Athena's birthday celebration. In Medusa's mind, Athena was second to none, not even to Zeus. She had such strength and wisdom, and the Charities were giving Medusa the opportunity to meet her. There was no way she could resist.

As soon as her mind was made up, she felt a queer stirring in her stomach. Fear? Excitement? She wasn't sure, but she did know that one way or another, she was going to Mount Olympus. She knew that her life was about to change.

"Do you think Eurynome will let me go?" Medusa asked timidly.

"Let you go where?" Eurynome's voice came from the door.

The foursome gasped collectively, and quite guiltily.

Facing Eurynome, Medusa spoke quietly, "To Mount Olympus for Panathenaia."

Once the words left her lips, Eurynome ceased to hear anything else. Somewhere in her mind, the arguments and commendations of her daughters tried to reach her, but the entire world melted away until none was left but she and Medusa, with their eyes locked.

Eurynome knew there was nothing she could do. Whether now, or tomorrow, or a year from now, this is a battle she would lose. Her daughters wanted this and, deep down, she knew Medusa did as well. Her girls were their father's daughters, and Gods at play will have their way.

BEAUTY RECOGNIZED

Eurynome gathered Medusa in her arms and kissed her forehead tenderly. "Swear to me you'll be careful," she whispered.

"I promise you," Medusa answered. She gave her an extra squeeze.

"Come **on** Little Cousin!" Thalia shouted dramatically. Throwing her hands up, she giggled and gave her mother a quick peck on the cheek.

Eurynome and Medusa stood embracing in the courtyard. Medusa hated to admit it, but she was actually nervous about leaving her home, even if it was only for a short while. She was going to Mount Olympus, out of her element and, quite possibly, out of her league.

Eurynome held Medusa, loathing letting her go. She didn't know what awaited Medusa on Mount Olympus, but she doubted it was anything good. For all intents and purposes, Medusa was a human. And the Gods did not always have humans' best interests at heart. Sometimes, she wondered if the Gods even had hearts.

Eurynome turned to face her daughters. "You are all responsible for her. You swear to me you will watch over her."

The three agreed, in unison.

With a brave smile, Eurynome stroked Medusa's cheek. "Have a good time, my love."

With a sniffle and a kiss and, of course, the last pleadings that she be careful, Eurynome let her go. She was rewarded with squeals and affection. Breaking away, she quickly turned, trying to hide the tears that were slipping from her eyes. The Gods will always have their way, and Medusa was about to enter their playground.

Her daughters blew her kisses and promised to take care of their little cousin. She stood there waving, until they finally disappeared from sight.

Mount Olympus

Medusa took in the sight before her, and almost found it difficult to breathe. They stood at the foot of the mountain, the top hidden above the clouds. Medusa knew at the top of the mountain was the palace of the Gods. Try as she might, though, she couldn't see it.

The Charities smiled at the obvious wonder etched on her face. Aglaea urged the mules on, and they began the slow ascension up the mountain.

Medusa let her mind wander. She thought of whom she would meet, what she would see. Her heart began to pound, echoing in her head. As they climbed higher, she lost sight of the rest of the world. Clouds surrounded her and a giddy euphoria filled her. Her breathing became shallower and her head spun. Her limbs felt heavy, and her eyes began to drift slowly closed.

Dragging her eyes open, Thalia came into view, like an apparition. Thalia tipped her chin up and gently set her lips on Medusa. Slowly, she breathed into her mouth. Her breath filled Medusa's mouth, filled her lungs. Backing away, Thalia smiled sweetly.

Medusa felt a hand on her hair. Euphrosyne stroked her cheek, turning her head towards her. Medusa found it hard to exert herself, so she rested on Euphrosyne's shoulder. Cradling her head, Euphrosyne clasped her mouth over Medusa's, exhaling into her. Medusa's chest rose with each breath. With a soft giggle, and a final stroke of her cheek, Euphrosyne disappeared from view.

Confused, Medusa swayed, trying to clear her head. She felt Aglaea's hands on her shoulders, steadying her. Sliding her hands up her neck, Aglaea held her face gently, pressing her lips to Medusa's. Medusa inhaled her deeply, as if she was life itself.

Suddenly she gasped, her breaths coming in a rush. Slowly the clouds dissipated, and she had command of her body, of her senses again. She looked up into Aglaea's eyes.

"Are you better now, little cousin?" Aglaea asked, still holding Medusa's face in her hands.

Medusa nodded slowly, gradually feeling like herself again. "Yes, I'm alright," she rasped.

Smiling brightly, Aglaea released her.

"Well then, welcome to Mount Olympus."

A lofty staircase extended before them. The first step was roughly hewn from the mountain rock. Each subsequent step was a little more finely crafted than the last, until a thin layer of fog began to cover them. Looking down, Medusa could no longer see her feet. It was as if she was walking on air.

The Charities stopped and, for the first time, Medusa looked around her. Once again, she felt unable to breathe. She had never seen anything more beautiful in her life. There in front of her, loomed an immense palace, etched from the finest marble. The palace was a stark white, as white as the clouds it seemed to reside on.

Ancient symbols in gleaming gold covered the ivory columns that reached skyward, and extended left and right, as far as the eye could see. The base of each column was nestled inside large pearl spheres that rested on the top step. This was truly a home for the Gods.

They stood in front of gilded double doors, reaching fifty feet into the air. The doors opened before them, revealing a grand foyer. The walls were a vibrant blue, feathered with white columns, and glossy tiles of sapphire trimmed in gold, covered the floors. Medusa stared in wonder, afraid, even to move. She dared not set foot in there. Just as she was ready to bolt back to the cart, Thalia leapt to her side, and threw an arm around her shoulder.

"Alright, little cousin, we need you to put this cloak on, so we can sneak you to our room," she giggled.

Medusa looked at her in shock. "Sneak?" she squeaked. "What do you mean, sneak?"

Euphrosyne smiled at her. "I'm sorry, darling, but we're not going to debut you to everyone wearing *that*." She rolled her eyes.

Medusa felt very self-conscious then. She had worn her very best chiton for the occasion, and her special pins. She'd spent hours in front of the looking glass, and thought she looked very fine indeed. Frowning, she closed the cloak around her and pulled the hood low over her head. She walked slowly, still having doubts about setting foot in the too fine palace.

Once her foot hit the first step, she had a strong sense of foreboding. Suddenly afraid, she quickened her steps. Once they crossed the entrance, it was as if she was had entered a completely different world. For all the beauty and serenity of the outside, there was equal chaos on the inside.

Ahead to the right was the great room, where the greatest commotion was coming from. There was no doubt that a festival was occurring. There were Gods, Demigods, and even humans, everywhere. The entire place pulsed with power.

Medusa suddenly felt suffocated. With each step, she picked up her pace, until she was practically running through the palace, with the Charities chasing after her. Medusa flashed past the Great Hall, her heart thudding in her chest.

"Daughters!" The exclamation brought with it a crash of thunder.

Medusa froze in her tracks. Just on the other side of the entrance to the great hall, she stood immobilized by the booming roar.

The threesome lined up in the entrance way, and joined hands. They'd always had to do that when using their powers, but often, it was a nervous habit, reassurance that no matter what they faced, they would face it together. Aglaea reached out her hand, seeking Medusa.

Medusa, trembling with fear, slowly offered her hand. Once their fingers touched, Aglaea pulled Medusa to her side with an unexpected force.

"Hello, Father," the three said in unison.

"Greetings. And just why are my offspring sneaking into their own home?" he teased.

"We were just going to get ready, Father. We did not feel appropriately dressed," Thalia spoke up.

Zeus smiled indulgently. "And has the number of my children increased without my knowledge?" He inclined a head towards Medusa.

Somewhere in the crowd, a fellow God made a jeer about the estimated number of Zeus' children, which made the entire hall explode into laughter.

Not to be swayed, Zeus turned his attention back to his daughters. "So, my dears, what is it you have brought to your sister's celebration?"

Aglaea stepped forward then. "We have brought our cousin, Father. Daughter of Ceto and Phorcys. Brought into the world by our own hands, and nurtured by our mother's breast." Reaching behind her again, she felt for Medusa. After a second, she felt a hand intertwine with her own. Grasping it, she pushed her into the great hall.

Gasping, Medusa stumbled forward into the middle of the room. She froze in her tracks, wishing she could melt into the floor. She stood there, feeling as if all eyes were upon her. Automatically, she bent her head lower. As she did, a lock of hair escaped the hood.

Intrigued, Zeus dismounted his throne and approached her. Medusa's stomach leapt into her throat. She kept her head lowered and her gaze on the floor. Before long, a pair of large feet came into view. Her chest was heaving with every breath, and she hoped that she could stay upright, at least until he lost interest.

Reaching out, Zeus pulled the tie on her cloak. As he slid the hood from her head, the cloak fluttered to the floor. Audible gasps could be heard throughout the room. Medusa even noticed the rise of Zeus's chest. Feeling even more like a freak, she kept her eyes glued on the ground.

Hearing the uncharacteristic silence, Poseidon turned away from the goddess he was courting and made his way towards the center of the great hall. He could see his brother, and moved to the side to see what had caught everyone's attention.

Zeus stared at the top of Medusa's head, taking her all in. Taking her chin in his hand, he raised her head. At the very last moment, their eyes met.

It could not be denied that Zeus was the King of the Gods. He towered over Medusa, with her head barely reaching his chest. He had broad shoulders, framing a chiseled, muscular torso. Every inch of him radiated power. His hand could easily wrap completely around her neck, and crush her throat. Instead, it gently cradled her chin.

Zeus looked much younger than she would've thought. She'd expected a great, hulking man, with flowing white hair. He was large, but with a tolerant control. He had thick, black hair, and a short, cropped beard. He had a strong jaw, and a rugged face, that housed the softest, blue eyes she'd ever seen.

Zeus was enjoying the perusal of the, obviously, intrigued little mortal who had fallen into their midst. She had the most interesting green eyes he'd ever seen. Her hair was like sunlight, and her presence was like a mother's bosom. Instinctively, Zeus leaned into her. Speaking lower than he intended Zeus said "What is your name, child?"

As she responded, from behind Zeus, a whisper escaped Poseidon's lips.

"......Medusa," he spoke in wonderment.

BEAUTY ACCEPTED

Remembering himself, Zeus took a step back from Medusa. Looking around, he noticed everyone's mesmerized faces.

"What an entrance you have made. It appears you will fit in quite well here. Welcome to Mount Olympus, Medusa." With a smile, Zeus returned to his throne.

Instantly, Medusa was surrounded by the Charities, who bustled her out of the great hall. Walking rapidly, she didn't notice any of the curious glances and yearning stares from male and female alike.

Poseidon finally cleared the fog in his mind. By Zeus! It was Medusa. How long had it been? When he had last visited Eurynome, he remembered a lovely mop of a child, lovely, sure, but still just a child. What he saw today was no child. But one thing was for sure, it was certainly Medusa. There was no mistaking that hair.

He slowly made his way back to the goddess he had abandoned. He smiled and apologized, but remained distracted. After every few words he spoke, he would avert his eyes to the entrance. He wanted to be the first to see her when she returned. This was a novel experience for him. And there was nothing more important to the Gods, than their next novel experience.

Finally, he saw his nieces. Each of them looked as beautiful as ever but, for once, he could hardly wait for them to get out of his sight. Ah… there she is. Poseidon saw and heard no one else. She wore a beautiful white gown, gathered by a simple golden rope belt. Smaller golden ropes attached the gown at her shoulders. Her hair was brushed away from her face, and gathered at her neck, to cascade down her back. He noticed she adorned her hair with the pins she wore earlier.

Medusa's senses were overloaded. Everywhere she looked, there were beautiful faces and well made bodies. Various raised platforms around the great hall were littered with cushions of every size and color. Against the far wall, a long table was lined with gleaming fruit, succulent meats, and any desire of man and God alike. Servants circulated, pouring fragrant wine into jeweled cups.

The threesome stopped at one group after the other, introducing Medusa to everyone. One by one, everyone would stop whatever he or she was doing, whatever they were saying, and drink in her beauty. Almost everyone felt the need to comment. Poseidon watched Medusa's response, and it was always the same. Her eyes would flash to the ground, and then with a sweet smile, she would press on.

It was just a slight lifting of her lips, imperceptible to most, a secret smile. But he saw it. That was the first secret he would share with her, the first of many, he was sure. Poseidon decided then and there that he would have her. Not just have her, he would possess her completely. She would die for him, and she would live for him. She would beg for the chance to be his.

Poseidon was nearly panting with his fantasy. His body hardened and throbbed. He could almost smell her scent, practically feel her beneath him, writhing. He closed his eyes, and could've sworn he heard his name on her lips. *Poseidon…Poseidon…*

"Poseidon!" Demeter barked.

He focused on her laughing face.

Demeter glanced at the object of his attention. "Ah… is it time for a new one already?" she teased. "Have you tired of your latest pet so soon, Poseidon?"

Poseidon had been attempting to woo Demeter this festival, but that would have to wait. After all, Demeter was immortal. Who knew how long Medusa's charms would last. He saw the foursome heading to Zeus' throne. "Why don't we go and pay our respects to Athena?" he said to Demeter. With a sly chuckle, he winked at her.

Nearing Zeus' throne, Medusa felt her legs turn to water. She was about to be face to face with Zeus again, and right beside him… was Athena. She could barely contain her excitement, or her fear. Medusa never believed this day was even possible. The one Goddess she had always worshipped, not just in deed, but also in mind and heart, and she was seconds away from meeting her.

As they approached, Medusa dropped into a deep bow.

Smiling Zeus bid her to stand.

"My wife, Hera," Zeus began.

Hera looked at the lovely new edition to Mount Olympus. As always, she quickly assessed the level of threat this new one possessed. She looked from Medusa to her husband.

"I thank you for allowing me, My Lord," she breathed.

Nodding, Zeus clucked, "Though you are mortal, you are still the offspring of Gods and, as such, you are welcome here as much as my daughters are."

He began to introduce her to the Gods around him, and one by one they inclined their head to her.

Hera exhaled and relaxed. Perhaps she could come to like this beautiful creature.

"Athena, I would like to present Medusa."

Medusa gazed at her fully for the first time. Her breath caught in her throat. Athena was extremely tall. She had wide, clear, gray eyes, so sharp they pierced. They were set in a full face punctuated by a bow mouth. Her braided hair was the color of wheat on a summer day, and coiled around her head like a serpent. Her neck curved down to broad shoulders and sinuous arms. Her every pore exuded strength.

Nearly breathless, Medusa spoke reverently. "I apologize for not bringing you a gift, My Lady. My visit here was…unexpected."

Athena extended a hand to her. "Come sit with me, little one."

Medusa nearly fainted from pleasure. Fighting the urge to giggle, she climbed the stairs, and lounged on a large cushion at Athena's side. The Charities chose a spot together, near their father. Medusa felt like she could die at this moment, for she could never be any happier.

They chatted amiably, all except for Medusa, who was trying to convince herself she wasn't dreaming. She spoke when comments were directed towards her, usually eliciting a smile or a laugh from everyone around her. They were impressed with her rapid wit.

Out of the corner of her eye, Medusa spotted Poseidon making his way over, with a Goddess in tow. Heaving a disgusted sigh, she tried to busy herself in conversation. It had been ten years since she had seen him.

Ten years, since he last visited Eurynome, accompanied by his latest conquest, letting her know she had been replaced. Ten years, since he'd set a gift of pearls in front of Eurynome, and tousled her own hair on his way out of their lives.

Medusa could still see the look on Eurynome's face; still hear her late night sobs. She had slept with her that night, singing to her softly. She'd even changed the words, just to make her laugh.

Poseidon had been very good at going away. Maybe, he would go away now.

Obviously, she'd underestimated the determination of a God on a mission, though what mission, she could not imagine. Either way, he made a line straight for her.

"Brother! Come to give Athena a blessing?" Zeus bellowed.

Poseidon stopped in his tracks. He spoke with his brother rapidly, still focused on his target.

"… Poseidon. I believe you may know each other," Zeus continued.

Poseidon affixed a charming smile on his handsome face. "Why, Medusa, how wonderful to see you again."

Raising an eyebrow, Medusa barely contained her contempt. "My Lord," she sniffed.

"Ah, a rose's beauty, and yet I get the thorn. Do you know, Medusa, that I gave you your first breath of life?" he asked.

Medusa raised her chin. "For *that*, I thank you, Great Poseidon," she said. There was no mistaking the disdain dripping in every word.

Many of the Gods and Goddesses exchanged glances. It was obvious by her response that the two *knew* each other. This would be the source of much speculation later. This young chit was all sorts of contradictions. She was seductive, yet innocent. She was shy, yet bold. And she was sweet, but had a sharp bite.

Intrigued, Poseidon slid to lounge beside her. She was reclined on her side, and he was memorizing the shape of her body, while she was very effectively ignoring him. He leaned opposite her, so he could gaze into her face.

Leaning in close, he whispered to her, "I do not recall what I've done to cause you pain, my beauty. I have not seen you in many years, but I would offer my apologies, and deeply… desire… to make it up to you." He pressed his lips against her ear.

Medusa turned her head to look at him. Shifting her body, she faced him. She leaned in close to him, so close they almost appeared to be embracing. She sighed against his ear.

"Your offense, Great God, was in the leaving. And the pain you caused was not mine. Therefore, I have no need for your apologies, nor your… desires."

With that, she rose from her position and asked if she could be of service to the guest of honor.

Not many people missed the interaction. There was a tension in the air. This was just what they needed. Life on Olympus had become stale. Now, here was this great beauty, and she promised to be a delicious bit of drama.

Hera decided she liked her after all… as did Athena.

As far as Poseidon, for the first time, he had been summarily dismissed, and by a mortal no less. He had never desired anything more.

BEAUTY EMBRACED

The festival carried on late into the night. Poseidon watched Medusa closely, but kept his distance. His prey had evaded him quite masterfully, and he would let her enjoy the small victory. Besides, it would make the moment that much sweeter when she begged him to take her.

Medusa kept with the Charities, and got close to Athena any chance she got. They all lounged together, laughing and talking of the latest gossip. Somewhere off in the distance, there was a flurry of chatter, and a rising of men's voices. That could only mean one thing. Aphrodite had arrived.

Medusa had always been curious to meet the Goddess. Growing up, comparisons had always been made between the two of them. Medusa didn't think anything too extraordinary about her own looks, so she couldn't imagine how Aphrodite would measure against any other goddess.

She could track Aphrodite's progression through the crowds by the raucous laughter and joviality she left in her wake. At this rate, she may never get to see her. As soon as she thought it, the crowd parted and she caught sight of her.

Medusa's lips parted on a sigh. How could anyone have ever

compared the two? It was impossible. Medusa knew she was fair on the eyes, but had still always thought Aglaea was the most beautiful woman to ever walk heaven and earth. She was wrong.

Aphrodite was of average height, but possessed a singularly unique body. She had small feet, and the hem of her gown swished around trim ankles. Her small waist was in direct contradiction to the flare of her hips and the curve of her breasts. She had a slender, delicate neck and a cheerful face, bearing thick, lush lips and flashing, Aqua eyes. Her hair, falling in thick waves down her back, caught Medusa's eye. She couldn't decide if it was the color of a sunrise, or a sunset. Maybe it was the color of hellfire itself.

Athena did not miss Medusa's fascination with Aphrodite. In fact, she had been waiting for it. Everyone had the same reaction when it came to the Goddess of beauty. But, she remembered, Medusa had admired **her** first, had worshipped **her**. She felt a familiar stab of jealousy. Jealousy became anger. Anger became sadness.

When given a choice, most would choose Aphrodite. Athena was worshipped by kings and soldiers, for her strategy and warfare. The elders worshipped her for her wisdom. She was not a goddess of the fair and beautiful. Most of the time, she was not even treated as a goddess. She was proud to be seen by the Gods as an equal. She had certainly gone to great lengths to prove her strength. Sometimes, however, strength itself was a weakness.

Medusa stared, looking positively smitten. She saw Aphrodite whispering to a young man, who then turned and pointed… to her. Aphrodite whirled around and, alarmed, Medusa quickly turned away and locked gazes with Athena. A soft, melodious voice found her.

"Well, I arrive just a little late, and I've been replaced," she teased. Chuckling, she continued, "I have not been able to take one step without hearing of this unbelievable beauty that has stumbled into Mount Olympus… quite literally from what I'm told."

Medusa felt her coming nearer and fought back the panic that was rising. She'd always been told about the jealousy of the Gods, and hoped beyond hope that Aphrodite did not take offense to her unexpected popularity.

She felt a strand of her hair lift.

"What lovely hair. Come dear, turn around and let me look at you," she said gently.

Shyly, Medusa turned and stood, facing Aphrodite. She was even more beautiful up close. Her eyes glittered like ocean jewels and her lips looked like ripened plums. Medusa felt herself being drawn into her, wanting to be held by her.

Aphrodite stared at Medusa in amazement. It was as if she had been created by her own hand. After a moment, Aphrodite smiled fully at her and clapped her hands, giggling in glee.

"Oh she is absolutely ravishing! How marvelous. Welcome to Mount Olympus, my dear. I daresay you will be very popular," she said.

Aphrodite fluttered onto a cushion, and patted the spot beside her. Medusa sat next to her and let out the breath she didn't realize she was holding. She turned, and met Athena's disapproving glare.

"I thought for sure you would come in here and smite her on the spot in a jealous rage, Ditie," she sneered.

Aphrodite rolled her eyes. "I am the Goddess of beauty… of love. Therefore, I appreciate everything beautiful," she explained. Linking her arm with Medusa's, she continued, "Not only is she beautiful, but so full of love, and humility."

Ah, so there it is, Athena thought. Medusa was humble and, therefore, posed no threat. If she ever made the mistake of thinking she compared to Aphrodite, Athena knew just how quickly the goddess would turn on her.

After much talking, they all decided to retire and take wine in one of the far courtyards. Medusa wandered around the courtyard, taking in the many trees and flowers. Looking up, it seemed as though she could reach up and touch the stars. It was so hard to believe that so much beauty could be confined to one place. She disappeared behind a hedge, and found a large fountain.

It enchanted her, the large basin, and out of the center, rose a large stone serpent. It posed straight and tall, with only its head bowed in silent homage. It was spectacular. She looked at it and envisioned a golden hue over the scales, and bright, green crystals in the eyes. She envisioned it was her mother.

"Beautiful, isn't it?"

Gasping, Medusa whirled to face Athena. "Yes, My Lady. It's quite beautiful." As she spoke to Athena, she noticed she had a sort of melancholy look. "Were you not enjoying your celebration, My Lady?" she asked.

Athena looked back towards the reverie and sighed. "Dionysus filled a fountain with some of his wine, and all of the goddesses decided to go bathing in the pool." She rolled her eyes, shaking her head.

"Did you not wish to join them?" Medusa shyly inquired.

Athena looked genuinely confused. "To what purpose?" she asked.

Medusa giggled. "Because it's fun, My Lady. Have you never bathed naked, with your hair spread around you, floating on water like it was air? Have you never sank beneath the water, hearing nothing, feeling as if time itself has stopped?"

Athena watched her as she spoke. She was so full of life and enjoyment. Hearing her talk of bathing, of how it made her feel, made Athena want to experience that feeling, if only once.

She smiled tenderly at Medusa. "Floating is for the delicate, and water and air, the home of beauty." Athena sat sadly on the side of the fountain. "I am afraid I am more suited for clay and stone."

Medusa did not know what to say. Athena was powerful, and wise. She needed no one. Oh, to not have the burden of needing! Physical beauty faded, but strength, that lasted. It was Athena's strength that made her beautiful to Medusa.

Medusa wished for strength more than anything. She would trade every ounce of her beauty, for just a fraction of Athena's strength. Medusa had not been prepared for the actuality that the Gods could ever be wrong. But Athena was wrong. And she would show her.

As Athena stared ahead across the fountain, she felt Medusa's approach. Medusa found the pin securing her hair and removed it. She slowly unwrapped her braid from around her head. Stealing a peek at her face, Medusa thought Athena now looked very young, having one long braid hanging down to her hips.

Smiling, she uncoiled the braid. Once it was loosened, she gently ran her fingers through Athena's hair, spreading it down her back and across her shoulders. Walking around, Medusa knelt in front of her, and noticed her eyes were moist. Slowly, she began to remove her sandals.

"You should wear your hair down more often, My Lady," she whispered.

Sitting beside her on the fountain, Medusa framed her face with her hair. Her hands poised on her shoulders, she began to slide Athena's gown off of her shoulders.

As she felt the fabric caress her arms, Athena thought she should protest. She should not allow a mortal such license with her. This was no way for a goddess to behave.

But, her voice would not come, and her gown pooled around her waist.

Medusa looked at her thoroughly, with an inscrutable expression. Her face softened and she rose on her knees, encouraging the goddess to follow her.

“Look, My Lady,” she breathed.

Medusa nudged her forward and Athena looked into the fountain. She could hardly believe what she saw. It should be her, but she hardly recognized her reflection.

Her hair raged wildly around her head. Her skin was flushed and full of color. Her breasts gently swayed with every movement. Though she tried to contain it, a small smile escaped, as did a couple of tears. Sitting back on her heels, she sighed and looked into Medusa’s smiling face.

Taking her face into her hands, she softly kissed one cheek, then the other. They looked at each other for a long moment.

“Thank you,” she said.

Nodding, Medusa rose. She untied the belt at her waist and laid it at her feet. As Athena sat dumbfounded, Medusa slid her own gown off her shoulders and let it fall. Athena drank in the perfection of her body, and felt nearly intoxicated by it.

Approaching her, Medusa took Athena’s hands and helped her to rise. Her gown fell to her feet. As they stood there naked, Medusa looked very deeply into her eyes, hoping she would not be harmed for what she was about to do.

Athena saw Medusa’s eyes take on an odd glint. Breathing heavily, Medusa smiled. She gripped her hand tightly and, with a squeaky giggle, she took off running, dragging Athena behind her.

Throwing her head back, Medusa laughed into the wind. She was running through a courtyard, naked, with Athena, on Mount Olympus. Even if she was dreaming she hoped it never ended.

Athena could not help but laugh, either. She could stop this at any time. But for some reason, she kept running. This little mortal made her feel stronger, and more alive than she'd ever been. She also made her feel more beautiful than she ever thought she could be.

The two came sprinting breathlessly and, with a shriek, jumped into the pool. Hands still joined, they surfaced in a symphony of laughter. They got more than one curious glance from the other goddesses. Athena dipped under the water and resurfaced. Swimming to the far side, she struck up a conversation with Demeter. Medusa noticed she looked so serene, and quite lovely.

"Well Medusa, you certainly have turned Mount Olympus upside down," Aphrodite chimed.

Smiling, Medusa lay on her back and floated in the pool. Her hair spread in the water, drawing the attention of everyone around her. Closing her eyes, she leaned her head back and let the water fill her ears, drowning out everything but her own heartbeat. This had been an intense day, and she'd hardly had a moment to herself.

Aphrodite watched her intensely. She was such a vibrant thing. She came streaking through Mount Olympus like a shooting star. She held the promise of fulfilled wishes, and they all wanted to grab a hold of her. Looking up, she caught Athena looking at her.

Then and there, a challenge was put forth, and accepted. Battle lines were drawn, and a silent war would ensue. Athena shot Aphrodite a triumphant smile. War is what Athena did best.

The other goddesses recognized the old rivalry, and began silently wagering on which of the goddesses would win the worship and devotion of fair Medusa.

BEAUTY PURSUED

Medusa rose out of the pool, oblivious to all who watched her progression. She had no way of knowing that a personal crusade had just begun, and she was the grand prize. She wrapped a large bath sheet around her body and lounged on a nearby chaise. A small yawn escaped and as her eyes fell closed. She realized what a long and exciting day she'd had.

Stepping out of the pool, Athena went to her side. She'd quickly formulated a strategy in her mind. She already had an advantage, and just needed to capitalize on it. She gently stroked Medusa's head, watching her eyes drift open slowly.

"Come, little one. Let's retrieve your clothes, so you can get some rest. Besides, I have a little present for you," she whispered.

Smiling drowsily, Medusa took her outstretched hand and trailed behind her into the hedges. Once they reached the fountain, Medusa dressed lazily, every muscle in her body feeling relaxed. Bending, she retrieved her rope belt from the ground. Gently, Athena took it from her hands. She looked up at her curiously.

"I've always loved this fountain," Athena said.

"It is very beautiful," Medusa sighed.

"It has meaning to you. You have an affinity towards serpents, don't you?" she asked.

Medusa glanced at her shyly. She was afraid to confess the fountain made her ache for her mother. It seemed such a childish thing. It made her feel weak, next to this paragon of strength.

"Yes, I admire serpents greatly," she carefully answered.

Smiling at her, Athena bent and placed Medusa's belt into the fountain. It floated gently for a moment, and then began to sink. As the water rippled, it seemed to move. Medusa leaned closer. Impossible. It was **moving**. Captivated, Medusa lowered her hand into the fountain. It was drawn to her, and before long, her fingers curled around a smooth body.

Her heart skipped a beat as a beautiful snake curled around her wrist, winding its way up her arm. She pulled it out of the water, and carefully uncoiled it. She'd never seen a serpent like it. It was the color of antique gold, striped with a deep onyx. It blinked at her, and her breathing halted. From its onyx head stared the most beautiful green eyes.

Medusa couldn't keep the tears from falling. Looking up at Athena, she sniffled. "Thank you, My Lady. You have no idea what it means to me," she said tearfully.

Athena placed her hands on Medusa's face, and tenderly kissed her forehead. "I'm glad you like it my dear. What will you name him?" she asked.

"...Erichthonius," she answered finally.

Athena nodded thoughtfully. "I like it. Well, he is yours, and he will always be here whenever you return to Olympus, which I hope will be often."

Completely content, Medusa lowered her pet back into the water.

Erichthonius floated gently to the bottom and swam away. Curling up at the base of the serpent statue, he fell asleep.

Athena made her way back to the courtyard, with Medusa dutifully following behind her with an enchanted smile on her face. Athena cut her eyes to Aphrodite's face and gave her a satisfied smile.

Aphrodite chuckled to herself. Athena had drawn first blood, very important for any battle. But, she was nonplussed. One good thing about being immortal was it made you very patient. She would give Athena this small victory, and they would see who would ultimately win the war.

The next morning came quickly, and Medusa was bursting with excitement. It hadn't been a dream. She was actually here on Mount Olympus. She had met Zeus, drank wine, and had been accepted by the Gods. She'd swam naked with the Goddesses and best of all, she had the favor of Athena. Stretching her tense muscles, she fell into a fit of giggles.

Medusa looked over and saw that her cousins were still sleeping. Quietly, she slid out of bed, and pad barefoot out of their chamber. No one seemed to be about. She walked silently through the halls, feeling just a little bit wicked for sneaking around, but she really wanted to see Erich. As she reached the courtyard, she broke out into a run, her hair streaming behind her.

Aphrodite caught a flash out the corner of her eye and smiled. Even if she was given an infinite amount of guesses, she was sure she knew whom it was. She plucked the last of the pomegranates she wanted to collect, and began to walk in Medusa's direction. She paused thoughtfully and, returning to the tree, picked a few of the flowers as well.

She rounded the hedge and came upon her. Medusa was leaning over the fountain, cooing. She looked lovely this morning. She was mussed and disheveled, like she had just crawled out of bed. She pulled something out of the water; a serpent; an unusual serpent with stripes!. Medusa was holding it close to her bosom. Interesting.

"Good morning, Medusa," Aphrodite said.

Gasping, Medusa whirled around. She always seemed to get frightened at this fountain.

"Good morning, My Lady," she stammered.

Aphrodite smiled as she walked towards her. "No need to be so formal, my darling. Please, call me Aphrodite." She continued, "What do you have there?"

Medusa couldn't believe how kind and gentle Aphrodite was, and how at ease she felt around her. She hadn't expected this from a Goddess, especially not a Goddess this beautiful. Finally, she remembered she had been asked a question.

"Oh, this is Erichthonius. I call him Erich. Athena gave him to me last night. She made him right out of my belt!" she exclaimed.

"Oh. How…lovely," Aphrodite replied. She had to stop herself from laughing. *So **that's** what the little tart was up to back here*, she thought. For a moment, Aphrodite had actually believed Athena had perhaps seduced the little beauty. She should have known better. She fought the urge to roll her eyes. Athena was completely out of her league.

Aphrodite and Medusa sat on the side of the fountain and played with Erich. They chatted about Medusa's first visit to Mount Olympus and, again, Medusa noticed how relaxed she felt around Aphrodite.

"How thoughtful of Athena to give you this present; I take it you favor serpents," Aphrodite probed.

"Yes," Medusa let Erich slide back into the water. She stared at the serpent statue wistfully. "They remind me of my mother."

She described her mother then, telling Aphrodite about the day of her birth, and how she'd never seen her mother since, but felt forever bound to her. The words flowed from her without reservation. She didn't sense any judgment for her mortal feelings, or feel weak for the pain she felt in missing her mother.

Aphrodite listened to her intently. Apparently, Athena had fortune on her side. She'd given Medusa something meaningful, that had really touched her heart, and she bet she didn't even know it. Aphrodite looked at Medusa tenderly. The little dear was so full of life and feeling. No creature felt love like mortals, and this little mortal was pulsing with it.

"Enough melancholy, it is a beautiful morning on Mount Olympus," she said, with a cheery smile. "Now tell me, my dear, have you ever had a pomegranate?"

Giggling, Medusa nodded.

"Well, I doubt you've ever had one like mine. I grow them myself." Aphrodite reached behind her and presented Medusa with the large fruit. Taking one for herself, she bit into it delicately.

Medusa stared at the pomegranate. This looked nothing like the ones she'd had at home. It was much larger, and the color seemed more vibrant. It looked almost like wine. She ran her fingers over the smooth texture. She bit into it vigorously, dripping juice all over her mouth, and down her chin. Wiping at her face, Medusa laughed. Flavor exploded in her mouth. The fruit was both sweet and sour at the same time.

Aphrodite laughed at her enthusiasm. "So messy," she tsked. Lowering her gaze to Medusa's mouth, she sighed. "Hmm. The fruit has darkened your lips," she whispered.

Leaning in, Aphrodite kissed her softly. She lingered, letting their mouths caress before gliding her tongue gently over Medusa's bottom lip. Her eyes drifted closed and her lips parted. Aphrodite cradled her head and let her tongue sweep inside in a gentle touch. Medusa shyly sought her out with her own tongue, pulling the goddess into an embrace.

Together they deepened the kiss. Aphrodite was moved by Medusa's innocence, and excited by her fervor. They nibbled at each other, their breaths mingling in sweet sighs. With a final caress, they parted from each other.

"You taste magnificent, my dear," Aphrodite breathed.

Medusa blushed, not quite sure what to say. She had never experienced anything like it. She felt warm and tingly… and desired. She not only felt desired, but desire itself.

Aphrodite knew that bewildered look well. She was the first to unlock Medusa's passion. She'd had just a small sample of what awaited her. But, Aphrodite wouldn't rush things. Admiration and even devotion could be given blindly. Love took time. She would gain Medusa's love, of that she was sure.

"Well, my darling, this is your final day on Mount Olympus. I think we should make you look extra special for the feast," she said. Aphrodite winked at her and helped her rise. Arm in arm, they walked back into the palace.

BEAUTY DIVIDED

Athena strode down the hall, slowing her pace as she saw the Charities coming out of their room. She also noticed Medusa was missing from the group. "Still abed, is she?" Athena asked, cheerfully. Shaking her head, Thaliana said, "No, she's not in there…" "When we woke, she was already gone…," Euphrosyne added. Aglaea shrugged. "We figured she might be with you."

With that, the threesome walked away, with no clue how upsetting this news was to Athena.

Deeply agitated, she fixed a nonchalant smile on her face, and trailed after the threesome. A thought entered her head and she broke off from them and headed out into the courtyard. She'd almost forgotten about Medusa's little pet. She probably couldn't wait to visit him this morning.

She approached the fountain and saw no Medusa. What she did see, was a half-eaten pomegranate. As her jaw tightened, thunder rumbled overhead. It seemed she had underestimated that clever little bitch. Had she been lying in wait for her? Or did she go and collect her straight from her bed?

Athena whirled around and stalked back into the palace, with purpose in every step.

"Daughter, Join me!" Zeus called.

Athena groaned. Her father's booming voice could not have come at a more inopportune time. As much as she was loathed to, she turned around and entered the great hall. There was no telling when she would find out exactly what Aphrodite was up to.

Almost finished," Aphrodite whispered.

With a clap of her hands, she led Medusa to a large looking glass. Standing beside her, she said "What do you think, my dear?"

Medusa could do nothing but stare. She didn't think she had ever looked so lovely. Her eyes were lined with kohl, which accented their luminous color. Her lips were stained and had a faint berry color. Her beautiful hair was pulled away from her face and gathered into a long braid over her shoulder, threaded with golden ribbons.

She looked like a Goddess, though she would never be caught saying that. Standing there, however, beside Aphrodite, the two were quite a pair. Medusa would never get used to how beautiful the goddess was. Aphrodite had fashioned her hair in the same way, with a ribbon of deep plum that matched her gown.

Aphrodite beckoned her attendant, Peitho. The young lady came forward with a package. She set it down and began to carefully unwrap it.

"Wow. I look…," Medusa started.

Silently, Peitho unclasped Medusa's gown. Setting her hands to Medusa's hips, she slid the gown down her body.

"…divine," Aphrodite finished.

Rising, Peitho held up an exact replica of Aphrodite's dress, except for the color. It was a muted gold that shimmered in the light, matching her ribbon perfectly.

"Raise your arms, My Lady," Peitho prompted.

Dazzled, Medusa held her hands above her head. She closed her eyes as the dress sheathed her. She twisted and turned, watching how it embraced her curves. Then, Aphrodite stood behind her and wrapped a belt around her waist. When she removed her hands, Medusa gasped.

The belt was a brilliant white, a startling contrast with the gold of her gown. It was the exact size of her waist, showing off her figure to perfection. But what she couldn't take her eyes off of was the clasp. It was made of two gilded serpents that interlocked together.

Aphrodite placed her braid over her shoulder, and let it fall over her right breast. "I'll bet you look very much like your mother tonight," she said.

Looking at her through the mirror, Medusa's eyes welled up.

Oh, no no no, my love. It's alright, don't cry… You'll streak," she tsked.

Medusa chuckled through the tears in her eyes. Nodding, she blinked rapidly, trying to clear her vision. She took a deep, shaky breath and smiled. She turned and embraced Aphrodite.

Aphrodite kissed her fully on the lips and stroked her cheek. "And now, we are ready to feast."

Athena sat on her father's right hand, trying to contain her fury. She had been with him since the morning, quite unnecessarily, in her opinion. What was worse, Medusa had been left unattended the entire time. There's no telling what Aphrodite had been up to during her absence.

She schooled her features to show no concern. No matter what, she would not let Aphrodite know that she had bothered her in the least. Still, she could not stop herself from searching for either one of them. The fact that they were both absent was deeply disturbing.

Laughter came from behind her. "Looking for your new toy, Athena?" Poseidon taunted. "Ah, and our little love goddess is missing as well. It looks like she would rather play with Aphrodite than you."

"And she would rather play with me than you, *Uncle*," she shot back. She loved to call him uncle to annoy him. She could tell by his thunderous expression that she'd hit her mark.

A slight commotion drew their attention. There was Aphrodite, in all her glory, as usual. The customary crowd was gathered around her, making it hard for Athena to see if Medusa was indeed with her. Finally, her devotees parted and she saw her.

Both Athena and Poseidon visibly straightened. They were utterly paralyzed by Medusa's beauty. Neither could mistake the reaction of the other. And neither would question the motives of the other. All they knew was that they both wanted her; wanted to possess her in some way.

Aphrodite approached them, with Medusa at her side, positively glowing. "Well, don't you two look cozy?" she teased.

"Good evening, My Lady," Medusa gave Athena a formal bow. Athena glared at Aphrodite smugly. "Good evening, Medusa. I must say, I did not think it possible, but you look even lovelier than last night."

Medusa beamed at the praise. She was so happy; she even bestowed a smile on Poseidon. "Good evening to you, My Lord."

"It truly is now that you have graced us Medusa. I am sorry for our misunderstanding yesterday. I hope, perhaps, we may begin again," he said.

Medusa was feeling particularly gracious tonight, so she bowed to him in acceptance.

"So, little one, what have you been up to today?" Athena asked, all the while looking at Aphrodite.

"Aphrodite and I had a wonderful time today. We ate pomegranates and sang and, obviously, she helped me to get ready," she giggled.

"Aphrodite?" Athena inquired.

Aphrodite laughed. "Yes. '*Aphrodite*'," she mocked. "Medusa is the offspring of ancient Gods. I don't feel the need for her to be so formal. As a matter of fact…" she draped an arm around Medusa's shoulder. "We have become… quite close."

Medusa smiled proudly. She felt so loved and respected on Mount Olympus. More than she ever thought possible.

Athena fumed silently, while Poseidon was infinitely intrigued. He imagined just how *close* the two of them had become that day. It did not matter. He had already made peace with Medusa. It was only a matter of time before he would have her *close* with him. He did have to admit though, Aphrodite had quite a pull.

Athena smiled serenely. "I'm very happy you enjoyed yourself today, my dear. Although, I did miss you terribly." She held her arms out. Happily, Medusa ran into her embrace. Aphrodite narrowed her eyes at the scene before her. "My darling, shall we go sample some of the feast?" she inquired politely.

Athena held onto Medusa's hands. "Awww, Ditie. I was hoping Medusa would sit with me for a while." She looked up into Medusa's eyes. "We could have a servant bring you a dish."

Medusa was torn. She wasn't used to being so popular and, of course, she never wanted to offend any of the Gods.

"You know Medusa, Athena really has missed you," Poseidon interjected. "Come and relax with her. Aphrodite, I'll be more than happy to accompany you."

Medusa exhaled and gave him a genuine smile.

Aphrodite's smile, however, was not so friendly. "Of course you're right, Poseidon. Have fun, my love." With that, she tipped Medusa's chin and kissed her softly on the lips.

Aphrodite cut her glance to Poseidon's salivating face. "Come Poseidon, you look positively ravenous."

Poseidon linked Aphrodite's arm in his and led her away. He did not know what was happening between the two of them, but he had definitely come out of that situation a winner. He'd just saved little Medusa's life, and she was sure to be grateful. He also helped Athena to keep her trophy by her side. And now, Athena owed him.

Athena watched their departure. She was sure Poseidon had not done that out of the goodness of his heart, but she would cross that bridge when it came. For now, she had won their little battle and, for now, she would be content. One thing still bothered her.

"Aphrodite is rather affectionate. Hopefully her kiss didn't make you uncomfortable," she said. She passed a comforting hand over

Medusa's head.
Medusa giggled. "Oh, no. Aphrodite always kisses me."

Athena nodded slowly. "Ah."

Medusa thought she heard the very faint sound of thunder overhead.

Aphrodite quickly glanced at the duo before returning her attention elsewhere. Her smug satisfaction was short lived. She had wanted to hit Athena with a double blow, spending the entire evening with Medusa. She was very determined to win.

More than that, though, she enjoyed spending time with her. Medusa was lovely, and charming, and had the most infallible spirit. Most mortal women only managed to annoy and enrage her. There was something very different about Medusa. Her very smile radiated love. Aphrodite would be sad to see her leave Olympus.

There was no question that she would return. They would see each other again. Still, she hated that Athena had her attention, again.

"What exactly do you hope to gain, for your part in all of this, Poseidon?" she asked her companion.

Poseidon did not attempt to pretend to misunderstand the question. "The same as you, fair Ditie. A lovely prized possession." That being said, he raised his glass to her in a silent toast.

Aphrodite felt his tone to her very core. Concern furrowed her brow, and she once again looked across the great hall. Suddenly, she felt almost happy that Medusa would be going home the next morning.

BEAUTY DEPARTS

I will miss you, Erich. But, I daresay I will return fairly soon."

Medusa held her beloved serpent close. As was his custom, Erich slowly curled himself around her arm, and nestled. Smiling, she uncoiled him and placed him gently back in the fountain. With a forlorn sigh, she made her way back into the palace.

"Mount Olympus will not be the same without you, Medusa."

Medusa looked up into Poseidon's smiling face. "I will miss it here," she said, casting a wistful look around. Turning back to him she said, "I want to thank you, My Lord, for what you did yesterday. I don't know what I would have done had you not intervened."

He grinned at her. "I intended it as an olive branch. I do not like the discord we've had between us. I cannot right the wrongs of the past, but I was hoping that we could... begin again?"

Medusa felt very silly holding a grudge that was not hers to bear, especially after ten years. Not to mention, Poseidon was a God. Who was she to judge him? She fell into a deep curtsey. Rising, she said "My Lord."

Poseidon took her hand and placed a chaste kiss on it. "My Lady," he replied. "You will be missed, and I eagerly await your return."

She smiled sweetly and took her leave of him.

As he watched her retreating steps, a triumphant smile filled his face.

Athena was waiting for her when she finally departed. Her face broke into a wide grin. Athena extended her arms, and Medusa, running into them, was caught up in a strong embrace.

"Now promise me you will visit again soon, little one," she said.

Medusa blinked away the tears that were starting to form. "Oh yes, My Lady. As soon as I'm able." She nodded vigorously.

Athena was smiling down at her, until something caught her eye. Her expression changed dramatically. Medusa followed her gaze.

"Aphrodite!" she giggled.

"Did you think I would miss seeing you off, my darling?" she chuckled. "I would've been here sooner had I not been detained by our Lord Poseidon." She leveled a pointed glare at Athena.

Aphrodite lovingly stroked Medusa's face. "Did you remember everything? You have your gown, yes?"

Medusa nodded "Oh, yes. It's much too fine for me to wear anywhere at home, but I will cherish it always. Thank you."

Aphrodite waved the thought away. "Nonsense. In fact, I have another gift for you. However, you must promise not to open it until right before your visit next year."

Athena raised an eyebrow. "Next year?" she asked.

Aphrodite didn't even spare her a glance. "Please tell me you'll come back for Aphrodisia, my love. It would not be the same without you." She ran a hand over Medusa's hair, and placed a soft kiss on her lips.

Medusa gasped. "Oh Aphrodite, really?! Well, of course, I would love to!"

Athena actually allowed herself a smile. She realized now why she disregarded Aphrodite. The woman was a novice. You never let your enemy know of even the smallest portion of your strategy.

"What a lovely invitation!" Athena said. "You know Aphrodite, Aphrodisia is not too long before the next Panathenaia. Medusa, you should stay straight through."

Medusa was so thrilled, she barely heard the Charities calling her. She allowed herself a moment to fantasize. "Amazing! I will be here," she glanced at Aphrodite. And I promise, I wont open this until it's time." Snapping out of her dream, she ran to join her family with a final wave to two Goddesses who meant so very much to her.

Athena and Aphrodite both displayed serene smiles, but the tension between them was palpable.

As they began their descent, Medusa could hardly believe her good fortune. She never believed she would ever be invited to Olympus. Not only invited, she seemed to have found favor with everyone. She let out a giddy laugh. Imagine that! Her, favored one of the Gods.

It was very heady being in the presence of such powerful beings. Mount Olympus was a magical place, where anything could happen, and most likely did. Everything was beautiful and pleasing to the senses. The entire time she was there, she felt like she was floating, beyond any realm of what she'd previously considered reality.

The Gods had it so easy. There was no desire beyond their accomplishment. There was nothing they could want that they couldn't have. What a life it was! She wondered if they even wanted anything anymore, or if they transcended the need to… well, need.

She mused the entire way, every now and then drifting off for a nap. Finally, she saw the familiarity of home. A small sigh escaped her lips, and she silently berated herself. This whole time, she had not once thought of home. Exiting the cart, she ran into the house, searching. Then, she set her eyes on Eurynome. They ran into each other's arms.

Eurynome thanked all of the Gods, even the ones she had been silently cursing for days. Her baby had returned safely. Eurynome rained kisses all over her face, then pulled away to examine her.

"Oh I've missed you so," she said. "Did you have a good time? Were you treated well?"

Medusa laughed. She could not answer one question, for being asked another.

"I had a wonderful time! I was treated exceptionally well. Everyone loved me, Eurynome," she said excitedly.

Eurynome's eyes filled up with tears. *Everyone had loved her.*

She was afraid of that. Eurynome knew what a special girl Medusa was. **She** loved her. She was sure the Gods noticed her qualities more than anyone else, but did they truly love her? Could a God truly love a mortal?

They sat and talked of the trip, with Medusa leaving out a few things she thought Eurynome might not approve of. She told her of being reacquainted with Poseidon and, at Eurynome's worried glance, explained how she effectively put him in his place. They had a good laugh at that. A mere scrap of a girl, had brought a God to a halt.

Eurynome's smile died on her face. "It sounds like a wonderful time, Medusa. I'm so glad that you were well received, and the Gods bestowed you with gifts," she let out a shaky breath. "I daresay you'll be invited back quite often. Just promise me you will always be careful. I don't… just promise me."

Medusa nodded solemnly, and Eurynome pulled her in to her arms once more, and hoped that the Gods' interest in her would leave her intact. Gods were magical and miraculous, and just like miracles and magic, they were unpredictable.

Medusa felt Eurynome's tears on her shoulder. She squeezed Eurynome tightly. "It's okay, Mother , I'm home now."

Hearing Medusa call her 'Mother' for the first time made her tears flow even harder.

BEAUTY SURRENDERED

Life returned to normal quickly for Medusa. Each day seemed to crawl by with maddening banality. Nightly, she had dreams of Olympus. She could feel her blood thrumming, her pulse soaring, only to awake in the morning and come crashing down to the reality that was home.

The way life was progressing, she didn't know if she would ever feel excited about anything again. At least, not until she was back on Mount Olympus. The day after her return, she broached the subject with Eurynome, telling her about her invitation to go back to Olympus. Eurynome seemed to digest the news with a quiet resignation.

So, Medusa began to count the days.

She missed Athena and, of course, Erichthonius. However, she realized she missed Aphrodite most of all. The past week had been filled with dreams of her, of the kiss they'd shared by the fountain. Aphrodite made her feel so accepted, so loved, and something else she couldn't quite name.

Feeling restless and anxious, Medusa began to walk through the courtyard. She thought about her admiration for Athena, and how it differed from the feelings she had for Aphrodite. Aphrodite was always so affectionate with her, and while Athena showed her great acceptance, she was still aloof in many ways.

Medusa felt extreme reverence while she was in Athena's presence, and an overwhelming sense of devotion. Athena was steady and solid. Athena was the earth, and the sky. She had always been, and she would always be. Without her, all would likely cease.

If Athena was the sky, Aphrodite was the sun. She was the moon and the stars, the thunder and lightning. They may be mercurial, but it brought purpose to all that could be. With Aphrodite, Medusa felt extreme inspiration, and was overwhelmed with sensation.

Medusa never knew she could feel so strongly in so many different directions.

She was walking by Eurynome's rose bushes, fingering the crimson buds. Leaning in, she inhaled their scent. She was distracted by her own thoughts, and unconsciously began to clip a few of the roses. Gathering them in a piece of fabric, she left a quick goodbye for Eurynome with a servant and began to make her way to the city.

While she strolled, her conflict tumbled around in her head. She had always believed devotion and loyalty to be single minded. How could she possibly feel what she was feeling for both Goddesses, especially given their obvious differences?

Medusa justified and rationalized. She condemned herself in one breath, then found exoneration in the next. When she thought her head might split, she decided that there was nothing wrong with devotion to them both, and perhaps their differences is what made it acceptable. Besides, all of the Gods should be worshipped. It was not as though she was forced to decide between the two.

The bustle of the marketplace shook her out of her thoughts. She needed a few more things for what she wanted to offer. She visited her favorite stands, chatting amiably with the merchants. In the end, she had purchased a small silken pillow, a few seashells, meat from a fatted calf, some scented oils and incense, and a couple of miniature statues.

With all of her purchases made, Medusa headed to the temple. It was very early and, likely, no one but the priestesses would be around. As she walked, she thought back and laughed at her self-inflicted dilemma. How silly she had been. She was perfectly capable of loving and worshipping the two goddesses, equally, albeit differently. At that thought, she turned and made her way to the shrine… of Aphrodite.

Kneeling at the feet of the Goddess, she marveled over her beauty. The statue before her, as well as the one in her hand, could never come close to doing her justice.

Medusa laid the silken pillow at her feet. She anchored the corners with four identical seashells, colored like the sunrise. She had chosen a small statue of Aphrodite in repose, lying on her side, the way she had been when they lounged and sang together in her chambers.

Medusa placed the statue in the center of the pillow, and scattered rose petals all around. She kept one rose in tact. It was a tight, unopened bud, of the deepest scarlet. Medusa had caught it just before the time of blossoming. Gently, she placed the bud on top of the statue.

Removing the stopper from the vial, she poured the oil over them. It was thick and smelled strongly of pomegranates. She lit the incense and, sitting back on her heels, closed her eyes and offered a prayer.

Adored Aphrodite, I open my heart to you.
I am blessed with the favor of your smile,
and treasure the gift of your embrace.
I am left hollow in faded sunlight,
obsessed with the rhythm of your heartbeat;
dizzy with the ecstasy resulting from your lips.
Too far are the days I beheld your beauty;
and felt the satin touch of your presence.
As recompense for your love bestowed,

Aphrodite, I offer my faith and devotion.

She sat there for several minutes in faint contemplation. Finally, she rose and walked to Athena's shrine.

Aphrodite let out the breath she had been holding. It had taken great strength not to go to Medusa. Her offering had touched the Goddess so deeply. Even from her position, the scent of pomegranates reached her, along with the image of her embracing with the virgin rose. Bathed in oil, the offering screamed of ecstasy and love. Medusa's voice, low and soft, speaking words of devotion to her, was almost more than Aphrodite could bear.

But Aphrodite would bear it. She had to. Athena was in quite a lather over Medusa, and though Aphrodite didn't know Poseidon's motives, she could guess. The battle for Medusa would prove to be a fierce one. And, as with all battles, there were bound to be casualties. She hoped if she admitted defeat, maybe Medusa would be treated kindly as a prisoner of war.

With a final sad smile, she turned away from the offering.

Medusa knelt at Athena's feet. She placed the fresh meat on the altar and unstopped the extra fine, extra virgin olive oil. After pouring it, she set her offering on fire and began her prayer.

I praise you, Athena, great goddess born of your own.
Most chaste and honorable of all maids,
loving defender and heroine of my existence.
I am blessed with the strength of your arm,

with the power of your majesty, I am awed.
Unfailing, in mind and eye, I desire to remain in your sight.
Skilled, in craft and deed, I beg to be stitched on your heart.
Strong one, I ask for the gift of your favor, to be useful in your service,
and held in your remembrance and in return, I offer my honor and devotion.

As she opened her eyes, Medusa beheld Athena, in her true form, standing before her. "My Lady!" she gasped. Athena held her arms open to her and, as always, Medusa ran into them. The goddess laughed fondly, as she folded her in a strong embrace. "That was an excellent offering, little one," she said proudly. "I cannot stay, but know you are in my thoughts, and I look forward to your visit." She placed a chaste kiss on Medusa's forehead, before vanishing.

Smiling, Medusa left the temple. As she descended the stairs, the smile died on her face. On her way home, only one thought ran through her mind. Aphrodite did not come to her.

In good spirits, Athena sank down next to a sullen Aphrodite.

"What a glorious day, don't you think, Ditie?" she smiled smugly.

Aphrodite was in a foul mood, and Athena's presence was not helping the situation. "Indeed. What has made it so glorious for you Athena?" She gave her a sigh of indulgence.

Turning, Athena lay back, resting her head on Aphrodite's lap. "Oh, not much. I just received the most lovely offering from Medusa."

Pushing her away, Aphrodite rose. "How very nice for you, Athena," she grumbled.

Athena giggled "Yes it is, isn't it? Oh, don't worry Ditie, mortals often can only focus on one thing at a time. I'm sure she'll make an offering for you."

Aphrodite's eyes narrowed at the condescending tone. She'd like nothing more than to tell the ***wise*** Goddess that Medusa **had** made an offering… and first. She bristled at Athena's freedom to go to her, and tried to take solace in the knowledge that she was doing the right thing.

But, there was no solace to be found.

Aphrodite excused herself and stomped out of the great hall. Athena looked after her with a pleased smile.

BEAUTY HEARTSICK

Medusa lie in her bed, a single tear sliding down her face. This was one of those days when she couldn't stop them no matter how hard she tried.

It had been months. Months, and no word. Medusa didn't know what to do. She didn't know what she had done. She regularly made trips to the temple, continued to give offerings to both Athena and Aphrodite. Each time, Athena made herself known to her, if not in her true form, then at least with some sort of sign. No matter what she did, Aphrodite would not come to her.

Confusion and despair filled her. She wracked her brain for what offense she could have caused, and how she could rectify it. Perhaps her offerings were unsatisfactory, which was disheartening, because she always put all of herself in each sacrifice. So, if her offerings were lacking, she must be lacking as well.

In light of everything, there was only one conclusion she could come to. Aphrodite had been struck by Medusa at the first, had her fun, and now that she had returned home, she was out of sight, as well as mind and heart. That is, if the Goddess had a heart. She had played with Medusa and, like all new toys, had tired of her. It was the way of the Gods. Even now, she probably had a new plaything on Olympus.

For that reason, Medusa had ceased making offerings to her. She was angry with the goddess. She was grieved and miserable, and she would show her. The one flaw in that plan was the fact that Aphrodite didn't seem to care. Secretly, Medusa knew she hoped for a reaction. She received none, not that it mattered. Aphrodite would just have to be deprived of a loyal and faithful servant. The Goddess of *Love* was denying herself of just that.

No matter how angrily Medusa said the words to herself, it could never end the rending of her heart. Hugging her knees to her chest, she felt choked with the pain. Medusa adored Aphrodite, and her dismissal burned. Did she not even deserve at least an explanation? Even Poseidon, in his callousness, had the decency to tell Eurynome when she was no longer wanted.

Still, despite the many times she rationalized and tried to reconcile the situation, Medusa still arrived to the same dead end. There was obviously something about her. And it ripped her soul.

She thought of Aphrodite then, of all they had shared, of the comfort she had felt with her, not to mention the warmth and excitement. In her heart, she knew she would do whatever she could to be what she needed. She would do anything to find favor with the goddess again.

Gathering herself, she left home, heading towards the temple. She strode with purpose, her hair streaming behind her. She stopped in the marketplace, picked up her customary offering for Athena and walked over to a jeweler.

Looking over his wares, Medusa found a stone the color of sea foam, nestled in a bed of gold. She paid him, then snatched the jewel from his hand and ran to the temple. She did not come to a stop until she stood before Aphrodite.

She fell down on her knees, placed the offering on the ground and slid it forward. Looking askance at the statue before her, she began a new prayer.

Aphrodite was lying in her bed resting her eyes, when she was jerked awake by a familiar voice.

Medusa, she thought to herself.

She had not been present at her temple for a month, Medusa's offerings and prayers becoming too much for her. It was harder and harder to resist. Without that sweet voice to hear, she lost her motivation to hear any others. Still, she kept an ear out for the well-known melody.

Glorious Aphrodite, I offer you my devotion.
O irresistible one, I am drawn as the tide to the moon.
I obey your desires, and bend to your wishes.
Show me my lover's eyes, let me see my beauty reflected in your smile.
New lovers unite through your will, and old loves find their passion ever rekindled. Aphrodite, I honor you Aphrodite, I worship you.

Taking a breath, she began again.

Aphrodite didn't know how, but her heart soared and broke simultaneously. There was such a mixture of love and pain in her voice, even the rational part wanted to run and soothe her. Instead, she paced in her chamber.

Still Medusa continued.

Again and again, she repeated the prayer, until her voice was hoarse. Each recitation became louder and more tearful. She seemed to slip into a trance, focused only on getting Aphrodite's attention. That she had. And she was driving her mad! Aphrodite covered her ears, her every movement agitated.

Shut up… shut up, she thought to herself. Finally, she could stand no more. She was going to the temple.

Then she saw her. Her presence was still undetected. Medusa was on her knees, her forehead touching the ground, rocking steadily. She looked up at Aphrodite's statue and revealed her tear-stained face. She looked confused and sick. Her chest rose and fell erratically, until it finally sank. Her voice rasping, she let out a final prayer.

Medusa shakily got to her feet. Aphrodite slipped behind a column to watch her, horrified. She seemed to be trembling all over. Misery was etched all over her face, as well as something she never thought she'd see… defeat. Aphrodite knew could end it all, but, at what cost?

With one final look to her likeness, Medusa whispered, "How did I wrong you?" Frowning, Medusa ran from the temple, completely forgetting her offering for Athena.

Aphrodite shook her head sadly. She didn't know what to do. She went back and forth with herself. On the one hand, it was very noble what she was doing. On the other, she was a goddess… why should she care?! Medusa is very special, so why should she not have her if she wishes?

Because she is special. And innocent. And quite young.

Because Athena would never let her go without a fight, and that snake Poseidon constantly slithers about. Aphrodite groaned loudly. *Oh this is ridiculous!* she thought. *She is just a girl. A mortal.* The world is full of them. This should not be an issue of utmost importance. In a few short years, she will no longer even be on this earth.

She is best left alone and forgotten. With that decided and firmly in mind and heart… she bent down and picked up the jewel, then vanished back to Olympus.

Medusa had never been so happy to see home in her life. She had held herself together on the journey home, practically running the entire way. She only had a little ways to go, just through the house, and into her chamber.

Making a dash, she barreled past Eurynome, not stopping when she called after her. Shutting her door, she dove onto the bed, and was finally able to sob freely, right into her pillow.

After that day, she made no more offerings to Aphrodite. Her offerings to Athena also declined, though she was still regularly making them.

Eurynome had questioned her about the day she ran home, but let the matter rest when Medusa refused to confide in her. She did notice, however, that Medusa was changed from that day on. She would always be a sweet and loving child but, since that day, her enthusiasm for life, and her optimistic vitality was slightly diminished.

She had become a woman. Gone was the naive little girl, and in her place, was someone wiser, someone who no longer viewed life with the same fascination and curiosity… because now, she **knew**.

Eurynome was grateful that whatever happened, Medusa seemed to have made it through alright. Still, it was sad. She knew firsthand how it felt when you no longer believe in magic, and the world is no longer solely beautiful.

Finally, Medusa fell into some semblance of a normal life. A constant worry in her mind was… what she would do about her invitation to return to Olympus. That decision was decided for her when Eurynome fell ill the week before she was to leave. Medusa sent her regrets to Athena, asking her to also convey her apologies to Aphrodite.

Each time she thought of her, a dull ache entered her chest and, once again, she would quickly squelch it. It would do her no good to think of what was, or what could have been. She must focus on what is, and what would never be.

Her birthday passed that year, almost nonexistent, with Eurynome being sick, and no one else but the servants around. One night, nearly a month later, Medusa sat in her room, looking up at the sky, the ever constant sky and, of course, what caught her eye was the moon, ever changing, but undeniably beautiful.

Reaching into her secret hiding place, Medusa pulled out a satin wrapped package. She knew she should put it right back, knew that whatever was in there would not lift her spirits. Still, in the darkness of her chamber, with the moon shining on her, her fingers went to the ties. The fabric fell open and Medusa gasped softly.

Inside was a smooth gold chain. On the end of the chain, was a blood red pomegranate, covered in rubies, except for the diamonds that depicted a bite mark. Wrapped around the fruit was a golden snake, with glittering peridot eyes.

Medusa placed the gift around her neck. The sparkling charm nestled itself perfectly between her breasts. Clasping the jewel in her hand, she curled up on her bed and fell into a melancholy slumber. Despite herself, she wondered what Aphrodite was doing at that moment.

Had she been facing the moon, she would've seen that the goddess was silently bidding her a happy birthday.

BEAUTY RETURNS

Time, whether fast or slow, always passes, even on Mount Olympus. It had been over a year since Medusa's last attempt to gain Aphrodite's favor. But, before long, it was only a month before another Aphrodisia would take place.

Aphrodite was terribly busy, seeing to plans for the festival. She had kept herself moderately distracted, with this lover and that but, now, it was time to immerse herself into a complete sensual stupor. She wanted wine, men and women, singing and dancing. She wanted to feed her senses and lose herself in the oblivion of ecstasy.

She was sitting with Dionysus, discussing these very plans, when an argument intruded on their conversation. Annoyed, she excused herself and went to seek out the offending voices. As she got farther down the hall, she made them out to be Athena and Poseidon. *Great.*

Athena had been nearly unbearable in her 'victory'. She considered Medusa her most prized possession and was always sure to keep Aphrodite abreast of all of her activities, namely Medusa's devoted worship of her.

When Medusa had not returned to Olympus, Aphrodite was convinced she had done the right thing. Obviously, now that Athena had won, she kept Medusa like all of her other possessions, at a safe distance, to be admired.

Still, she did miss the little darling's vibrant presence.

Aphrodite was ready to barge in and tell them to take their noise elsewhere when Poseidon's words stopped her.

"I have waited long enough Athena. Now, ***where*** is she?!" he shouted.

Athena shot him an unruffled glance. "She will be here for Panathenaia, not that she'll be available to you while she serves me. If you are so enamored of her Poseidon, why not just go to her? Or you could have Aphrodite force her love for you, although, she could not even accomplish that for herself," she taunted.

Aphrodite balled her fists and breathed through clenched jaws.

"It is too difficult to woo her in her home, with Eurynome still there."

She gave him a look of disgust. "You are lower than a pig. This is why I will be a virgin, eternally."

"You will remain a virgin, because no man will have you," he shot back.

Ever the strategist, she'd anticipated that particular comment. "You may be right, although ***I*** seem to do well with women."

Poseidon slammed his fists on the table. "Damn you, Athena. You owe me! I helped you claim your little prize."

Athena finally let her temper show. Standing up, she faced him squarely. "Owe you? You've taken leave of your senses. Medusa is mine, and by my own doing. I've asked you for nothing, so I owe you ***nothing***."

A devious smile crossed his face. "Perhaps I should have Ditie invite her for Aphrodisia, and have her come here sooner."

Athena laughed at that. "You would try to ally yourself with Aphrodite? What do you think that would accomplish?"

She sobered and stared at him seriously. "You would do well not to cross me, Poseidon. It has not worked for you yet."

Poseidon straightened and turned to leave. "I **will** have her, Athena."

Aphrodite stood outside of the door, in shock.

After all she had done to avoid this exact situation; Medusa was right back in the middle of a battle of wills. She should have known. Even the Gods are bound by the will of Fate.

This time, though, Medusa was in a lot more danger. Poseidon and Athena were the fiercest of rivals. Who knew how she would fare in the crossfire. Poseidon had given her a good idea, though. If she could get Medusa here for Aphrodisia, she could have more control over the situation. Zeus would not deny her the deference she would need during this time.

There was much to do. Her duties had just doubled, and her timeline had not changed. She was afraid and apprehensive and… oddly excited.

Medusa was coming back to Mount Olympus.

Medusa paced in her chambers, her necklace bouncing against her bosom with each step. She knew she couldn't escape it forever but, apparently, she didn't even have another year.

She had made her offering to Athena and, as usual, the Goddess came to her. She's been summoned to Olympus for Panathenaia. It was only a month away. Of course, it was a great honor, but still. She shook an errant thought from her head.

Aphrodite probably wouldn't even be there.

So what if she was? she thought to herself. She was not the same Medusa she had been two years ago. She was a woman of nearly nineteen years. She could handle seeing Aphrodite again.

Hopefully, Aphrodite won't even be there.

A soft coo caught her attention. She looked towards her window, and there, on the sill, was a beautiful white dove, an olive branch perched in its beak. Her breath caught in her throat. *It couldn't be,* she thought. Medusa backed away from the window, only to have the dove fly in. Landing on her bed, it dropped the olive branch and looked at her curiously, before flying off.

Medusa exhaled, trying to get a grip on her imagination. Yes, it was from Aphrodite but, realistically, it was only an olive branch. A symbol of peace, or treaty. All she had, really, was some sort of an apology. Nothing to fret over. It was good that Aphrodite was apologizing, since an apology was due. In fact, this olive branch was nearly two years late. *The dove must've gotten lost*, she mused.

She chuckled to herself, then straightened, very proud of how mature she was being. She felt very much like an adult, all of a sudden. She was preening when Eurynome came knocking on her door.

"You have a visitor, my darling."

Medusa instantly deflated. ***No,*** she thought. Shrinking, she backed herself against a wall.

At Eurynome's confused look she hesitantly began to make her way down to the aule. There she set eyes on Peitho. ***No.*** It was the only word that would formulate in Medusa's mind. Medusa tried for what she assumed was a very mature, self-assured smile.

She failed.

She looked like she had been hit both in the head and in the stomach, and couldn't decide which hurt worse. Peitho didn't seem to notice. Her grin filled her entire face before she launched herself at Medusa and hugged her tightly.

"My lady, it is so good to see you! It has been so long."

Despite everything, Medusa couldn't help but smile. She hugged Peitho and sighed. "Is all well, Peitho?"

Remembering herself, Peitho straightened. "Yes, my lady. I come, my lady, because my mistress summons you to Olympus for Aphrodisia."

No, Medusa thought again.

Her mouth sat agape, and she tried to force the word past her lips but, deep down, she knew there was only one response she could give.

"Well… uh yes, of course," she said. "When am I needed?"

Medusa had to give Peitho credit. She, at least, had the forethought to look chagrined. "Why… now, my lady. We are to leave immediately."

Medusa sighed. *Of course she was expected to leave immediately.* That way, there was no excuse that could be made, no way to get out of it, no way to postpone the inevitable.

With the help of Pietho, she was quickly able to pack what she needed for her extended trip on Olympus. Medusa prepared rather dazedly, still shocked that she was going back. Even more shocking was that, after all this time, she was going to see Aphrodite, and at Aphrodite's request.

They were on their way in record time. Still, none of it felt real to Medusa. Surely, she was dreaming. Peitho kept her well entertained with innocuous stories of life on Olympus. She kept mentioning everyone and everything… except for Aphrodite. Medusa thought she would lose her mind from it.

Aphrodite was surrounded by beautiful men and women, in various states of undress and, still, she could not contain her agitation. She reclined with her entourage, but kept a watchful eye.

She let the hands roaming over her body ease some of her tension. The last few days had been so nerve wracking. And she had a distinct feeling the next few would be no better. Athena and Poseidon had been visibly at odds since their argument, and both were suddenly more interested in her and her activities.

Things seemed to be nearing the boiling point. Aphrodite was sure that point would escalate when Medusa arrived, but at least she could retain some kind of control. She didn't know how, but she was determined to end this battle once and for all.

Medusa could take no more of this inane talk. "So, why am I being summoned, Peitho? Has your mistress tired of her latest plaything? Is she feeling nostalgic?" Medusa herself abhorred her bitter tone, but she could no longer pretend to be unaffected.

Peitho gave her a wounded look. "My lady, you…" She looked as though she wanted to speak, then thought better of it. "…you have been missed."

Nodding, Medusa rolled her eyes.

Peitho didn't quite know what was going through Medusa's mind, but it was not her place to speak for her mistress. They passed the rest of the ride in silence. Medusa was ready to scream by the time they arrived.

Medusa stared at the palace in front of her. It looked different than it did before. It wasn't as large, wasn't as grand, and she no longer feared climbing the stairs. Without waiting for Peitho, she entered the palace and headed straight into the great hall.

Aphrodite was stroking the hair of a beautiful olive-skinned girl who was draped across her. She wondered what was keeping Peitho. Looking around the hall, she spotted Poseidon. She had sent a young lady to occupy him, and it looked like the little dear was doing a good job.

With that handled, she turned to the handsome young man at her side and engaged him in conversation. Feeling Athena's eyes on her, she smiled and flirted, as if she hadn't a care in the world. She placed a distracted kiss on his beautiful mouth.

The emotion that hit Medusa at that sight was not only unexpected, but unidentifiable. It was the oddest mixture, and she didn't have time to delve into it. She quickly backed up, right into Peitho. By her reddened cheeks, Medusa assumed she had caught the indelicate situation.

Medusa took a deep, calming breath, and tightened her jaw until she felt physical pain. "Peitho, I need to change," she said resolutely.

Peitho suddenly flashed her knowing grin. "Yes, my lady. Follow me."

Medusa trailed after her, thankful that she escaped the hall without anyone noticing her presence… except, of course, Poseidon.

The girl in front of him chatted continuously, but she no longer existed. A broad smile broke on his face.

Beauty had returned.

BEAUTY RECONCILED

Poseidon did not even bother to excuse himself from the girl in front of him. He was on a mission. With purpose, he strode towards the entrance. "Brother, Join us!"

Zeus's voice was most unwelcome. He was well into his cups and no doubt in a friendly and jovial mood. It would not be easy to get away from him. It didn't matter. Medusa was here now. There was plenty of time.

Medusa tossed another gown on the floor. None of them would do. Frustrated, she sank down on the bed, her head in her hands. She felt someone's presence and looked up. Peitho entered shyly, with something in her arms. "Try this, my lady."

Medusa took the gown from her and held it up. It was a deep turquoise color, and as she turned towards the light, she realized it was very sheer. Beyond that, it was the most daring scrap of material she had ever seen.

It was perfect.

Squealing, she yanked Peitho up in a gripping hug. With a newfound confidence, she stripped her clothes off. She looked at her reflection, and a far-off look passed over her face. Slowly, she unclasped the necklace she was wearing and placed it on a table.

Poseidon was trying to pay attention to what his brother was saying. Zeus just couldn't seem to shut his mouth. It was becoming harder to come up with appropriate responses, with his focus always at the entrance. He had to get away somehow. He wanted to intercept Medusa before the others saw her. Since his brother had first waylaid him, they had been joined by Athena, Aphrodite, and her simpering little pet.

He was trying to figure out a solution to his dilemma, when a hush descended over the room. He was too late. The group at large turned towards the entrance and, one by one, jaws dropped.

This was not the Medusa they remembered. This was the Medusa they would never forget. She was barefoot, and walked with confidence and self-assurance, a far cry from the way she stumbled in two years ago. Her amber hair flowed freely in a curly riot.

The sheer, turquoise sheath was molded to her body, displaying her tanned skin to perfection. The top consisted of two panels at the front, from neck to waist, that barely covered her breasts, and two in the back, the pairs joined at the top by golden bands that rested on her shoulders.

The bottom was over long, embracing her hips, and then split in front, so that the garment exposed her long legs, and trailed behind her as she walked. Everyone she passed greeted her breathlessly, and was met with a silent smile.

She approached the group with a serene gaze and a bow for Zeus.

"Well, my dear. You always did know how to make an entrance. I believe, however, this one overshadows your last." Zeus cheerfully kissed both of her cheeks.

Poseidon finally found his voice. "As always, you are most welcome, Medusa. You have been sorely missed." He also kissed her on both cheeks, and then pulled her in for a friendly hug.

"What are you doing here?" Athena barked.

Medusa frowned at her. "I was invited here for Aphrodisia."

Athena quickly remembered herself. She would not allow herself to be perceived as being caught off guard, so she wrapped Medusa up in her own embrace. "I'm sorry, my dear. I just was not expecting you so early. But I am so pleased to see you."

Medusa squeezed her tightly.

Athena held her at arm's length then, and looked at her thoroughly. "I must say, you look very different."

Medusa smiled fondly. "Well, I actually arrived some time ago. I came into the great hall and, upon looking around, I realized I was…" She shot a look of disgust at Aphrodite, and the scantily clad girl hanging on her arm, "… inappropriately attired."

The gesture pleased Athena greatly.

Then, Medusa turned to Aphrodite, and gave her a formal bow. "My Lady, blessings on your festival." Medusa rejoiced at seeing her jaw tighten. Someone should've told her to be careful what she asked for. She had wanted her here, and now, she had her.

In Medusa's opinion, it served Aphrodite right for ignoring her all this time, and then thinking she could just snap her fingers, and everything would be like it was. Damn her arrogance. Damn her ego.

Damn her for looking so incredible.

They all lounged, chatting idly, enjoying the wine and dancing. With each cup of wine, Aphrodite's little kitten pawed at her more and more, causing Medusa to feel her nerves stretch to the breaking point. When the girl went to unclasp Aphrodite's gown, Medusa decided she'd had enough.

Rising abruptly, she excused herself. "I just realized I haven't seen Erich yet, so if you all will…" Her eyes dropped to Aphrodite's cleavage. Her eyes widened. "… that jewel…"

Athena scoffed. "Oh ***that*** thing? She's always wearing it. I don't know why, but she keeps it tucked away between her breasts. I think she likes her pets to play hide and seek with it," she teased.

Suddenly, the great hall seemed to be getting smaller. She politely excused herself, a great feat for someone who couldn't breathe. She calmly sauntered to the entry, and then broke into a run for the courtyard.

She arrived, gasping for air, and dropped to her knees in front of the fountain. She knew the exact moment Aphrodite had arrived. She whirled on her fiercely. She stared at her, as she paced in agitation. Aphrodite couldn't help but notice that she looked like an angel of vengeance.

"That's a beautiful necklace, My Lady. Such a lovely jewel. Where did you get it?" Medusa sounded deceptively polite.

"Medusa…" Aphrodite began.

A sardonic chuckle escaped her. "I recall seeing something similar years ago. When did you get it?" She was getting more and more angry.

Aphrodite sighed. "I got it the day you left it. I was there."

Her pacing turned frantic, until she was nearly panting. "Why didn't you come to me? Months and months, and you never came to me. Not one word. Why wouldn't you come to me?!" Ending on a shriek, the tears she was holding back finally began to fall.

Aphrodite ran to her, and held her tightly.

"What did I do?" she sobbed.

Cupping her face, Aphrodite looked into her misty eyes. "You did nothing, my love. I did not want to stay away. I promise you, my only thought was to protect you…"

"Protect me? From…"

Aphrodite hushed her. She held the jewel up. "… Know you have always been near my heart." Slowly, she kissed away her tears, then gently brushed across her mouth.

Medusa put her hands on her waist and leaned into her. She'd forgotten how soft her lips were. Their mouths opened of their own accord, and two tongues sought each other out. They both tasted of pomegranates to the other.

Pulling closer, Aphrodite explored the satin texture of her back. She trailed kisses down her neck, nibbling at her collarbone. Medusa shivered and stroked her cheek, bringing her back for another kiss. Aphrodite cradled her neck, as she caressed the valley between her breasts. Medusa could feel her breasts swell, and the peaks tighten. Sighing, she took Aphrodite's wrist and guided her hand to her breast. Aphrodite smiled as she stroked it fondly. She heard a faint whimper and felt her nipple harden in her palm. Wrapping Medusa in her arms, she flashed them out of the courtyard.

When Medusa opened her eyes, they were in Aphrodite's chamber. Circling her, Medusa unclasped her gown and guided it to the floor.

And there was her Goddess. Her Moon. She ran her fingers down the length of her spine, and placed a kiss on her shoulder. Reaching up, she slipped her own gown off of her shoulders. Holding her hips, she stroked Aphrodite's stomach, up to her breasts. Holding them tenderly, she pulled Aphrodite to her.

The sensation was shocking. Warm, soft skin against warm, soft skin, and Medusa's breasts pressed against her back. Turning, Aphrodite looked at her naked body like it was the first time. Medusa caressed her neck, down to her breasts, letting her fingertips lightly brush the tips. She leaned closer to kiss each, her breath warming them, her tongue darting out at the last moment, eliciting a small moan from Aphrodite.

Medusa was aroused by the power she held over her. Taking her hand, she led her to the bed, and they fell onto it in a tangle, kissing and touching, exploring every inch of each other's bodies. Aphrodite moved down her body, insatiable for the taste of her, suckling her every curve. She inspected the softness of her thighs, and discovered the warmth in between.

At the slightest touch, Medusa's back arched and she bit her lip against the pleasure. She throbbed and pulsed until her entire body trembled. Aphrodite came beside her, touching her, loving her. She kissed her slowly and passionately, penetrating her body as gently as she penetrated her mouth.

Medusa felt the tension rise until she broke away from the kiss, moaning and gasping. Pressing her thighs together, she burst from the inside, crying out. She threw her arms around Aphrodite and kissed her. Rolling over her, she ran her hands all over her body, making up for two long years lost.

Medusa knelt between her legs, her hair caressing her, softly tickling her skin. Trailing her hand over her stomach, she rested her head between her thighs, and stroked the silky red curls there. Medusa kissed her softly and was rewarded with a shaky pant. She held her hips and pulled Aphrodite to her, kissing her deeply. Aphrodite stroked her hair and held her there, never wanting her to leave. In a quivering explosion, she finally found the oblivion of ecstasy she had been looking for.

They laid together in a drowsy tangle, legs and arms entwined, enjoying unhurried kisses and soft touches. They talked in hushed tones and stifled giggles, like two children up past their bedtime. Medusa once more resembled the young lady Aphrodite remembered.

Still, she couldn't deny the woman she was today. A vibrant, passionate woman whose enthusiasm had brought Aphrodite countless pleasures that night. She looked at Medusa drifting off and smiled. She really did love the little darling. No matter what it took, she would do anything to keep her safe.

Though she had no idea how.

They had been there for several hours. No doubt they had been missed. Oh well, there was nothing that could be done about it now. They were on the cusp of a battle; she might as well be ready for it. She kissed Medusa softly on the lips, careful not to wake her. Laying her head down, she closed her eyes and let herself float away. She was not ready to come down off of her sensual cloud. The battle would have to wait.

BEAUTY IN BLISS

Aphrodite made her way to the Great Hall, to find that many of the guests were still enjoying themselves, all except Athena. She was present, but was most certainly not enjoying herself. She noticed Aphrodite as soon as she entered.

Handling this situation was going to be a task. Athena had always been competitive, and very possessive. Medusa was her crowning jewel, her most precious trophy and, as such, was guarded jealously. Athena had very little personal interest in Medusa; save from the fact the little dear worshipped her unconditionally. As always, whenever Aphrodite thought of this problem, she came to the same dilemma.

Athena didn't care, but Athena didn't share.

None of that mattered. Athena posed no threat to her. They wanted very different things from Medusa. It was Poseidon who was the problem. For Medusa's sake, they would have to reach some sort of compromise.

She approached Athena cautiously, and as nonchalantly as possible.

"And *where* have you been?" Athena queried.

"I've been thinking. And I think we need to talk about Medusa,"

Aphrodite responded.

Athena raised an eyebrow at her. "Why is Medusa any of your concern?" she asked haughtily.

Aphrodite had to bite her tongue against the remark that begged to leave her lips. "Poseidon shows an unhealthy interest in her…," she began.

"No, Ditie! I believe it is ***you*** who shows an unhealthy interest in her. I know how to secure what is mine. And I also know how to handle my uncle," she hissed. Without another word, she stalked off.

Medusa awoke and stretched her aching muscles. Smiling drowsily, she reached over, feeling nothing. Sitting up, she focused on the room, and discovered she was alone. She wondered how long she had been asleep, and what time it was. It was still dark outside. She looked around, and found a dressing robe. Putting it on, she tiptoed out of the room.

Sneaking past the Great Hall, she noticed there was still a fair amount of people partying. Quickly, she made her way to the courtyard. Once there, she began to breathe easier. She grabbed a pitcher of wine from a nearby table and headed to see Erich.

One thing that would never change, was how she felt every time she laid her eyes on that fountain. So many memories and emotions bubbled forth from this place. She smiled as her mind took her on a journey throughout the years.

Finally, running over to the fountain, she ducked down beside it and slowly slipped her hand in the water. This was Erich's favorite game. Mere seconds had passed, before she felt the familiar coiling around her arm. Rising, she began to lift Erich out of the water.

"You're getting faster," she giggled. "… and **bigger**! Oh my, look how you've grown, my love."

She uncoiled him from her arm and placed him back in the fountain. Lifting the folds of her robe, she stepped into the fountain. She sat on the side and could hardly believe her eyes. Her little Erichthonius, now full grown, moved swiftly and adeptly in the water, coming to a stop at her ankles.

"Come then, let's have a look at you."

Erich reared up then, slowly rising from the water. With an affectionate hiss, he lowered back into the water, to wind around Medusa's leg, and come to rest his head in her lap. She stroked him gently and began to hum, sipping at the wine, and feeling utterly at peace.

"Uh…Me-Medusa?" spoke a deep voice.

She gasped as she turned to face the stranger shyly approaching her. She gave him a friendly smile. "Yes?" she said warmly. "Wo… Would you mmm-mind if I joined y-you?"

Medusa cocked her head. "Not at all." She patted the space next to her. She tried to place his face, but it wasn't familiar to her. She didn't know him. But he obviously knew her. "I'm sorry, but I'm afraid your name escapes me."

He smiled and shook his head. "We've n-n-never m-met. I'm Glaucus, sss-ss-son of M-Minos and P-P-P-Pasiphaë." He ended on a sort of shout. Glaucus never hated his stutter any more than at this moment. He had spent all night practicing, and had been able to make it through several flawless recitations. Now, here, in front of her, he sounded like a stammering fool.

Medusa held her hand out to him. "It's very nice to meet you Glaucus."

He took her hand and exhaled in relief. She didn't berate his speech but, instead, smiled fondly at him. Glaucus really wished he'd had more time to prepare, but it was such a shock to see her again.

He would never forget the first time he saw her walk, or rather fall, into the Great Hall. He thought she was the most beautiful woman he'd ever seen, but did not have the courage to approach her. Plus, she was favored of the Gods, which was always a reason to tread lightly. He had visited Olympus several times since that day, but had not seen her since. Then, suddenly, she was there. He knew, it was now or never.

"I rem-mmm-ember you. Two years ag-g-go. I th-thhhh-ink you're sssss-ss-so……sorry." He frowned deeply.

Medusa gasped dramatically. "You think… I'm sorry?"

He groaned in frustration.

Laughing, she shushed him. "I'm only kidding. It's okay. Speak slowly… very, very slowly."

He took a deep breath and enunciated. "I… think… you're… ssss-so… beautiful. Mmm-more beautiful than any gggg-gggoddess."

She blushed prettily. "Why thank you, Glaucus. And…" A small giggle escaped. "I really like the way you talk."

He smiled proudly then, and sat a little straighter. "Mmm-my mmm-mmmm-mothhh-ther said I d-d-died in honey. Shhhhhsh-she said the honey st-st-sticks my tongue." He was quiet for a few moments, then quietly added, "Y-yyy-your hair remmm-mmminds me of honey."

Medusa stroked Erich's head slowly. "How is it we've never met Glaucus? You obviously know me. I do not remember you at all."

"I d-d-do nnn-not speak mm-mmm-much," he shrugged.

Medusa looked past him and saw Aphrodite leaning casually against a nearby tree. She waved and winked, before dipping back into the trees. Grabbing the pitcher of wine, she slipped Erich back into the water.

"Well, you are always welcome to speak to me. I'm very glad we met, Glaucus. I have to go now, but I will see you again." She went to leave.

Seeing his opportunity slip away, his heart pounded as he called after her.

"Mmmm-mmm-mmmeddd-ddd…," he stammered.

Looking back, she stroked his cheek. She knew how hard it must be for him. The Gods rarely had any tolerance for imperfections. He spoke much better when he spoke slowly, but he was likely too embarrassed to ever speak as slowly as he needed to. The more he stammered, the more frustrated he became. The more frustrated he became, well, the more he stammered. It was a vicious cycle.

He was very sweet and quite handsome. He had soft blue eyes that were very open and inviting. His dark hair brushed his narrow shoulders, and his mouth was full and blushed. She assumed their ages were close, though he looked very young, almost boyish. She enjoyed his company very much.

"We will talk again soon, I promise you." She turned to walk away, and then stopped. "And from now on," she flicked a strand of her hair, "… you can just call me Honey. Is that easier?"

Smiling, he nodded furiously. She gave him a final wave and followed the path Aphrodite had taken. She ran breathlessly, wondering where she was, until finally she came across a small opening in the trees. There was her Goddess, beautiful and naked, lying in a pool. It reminded her of the night they first met. She unknotted the belt of her robe and let it fall to the ground. Carrying the pitcher of wine, she set it on a rock on the edge of the pool, and went to join

Aphrodite.

Glaucus sighed and lay down on the side of the fountain. Dipping his hand into the water, he felt Erich slide under his fingers. He let his mind wander with thoughts and fantasies of Medusa, the latter causing his body to tighten and throb. Nearby footsteps jerked him to the present.

Athena burst around the tree and stopped when she saw Glaucus. She put on a mask of regal indifference.

He scrambled into a hasty bow. "Oh! Evening, Mmm-mmmmmy Lady."

Athena smiled generically. "I didn't mean to frighten you. I expected I would find the Goddess Aphrodite. You haven't seen her by any chance, have you? Or perhaps a young lady with sunrise hair?"

Glaucus took a calming breath and spoke slowly. "I have not sss-ss-seen the God-ddess Aphrodite, but Hon… the lady Mmm-mm…med-duss-sssa went fff-farther into the yard… that way."

Athena looked at him oddly. There was obviously something wrong with that boy. Inclining her head, she took off in the way he indicated. This was actually going to be perfect. She'd been enduring Aphrodisia long enough. She tired of everyone fawning over Aphrodite, not to mention her nerve in summoning Medusa here. She'd always coveted Medusa's worship. As she quickened her stride, a genuine smile lit across her face. Wherever Aphrodite was, Athena would finally get some time alone with Medusa.

BEAUTY BETRAYED

Aphrodite and Medusa splashed around in the pool like children. When they had their fill of playing, they laid on the large rock at the pool's edge. With their hands joined, they let the night air dry their bodies.

"So, your new friend is very handsome. I daresay I will be replaced within the week," Aphrodite teased.

Medusa looked aghast. "How can you say that? You know I've always loved you. I could never love another. I definitely couldn't…" She shook her head against the thought.

"I love you too, my darling Medusa." Squeezing her hand, she continued sadly, "But, a love like ours is not meant to last."

"What? But, why?" she whimpered.

Aphrodite smiled at her naivety. She had grown, but still had very much to learn. "So it goes with Gods and mortals. By our very natures, we are bound to take each other for granted, and I would see it end, before that ever happens… but, whether by death, or disappointment, a time will come, when we will part."

Medusa frowned, trying to wrap her mind around the concept.

"Oh don't fret, my love. We will live, and we will love more times than either of us will have thought possible. And, right now, we are alive…" Aphrodite propped herself on one arm and looked down at Medusa. Stroking her stomach softly, she smiled at the shiver it caused. She lifted the pitcher, and poured a tiny bit of wine into the indention of her belly.

"And, right now, we love each other." Leaning over her, she sipped the wine from her, and laved her stomach, kissing her ribs softly. "You make the wine taste better," she whispered.

Medusa moaned quietly, and all thoughts of separations drifted from her mind.

"So now, my dear. Tell me of your new friend."

Medusa's mind cleared slowly. "Oh, you mean Glaucus? Well, I don't really know him. You see, I just met him tonight."

Aphrodite smiled. "Well he is cert…ttt…ttainly hhh…hhh-hand…sss…sssome," she mocked.

Medusa gasped. "Oh, Ditie, don't make fun! I like the way he talks."

Aphrodite kissed the little pout from her face. It was nice to see her happy once again. "I'm only joking, my love. He seems like a very nice young man. And he is very handsome."

Medusa shrugged. "I suppose he is."

"And he *certainly* seemed taken with you…," she teased.

Medusa blushed. "Well, he did say I was beautiful," she continued shyly, "more beautiful than any goddess, even."

Sitting up abruptly, Aphrodite gasped in mock affront. "How **dare** he!…"

Grabbing the pitcher, Medusa knelt between her knees. "Shall I make amends, My Lady?"

Athena's patience was running thin. She wanted to surprise Medusa, but it looked like she would never find the chit. Up ahead, she heard bits of a conversation. It seemed Medusa wasn't alone after all. Finally, she came to a break in the trees.

What she saw, made her blood boil. Aphrodite was perched on a rock, with Medusa kneeling before her. They were both naked, and they were *kissing*. Just when she thought she might be sick, they pulled away from each other.

Aphrodite grabbed a fistful of Medusa's hair. "So, you are more beautiful than any goddess, are you?"

Medusa looked at her defiantly. "Yes, I am."

Aphrodite stroked the side of her breast. "More beautiful than me?" She gave her nipple a squeeze.

"Yes, I am," she growled.

Aphrodite slowly brushed her lips across Medusa's mouth. "More beautiful than your precious Athena?"

"Yes, I am," she breathed.

Aphrodite released her and leaned back. "So, am I to assume that you will no longer be content to worship at my feet?" she teased.

Medusa lifted the pitcher, and poured wine over her chest. "My Lady, I worship at the tips of your breasts."

They laughed together, neither noticing the thunder rumbling overhead.

Athena stormed back to the castle in a rage. Aphrodite had stolen what was rightfully hers. And now, her most prize possession was tainted. *Did her jealousy know no bounds?* Aphrodite had seduced her, and turned her into an immodest creature, a slave to decadence. Athena would make her pay, no matter what it took. As for Medusa, she would no longer be able to stand the sight of her. Her very presence was an insult. She would have to leave at once!

Medusa and Aphrodite strolled into the palace some time later. As soon as they entered the great hall, Medusa began to look around. She was hoping to see Glaucus, thinking that he really was a very pleasant boy. She spotted him over in a corner, off to himself. No wonder she hadn't met him before. With a wink for Aphrodite, she began to walk towards him. A bright smile lit his face as she neared. She blushed and before she could speak, a bellow caught her attention.

"Medusa!"

Confused by the harsh tone of Athena's voice, she immediately sought out the Goddess.

"…Yes, My Lady?" Medusa approached the center of the room cautiously. She didn't quite understand the thunderous expression on Athena's face.

"It is time for you to return to your home," Athena responded with no emotion.

"My Lady?"

Poseidon did not know what was happening, but he could not allow Medusa to be taken from him so quickly.

"Here now, Athena! The festival would not be the same without Medusa. Surely, she doesn't need to return home ***right*** now."

Athena barely spared him a glance, and continued to glare daggers at Medusa. "Indeed she does, *Uncle.* And the decision is final."

Glaucus made his way to Medusa's side. His concern for her outweighed his need to blend into the shadows. She looked completely desolated and his heart went out to her. Aphrodite took one look at Medusa's wounded face and became enraged. Storming up to Athena, she let the full force of her fury show.

"Medusa is **my** guest for **my** festival. You have no right…"

Athena looked at her haughtily and lowered her voice. "She will go home……… or she will go to Hades. Either way, she will go there ***now***." She smiled deviously as Aphrodite deflated.

Aphrodite had no doubt that she meant it. If she didn't get her way, she would kill Medusa without thinking twice. This was getting way out of hand. All she wanted was Medusa safely away.

"Medusa, I think it would be a good idea for you to return home," Aphrodite sighed.

Medusa found it hard to breathe and a stray tear rolled down her cheek. "But…Ditie…"

Athena narrowed her eyes at the endearment. "You will leave Mount Olympus, **now**," she ground out.

Medusa stood staring dazedly. All around her she could hear confused whispering and uneasy shuffling. Then, she felt an arm around her shoulder. Glaucus began to move her. "Come Honey… I'll sss-ss-see you home," he whispered.

Finally, her feet began to move. She turned to glance at Aphrodite, but the Goddess would not meet her eyes. She felt as if everything around her was moving slowly. Her chest ached and her eyes burned, and only one thing blazed through her mind. ***Why?***

Once outside the great hall, she sank against Glaucus. He supported her easily, and she discovered he was obviously stronger than he looked. Suddenly, she noticed she was trembling. "I don't understand any of this…"

He embraced her and placed a kiss on her forehead. "Let mmmmm-me help you g-g-g-get your thhhh-thhh-things."

"No! I just want to get out of here. I have to get out of here. Let's just go."

Glaucus didn't argue. He just followed after her.

Aphrodite was livid. She would have to straighten out all of this once and for all but, first, she would see Medusa safely off of Olympus. If Athena wanted a war, she would get one. Striding purposefully through the halls, she ran into Peitho on the way to Medusa's chamber.

"Is she packing, Peitho?"

Peitho was instantly confused. "Packing, My Lady?"

"Yes. Medusa. Is she packing?"

"I have not seen the lady Medusa…"

Aphrodite slammed the door open to Medusa's room. Everything was still there, everything in its place. Everything… except Medusa.

Aphrodite paced worriedly, and a flash caught her eye. On a nearby table, sat a jeweled pomegranate embraced by a golden serpent. Picking it up, Aphrodite held it tightly and sighed.

BEAUTY VIOLATED

Medusa's hand went to her neck in an unconscious gesture. She frowned and sighed as her memory sharpened. Watching her, Glaucus put a hand on her shoulder.

"Sss-ss-sssomething wrong Honey?"

She shook her head sadly. "I left my necklace."

"D-ddd-do you want t-t-to go b-b-back?"

"No. I just want this night to be over."

Glaucus slid closer to her and took her hand. Medusa laid her head on his shoulder and let herself drift away.

Aphrodite could barely see, as rage clouded her vision. "You had no right," she growled.

"Neither did you… *darling* Ditie."

"What are you talking about?"

"You just couldn't accept defeat, could you? I've always ignored your immodest ways, but when you poach what is mine…"

Aphrodite's face softened. "Athena, I had no idea you desired her…"

"…Desired her?! I am not burdened with such trivialities. The war was fairly won… the spoils were mine," she continued haughtily. "You seduced her into your service, so I spared her my wrath. Such a display is beneath me, anyway. Be grateful, Aphrodite; for her and for yourself." Athena whirled away in righteous piety.

Out in the hall, a look of pure ecstasy passed over Poseidon's face. Athena would no longer stand in his way, and Aphrodite could not possibly leave her own festival. He knew this was his chance, that all of his waiting was finally over.

He knew exactly where she would be going.

Medusa opened her eyes and immediately cringed at the sun. She had been crying all through the night, and her eyes were sore and reddened.

"Have we reached Athens?"

Glaucus stroked her cheek. "Yes, we've j-j-just arrived. I fff-ffffigure we can sss-stop for a night…"

"I have to go to the temple. I must speak with her."

Glaucus sighed. "Honey, you need pp-pp-proper rest. You need fff-ff-food, a bbb-bb-bath!"

Medusa nodded. "I know, but, please understand that I don't understand what happened. If I did offend My Lady, I must beg forgiveness. Take me to the temple, and you go and get lodging for the night. Once I've made my prayers, I will come, I promise."

Glaucus looked at her, skeptically.

"And… If I have not returned in an hour, you may come and drag me away." She smiled reassuringly.

Glaucus chuckled and nodded at her. He tried to ignore how his heart pounded at the mere thought of time alone with her. Maybe he could find a way to tell her how special he felt she was. Maybe…

He couldn't think that far ahead. If he got himself too excited, he wouldn't be able to string a sentence together.

"One hour," he reminded.

Poseidon strolled through the temple, excitement thrumming through every fiber of his being. All of his patience would finally be rewarded. Ever the hunter, he knew the moment his prey arrived.

Running into the temple, Medusa was so absorbed, she failed to notice the absence of priests, or any life other than hers. She fell to her knees in front of the great statue of Athena and looked at her idol.

There she stood, tall and proud, spear and shield in hand.

I praise you, Athena, great goddess born of your own.
Most chaste and honorable of all maids,
loving defender and heroine of my existence.

Bless me again with the strength of your arm,
Bestow, once more, the power of your majesty.
Unfailing, in mind and eye, I desire to remain in your sight.
Skilled, in craft and deed, I beg to be stitched on your heart.
Strong one, I ask for your forgiveness;
For your favor once again.
I am your humble servant.

Medusa immediately felt her heart break and she wept, brokenly.

As she pad through the courtyard, Athena heard Medusa's voice faintly. She felt a swell of pride that Medusa had not been gone a full day before she was begging at her feet. The prayer wrapped around her as she dipped her hand into the fountain.

She let her mind go back to the night a young girl had looked at her with admiration and love, and had made her feel admired… and loved. Picking up Erichthonius, she made her way out of the courtyard. Maybe Medusa was not completely lost. And wouldn't it be a coup to have defeated Aphrodite not once, but twice.

"My Lady, I beg your forgiveness. Please tell me how I've offended you. Allow me to make amends." She was whispering fervently when she heard someone behind her.

"Oh my poor darling, I came as soon as I could," Poseidon said smoothly. He opened his arms to her.

Sinking into his arms, she allowed him to embrace her, as the sobs wracked her body. "Oh My Lord, I do not understand. I swear I would never knowingly offend My Lady."

"I know my sweet, I know." He cradled her tightly, enjoying the feel of her soft, supple body against his. Distracted, he stroked her hair, loving the silky texture of each curl, admiring how the light reflected each drop of honey. Softly he whispered, "I will speak to her for you, all will be well."

Medusa looked up at him in pure gratitude through a veil of tears. She let out a relieved sigh and wrapped her arms around him fully, squeezing him tightly. "Oh, thank you My Lord! You cannot know what this means to me."

Poseidon instantly hardened. Caressing her back, he dipped lower, to pull her nearer. He placed a kiss at her temple, then her cheek. Her hands fell away, and she moved to end the embrace. Poseidon held her tightly, placing another kiss on her neck.

"My Lord, please."

"Yes, my love." Poseidon took her mouth in a passionate kiss, grasping her beautiful hair in his hand.

"No…" Turning her face away, she tried to figure a way out. She pressed against his chest and tried to back away.

Poseidon was deaf to all but his body's need for the golden haired beauty in his arms. He'd wanted her for so long, and he would finally have her. Poseidon lifted her off of her feet, his arms wrapped around her waist, kissing her chest, down to her breasts.

Medusa began to fight in earnest, not that it did any good. Everything about this felt wrong. She pushed and clawed at his shoulders, which only seemed to enflame him further. He took her down to the floor, landing heavily on top of her. She tried to scramble backwards, but he held her hips firmly, as he tore at her gown to reveal her breasts.

"Perfection...," he sighed.

She looked up and they were at the feet of Athena's statue. She silently asked the Goddess for help, not sure she could hear her, not sure she would listen. Tears blurred her vision when she felt the hem of her gown edge up around her thighs.

"Please don't, My Lord. I beg you," she whimpered. She grabbed his wrists and tried to force him away.

He raised her arms above her head and held them there. "Shhh. Don't be nervous, my beauty."

She had not known she was inviting this when she embraced him. She had just been so grateful that he would help her. Medusa cried out in pain as he entered her. She didn't mean for this to happen. She hadn't wanted any of this.

"Ohhh, you were untried, my love. It will not hurt the next time, I promise."

Medusa shut her eyes as he thrust into her again and again. She left her body through her mind. She thought of home, of Eurynome. She thought of swimming and Aphrodite. She thought of herself sharing a meal with Glaucus.

She did not hear Poseidon's moans.

She did not feel him bury his face in her glorious hair.

She did not see... when Athena arrived.

BEAUTY'S CURSE

Athena took in the scene before her and, dropping Erichthonius, immediately shielded her eyes. She panted in rage, just as Poseidon was panting in lust. She had been ready to show Medusa mercy, thinking she had been seduced by Aphrodite's legendary charms, but here she finds her, mating like a common animal, with her uncle, desecrating her most sacred of places. She had no concept of devotion and loyalty. She had no concept of love.

While Poseidon hoarsely groaned his release, Athena felt the bile rise in her throat. He praised everything about Medusa, nothing more so than her hair. He spoke of how every time he looked at her, his body hardened to stone. All of this, in her sacred temple. Medusa would pay for this affront, and she would pay eternally, for death was far too lenient.

Poseidon smiled down at Medusa's still form, at the blood that stained her thighs. She would be his most prized possession, his perfect virgin sacrifice. He would lament the day her beauty faded.

Athena's scream made the walls tremble. She faced them with fire in her eyes. "You **dare** defile my temple?!"

Medusa crawled hastily to her, attempting to cover herself. "My Lady…"

Athena yanked her by her hair, and wrapped her hand around her throat. She put her face close to Medusa's. "You do not address me, Whore!" she hissed, tossing Medusa down to the ground.

Sobbing in earnest, Medusa shook her head, trying to explain through her gasps.

Poseidon, bored with Athena's dramatics, decided to try a bargain. "Give her to me Athena. You won Athens, you won your temple. You even won Medusa. We all know you are the best. You obviously did not want her, so I have every right to claim her."

Athena glared at him. "I would send you to Hades if I could. Be warned though, I shall not forget this, *Uncle*." She turned to Medusa then. "And as for your harlot, she has been a serpent in our midst from the very beginning, and she will suffer like no one else."

Medusa felt as if she couldn't breathe. "Please…," she begged.

"This is my word," she pointed to Medusa. "Be as your mother, until to her womb you're returned. Let man never behold you, lest his body to stone be turned. Live in shame and misery, and in dank shelters make your home." She narrowed her eyes. "…And your crowning glory, forever, be the viper you've become."

Medusa was assaulted by agony. She tried to run, but her legs would not part. The skin between them seamed, and fused. Scales began to cover her skin and her nails grew long, and hardened to sharp points.

Suddenly, a searing pain seemed to split her head. She screamed loudly as her hair fell away from her head, and angry vipers tore through her scalp. The snakes began to strike at her shoulders and face, hissing ferociously. She clawed at them, ripping them apart, only to have them replaced.

Medusa dragged herself over to the base of Athena's statue, cowering. She covered her face with her hands and begged for the painful bites to cease. Her eyes began to sting, and without warning, a bright light burst out from them, sending the snakes shrieking. As her vision cleared, the world looked different.

The snakes, enraged, reared in unison, poised to strike. A deep hiss halted their attack, and Medusa looked up, into the eyes of Erichthonius. He was reared up, at the feet of Athena's statue, in defense of his master, before his body became stone.

"No!" Medusa cried.

Athena felt her heartsick cry down to her toes. "Get out of my sight," she whispered shakily. "To Crete with you!" she shouted and vanished.

"Damn you, Athena!" Poseidon bellowed. He looked sadly at what Medusa had become. As she disappeared, he picked up a lock of her fallen hair, and left the temple.

Glaucus looked at the spread with satisfaction. He didn't know what Medusa's favorite foods were, so he tried to get a wide variety. He wanted to learn everything about her. He had been practicing what he would say to her, and was confident he could get through a fair amount of it without stuttering. Too excited to do anything else, he decided to go to the temple to meet her.

Aphrodite paced the Great Hall. *Fine time for everyone to disappear.* Just as she was going to turn, she saw Poseidon stride past, purposefully.

"Poseidon!" she ran after him. "Where is she?"

"Where is who?" he asked cautiously.

"Why, Ath.." She saw the strand of hair before he could tuck it away completely. Her breath rushed out in a whoosh and she stared up at him in shock. "What…did you DO?!"

Poseidon backed away from her. "Not me… Athena."

Aphrodite covered her mouth with her hands and tried to shake the thoughts out of her head. "Where is she? Where is Medusa."

"…Crete," he answered.

Aphrodite let out a relieved sigh. *She's still alive.* Her joy turned to hatred and she glared at him. "I'll kill her."

Poseidon walked past her to head for his chariot. "You won't have to."

Glaucus approached the temple, and was uneasy by how eerily quiet it was. He didn't see any priests… he didn't see anyone.

"Honey?" he called out. Walking through, his pace increased, as did his worry. "Mmm-mmm-mmedusa!" His voice echoed back to him. Maybe, she had left earlier. Maybe, he had just missed her. Still, something felt very wrong. He approached the great statue of Athena and paced back and forth, thinking of his next move.

He glanced up and stopped in his tracks. Stepping closer, he frowned in confusion. There was something different. He hadn't remembered the serpent before. He tilted his head back and forth. It couldn't be.

"Is that…"

Poseidon's chariot sliced through the water like a blade. No speed was fast enough to satisfy him. He had to get to his destination as quickly as possible. Athena needed to pay for her insolence.

Just as soon as he had his desire firmly in hand, she took it away. He arrived in the dark, murky depths and awaited the familiar rumble. With a deep bow, he let the urgency show on his face. "Phorcys. I need to speak with you and Ceto. It concerns Medusa."

Medusa half slithered along the bank. Unused to her new body, she floundered clumsily, relying heavily on her arms. A nearby scream frightened her.

"A… GORGON!" someone shouted. More shouts came from everywhere, seeming to surround her. Something came rapidly towards her. Without thought she looked up, and the man that was standing over her, froze in mid-strike. She turned away and closed her eyes, but she already knew his fate.

"Kill it!"

Medusa curled up and awaited death, hoping it came swiftly. The angry voices crept in closer… and the serpents in her head hissed…

"Get away from her!"

Medusa would never forget how Aphrodite's voice sounded, and nearly wept with the beauty of it. A collective gasp sounded all around her as everyone fell to their knees.

Aphrodite knelt down and looked softly at the wounded creature at her feet. Medusa had yet to meet her gaze. She tried to raise Medusa's chin. Medusa turned away, keeping her gaze on the ground. "Don't, you'll turn to stone."

Aphrodite smiled gently. "You cannot harm me, darling. Look at me." Medusa raised her eye, still wet with tears and beheld her Goddess.

"Oh, my love. What has she done to you?" Taking Medusa in her arms, they both vanished to a far-off cave, away from the threats, away from the pain.

The onlookers all stared stunned at their disappearance. Then, there was a tremble, and a loud roar shook the ground around them, as out of the sea climbed a giant, golden monster.

BEAUTY RESTORED

Medusa lie coiled, and still, on the cave floor. Face down, in the rock and dust, silently, she prayed for death.

"Tell me what happened, darling," Aphrodite said gently.

Medusa was so motionless, Aphrodite did not think she would speak.

"I could not bear her displeasure. I did not understand her fury, so I went to her temple. I offered and prayed, but she didn't come to me… *he* came to me."

Aphrodite felt the blood drain from her heart. "Who?… who came to you?"

"He was going to make it all better. I didn't know… I was just… so thankful… it was my fault… I shouldn't have embraced him… ," she ended on a sob.

Aphrodite closed her eyes against the sickening rage that threatened to overtake her. "Poseidon…" she whispered.

"Right there, in her temple… I didn't mean for it, I swear. Now look at me… look at what I did to that poor man."

Aphrodite swallowed down the rising bile and took Medusa's face in her hand. "Darling, it's not your fault… none of it."

Medusa shook her head. "Then why is this happening to me?"

"… Because we all wanted you. Because you could find no fault in the Gods… could not fathom us as jealous and self-serving. … Because you loved me."

"I am hated for love, and cursed for a blessing… hated for love, cursed…" Medusa weakly murmured.

"Not for long, my love. Now, tell me *exactly* what Athena said to you.

Athena sat in silence, staring off into nothingness. She tried to understand what she was feeling, but so many emotions coursed through her.

Suddenly, she was assaulted by voices. An endless number of cries seemed to fill the chamber. She jumped up and ran through the halls, but they followed her. Cries of pain… of fear. Covering her ears, she nearly fell to her knees, when Zeus burst into the room.

"What has happened?!" he shouted.

Athena let out a relieved sigh. "You can hear them too?"

"Of course I can hear them; there is mass panic in the streets! All I can gather from them, is there is a monster of sorts threatening to destroy everything. Come daughter, we go to Crete."

Athena visibly paled. "… To Crete?"

Be as your mother until to her womb you're returned.

Let man never behold you lest his body to stone be turned.
Live in shame and misery and in dank shelters make your home.
And your crowning glory forever, be the viper you've become.

Medusa would never forget those words as long as she lived. Aphrodite puzzled through them, not seeing any release for Medusa. She would not give up, though, no matter what she had to do.

Stopping, Aphrodite looked around, a frown knotting her brow. Something was wrong. "Stay here, darling. I promise, I'll return soon."

Zeus arrived in Crete with Athena at his side. His jaw tightened at the amount of destruction he saw. He did not know who, or what, was responsible, but they would be in the hands of Hades by day's end. Turning towards a fresh wave of screams, confusion marred his face.

"…Ceto?" he breathed.

Athena gasped quietly. *Ceto?! Oh no*, she thought.

Zeus walked, purposefully, into the melee. He didn't know what could have happened for Ceto to attack his city, but he could not allow it to continue.

"Ceto, Stop This!" he shouted.

Zeus looked into pale, green eyes, blazing with fury. As Ceto took notice of Zeus, they tilted in despair.

"Give it back," she cried.

"Give **what** back, Mighty Ceto? What do I have?"

Athena felt her pulse race. She had to figure a way out of this situation. As she stepped forward, Aphrodite called out her name, and Ceto took notice of her for the first time.

Eyes narrowing, she let out a piercing roar and rushed towards them. Charging past Zeus, the only thought in her mind was to crush Athena's head in her mighty claws.

Ceto snatched up Athena and headed towards the sea. Zeus chased after them, sending bolts of thunder raining down on Ceto. Athena also raged against the beast, eventually earning her release. Father and daughter worked together to back the monster into the sea.

Despite enduring blow after crushing blow, Ceto would not give up her endeavor to rip Athena to shreds. She weakened, buckled, and finally fell into the sea. Laying there, her breathing labored, she lamented her failure to her child.

Zeus clenched a white-hot thunderbolt, and raised it, poised to strike. Suddenly, Aphrodite caught his eye. Stepping out across the water, she approached Ceto.

"Aphrodite, leave her!" Zeus shouted.

Ceto flinched at her approach, too weary to strike out.

"Mighty Ceto…," she began, "I know, and love your daughter, and I will keep her safe, with your help."

Strike her, father. What are you waiting for?" Athena panted.

"She is weak and defeated, daughter. The life of an ancient is not to be taken lightly."

"She will not stop, father. We both know this," she reasoned.

Open yourself to me, Mighty Ceto. I swear to you I will care for her throughout her days," Aphrodite crooned.

With a shriek, Ceto's skin began to split and spread.

Bursting through the waves, Poseidon scooped up Aphrodite and sped away on his chariot. Her screams of protest echoed to the horizon.

"Strike, father! Now!" Athena shouted.

With one final blow, Zeus ended Ceto's life. Her body began to seam itself, until her scales hardened, dense and rock-like.

As they neared the shore, Aphrodite was jerked back to reality by the cheers of the citizens of Crete. The four of them gathered there, silent slaves to their own thoughts. Zeus was the most pensive of them all.

Aphrodite broke the silence. "She was defeated, she was no longer a threat."

A pained look passed over Zeus's face. "We cannot know that."

Aphrodite looked between Athena and Poseidon. "And, I suppose we never will."

Thunder rumbled overhead, and Zeus vanished back to Olympus. The trio looked at each other as the sun set, each glance speaking volumes.

As the sky streaked blood red and plum, once again, it was

Aphrodite who refused to stand silent. "Is there no length to which you will not go?" she asked.

Athena raised her chin defiantly. "It is done now. It is over."

Aphrodite laughed bitterly. "It is far from over. What do you think Zeus would say to what you did to Medusa, Athena? Or to you sending Ceto here bent on destruction, Poseidon?"

Athena pushed Poseidon roughly. "**You** sent her here?!"

Poseidon grabbed her wrist and squeezed. "I merely told her what you did to her daughter."

Aphrodite drew back and slapped him across his face. "Did you tell her what **you** did to her daughter?"

"Enough!" Poseidon yelled. "As we've said, it is done now."

Aphrodite let a devious smile light up her face. "True. It is done. Medusa is cursed, Ceto is dead, and we are all saved…for now. "I cannot end either of you, for believe me, if I could, your bodies would join Ceto's." Aphrodite moved to walk away. "Remember though, darlings. The one thing unavoidable by man and God alike is fate."

She stopped and turned to Poseidon. "I pray Zeus never learns the truth of what happened here." Reaching out, she stroked his cheek. "Even more, I pray Phorcys is not overly grieved about his wife's death."

She faced Athena next. "And as for you, beauty cannot be given, or taken away, not by you. Through all your trying, you destroyed nothing, and only accomplished one thing."

She took Athena's face in both her hands. "Beauty and love, the only things you've ever wanted. These are mine to give, and these, you shall be **forever** denied." She pressed a rough kiss on Athena's frozen lips, before pushing her face away.

With a wink for both of them, she vanished on the wind.

Medusa tried to lie very still, afraid of angering her hair. The low hissing that began when Aphrodite left, was starting to increase. She had barely breathed when she felt Aphrodite's hand at her back.

"Come, my love. I'm taking you somewhere safe," she whispered.

When Medusa's vision cleared, she looked around. The walls around her seemed warm, oddly protective in a way. She closed her eyes and, for the first time that day, she felt at peace.

"Aphrodite, where are we?" she asked.

"Somewhere where you should feel safe," she answered, cryptically.

Aphrodite was torn as to how much to tell Medusa. The poor darling had been through so much that day. She just wanted to give her a little tranquility.

"I cannot undo everything that has been done to you, but I will do what I can."

Starting with her face, Aphrodite ran her hands all over Medusa. Inch by inch, her scales gave way to flawless skin. As they separated, she stretched her legs and moved around. She looked at the body she was used to, and her appreciation at that small bit of normalcy nearly moved her to tears.

"Thank you, Ditie," she smiled.

The night was quiet, as Aphrodite kissed each of the bite marks that marred Medusa's face and shoulders, watching them fade away. Holding Medusa's face in her hands, she sighed.

"I wish I could bring your beautiful hair back. I can, however, bring back an old friend."

She moved her hands up, grasping the serpents, massaging Medusa's scalp. Medusa felt a dull ache and groaned quietly. Aphrodite took a step back, looked at her finished product, and smiled. Intrigued, Medusa reached up to touch her head. A smooth, familiar body wrapped around her wrist. She closed her eyes in disbelief.

"Not Erichthonius," Aphrodite said sadly.

Aphrodite looked at her Medusa. Everything was as in place as she could manage. She looked at Medusa's eyes, no longer the narrow, slit eyes of a serpent. They were round and full, but still possessed an unearthly glow.

"Erichthonia may be more proper… they're female. I'm sorry, my love, but you will not be able to look at any mortal male, without him turning into stone."

"It's alright, Ditie. I can't imagine a man I would want to set my sights on," Medusa bitterly replied.

Aphrodite stroked her cheek tenderly. "What happened to you was wrong, Medusa. That is not the way it should have been, and it is not the way it will always be." Aphrodite hated to see one so young so jaded. She hated for anyone to place limits on love, even the ones whose love she wanted for her own.

Medusa pasted a cheerful smile on her face. "No matter. I am restored… as it were, and I'm grateful, and alive, and happy." Giggling, she spun around on the legs she had begun to miss.

"If I never laid eyes on another man, I would be only too happy."

THE SEARCH FOR BEAUTY

Glaucus looked up into the blinding sun. He could faintly make out the outline of the palace. He had finally made it. He was exhausted and sick with worry for Medusa. Already, more than two days had passed. He had searched Athens like a madman, and had no idea where she was. No one had seen her. It was as though she had simply vanished. He would need some help, and fast. He had to find her.

Medusa and Aphrodite flitted around like woodland nymphs. Before long, with much giggling, and largely part to Aphrodite's powers, they were able to turn the small opening into an intricate system of caves, and make them into a fairly inhabitable home.

Medusa leaned back on her newly created bed and sighed. She thought of how funny life was. She couldn't tell if time was standing still, or flying by. She had been cursed, her life would never be the same, would never travel the course she had laid out for herself, and yet she was overjoyed.

She was alive, relatively healthy and sheltered. She was loved and cared for, and that made everything right with the world.

Almost everything.

Medusa frowned. Looking at her newly made home, a frightening thought entered her mind.

This was her home.

She would never have a normal life again. She could never go home. She glanced at her enchanting Goddess. She could never go anywhere. She would take her curse with her wherever she went. She would hurt people, anywhere she ventured. People would fear her in every village. They would hate her and hurt her, just like on the beach. For the safety of herself and everyone else, she would have to stay in the protection of the caves. Suddenly very weary, she curled up on her side.

Aphrodite noticed the shift in her mood and came to lie beside her.

"What is wrong, my love?"

Medusa shook her head. "Nothing. Just very tired. The last few days… long days," she gave Aphrodite a wan smile.

Nodding, Aphrodite wrapped her arm around Medusa and held her tightly. "Of course, darling. You must be exhausted."

Medusa turned slightly, and placed a soft, warm kiss on her lips. "I thank you, My Lady, my love. For everything."

As she lay there, the serpents on her head rested in the curve of her neck. They were so docile and loving, just like her beloved Erich. Another gift given to her by her Goddess.

Sighing, she decided to focus on all she was given, and not what had been taken away. Before long, she decided not to focus on anything. The day, along with its trials, was quickly coming to an end, and tomorrow would provide its own.

Closing her eyes, she cleared her mind and deafened her ears. She heard the world as she did in her bath. She drifted on time and her spirit was carried everywhere, and nowhere. Faintly, she felt warmth engulf her body, and heard the gentle hum of a far-off lullaby. A golden glow filled her as the afternoon sun wrapped itself around her. She slept soundly like a babe, cradled by its mother.

The tension in the palace was palpable. Zeus had locked himself away for hours, seeing no one. Poseidon and Athena were visibly agitated. They were seen pacing and, often times, in the middle of a heated exchange.

"Where is she? Where has she been?" Poseidon puzzled.

"We've waited long enough. What is her game?" he growled.

"Fine question coming from you. This situation is your doing. You meant for Ceto to kill me, which she very nearly did!"

Poseidon narrowed his eyes at her. "**You** started this situation, poisoned by envy when you cursed Medusa. Ceto was well in her rights to kill you. I wish she had."

Athena stood toe to toe with him. "Why send an ancient to carry out your wishes? I am right here, *Uncle.* Why not dispatch me yourself?"

Poseidon grabbed her throat and squeezed. "This… is getting us nowhere." He punctuated the thought by applying more pressure.

She was determined not to show any fear, but she could not mask the audible gulp that escaped. "Agreed. We must figure out Aphrodite's plan."

"I know her plan. Her plan is to ruin us. If Zeus finds out Ceto's attack on Crete was my doing, he'll kill me. If he finds out my doing was your doing, he'll likely kill you. And if Phorcys finds out what we've done to his child, he'll kill us both."

Athena contemplated this for a moment. Finally, she sighed. "We must find Aphrodite… quickly."

Hidden in an alcove, Glaucus thought he would be sick. Cities attacked, Poseidon and Athena at each other's throats, the ancients? What had they done to his Honey? He wanted to rage out, demand they take him to her. With a strength he did not know he possessed, he wanted badly to kill them both.

The reality of the situation quickly hit him, and he realized there was nothing he could do to them. He did not even know everything that had happened. He didn't know if Medusa was dead or alive. There was only one thing he did know.

He had to find Aphrodite… quickly.

Aphrodite awoke and found herself alone. After a bit of searching, she found Medusa in a lower cavern, sitting by a large pool.

"Amazing…," she exclaimed. Aphrodite looked around and the glowing silver walls, bathed by the light of the moon coming through above openings. The area was surprisingly comforting and soft, despite being made completely of rock.

"I stumbled upon it, accidentally. I've never been in a more beautiful place," Medusa said, stroking her hair absently.

She had been up all night, her mind racing, until if finally drove her from her bed. She began exploring her new home. Each new passage she found, each hidden alcove, was familiar to her in some strange way. Every bone in her body shouted that this was her home. The more she thought about it, the more she knew she belonged here.

The more she thought about it, the more she knew Aphrodite didn't.

They hadn't discussed how long Aphrodite would stay, but Medusa noticed she made no moves to leave. She knew that she herself craved freedom, so how much more must a vibrant spirit, like Aphrodite, desperately wish to be elsewhere. This curse was hers to bear, no one else's.

She would have to let her go.

Aphrodite looked at Medusa cautiously. She had been melancholy earlier that afternoon, and it didn't seem to be coming to an end anytime soon. Sitting beside her, she lightly stroked her back.

"Tell me how I can make you happy, my love."

Medusa sighed, and turned to her. This was her chance. She would simply spit the words out, and be done with it. There was no more use holding onto Aphrodite as there is holding onto a burning, hot star. She would simply tell her.

"... Will you go... will you go to Eurynome. I do not want her to hear from someone else. I do not want her to worry."

She berated herself for her cowardice. Still, though her palms may forever bear the scars, she could not release her star just yet.

Aphrodite smiled brightly and patted her cheek. "Of course, my darling." She felt a renewed sense of purpose. She could do something to make Medusa smile. She supposed she should also see what the mood was on Olympus. As much as she hated to admit it, she was glad to have a break from the cave for a while. Turning back, she also admitted she would miss Medusa terribly.

Once Medusa was sure she was gone, she let out the breath she had been holding. Slipping slowly into the pool, she let the water envelope her. As she floated under the opening, and stared up at the stars, she remembered another night where she floated under the night sky. How different it was… how long ago.

Maybe she should've talked with Aphrodite, but she was feeling selfish. She'd lost so much in the last days, and she was not prepared to lose anything else right now. She floated, carefree, her eyes drifting closed, as she swayed to the sound of a faint humming.

Glaucus, once again, looked up from the base of Mount Olympus. He couldn't tell if the sun was rising or setting. He couldn't remember when he last slept, or the last time he ate. All he could think of was how long it had been since he'd seen her. He rubbed his eyes, and took a fortifying breath. He had no idea where she was, but he did know where they had been heading, and that was as good a place as any to start.

Aphrodite materialized in Medusa's home, in her room. She smiled as she looked around the neat room. There was no doubt in her mind that this was Medusa's room. The more she explored, the more her mind worked, until she got a wonderful idea.

Eurynome sat in the courtyard, enjoying the morning. As she often did these days, she kept an eye on the road. She experienced the strangest dreams as she slept and, more often, nagging feelings of dread had plagued her while she was awake. She hated how the Gods could just come and whisk her away like that. She would be much happier once Medusa was safe at home again.

"Greetings Eurynome," a smooth voice said.

Eurynome closed her eyes as her heart sank. She sighed in resignation. She knew what went on between mortals and Gods. Aphrodite's velvet voice could only mean one thing.

Medusa was not coming home.

Turning, she let the fury show on her face, even as she dipped into a bow. "My Lady."

"It has been many years, Eurynome. You are looking lovely as always."

Eurynome scoffed. "You are too kind, Goddess. It has, in fact, been many years since I've been *graced* with the presence of a God."

"You have a beautiful home. Shall we sit…"

"Is she alive?" Eurynome interrupted.

Aphrodite looked at her and saw the heart-wrenching trembling of her lips. "Yes, she's alive." The look of relief on Eurynome's face made what she had come to say that much harder.

Eurynome frowned deeply, on the verge of tears. "What did you do to her?" she pleaded.

"Please…sit."

All appears to be quiet," Athena said.

"Yes. There haven't been any disturbances since the battle with Ceto," Poseidon replied.

They had stopped in Crete first, the last place they had seen Aphrodite, and the last place Medusa was seen. Other than rebuilding what was destroyed, everything appeared to be back to normal. There were no reports of a monster roaming the beaches of Crete.

"She couldn't have gone too far," Athena murmured.

"Who?" Poseidon asked.

"Who?! **Medusa,** you fool!"

Poseidon gritted his teeth. "She may not have, on her own. But, have you forgotten, Aphrodite is likely with her. They could be *anywhere.*"

"That is true," Athena sighed. "Well, we are doing no good standing here. Let us go back to Olympus and formulate a plan."

THE RACE FOR BEAUTY

Eurynome screamed in impotent outrage. Her baby, her beautiful baby, ravaged, abused, and turned into a monster. "You did this to her… ***all*** of you! We're nothing but toys to you," she shouted.

"Eurynome, I love Medusa. I would never do anything to harm her. In fact, I've done everything I can to fix the situation."

Eurynome fixed her with an incredulous look. "***Fix*** the situation? You cannot fix **this**."

"I held her while she cried. I kept her safe. I **love** her," she said.

Eurynome gazed at her in disdain. "Yes. But for how long?" she asked quietly. "We both know one day you'll simply leave her to her fate. She will live out the rest of her life as this… thing."

Aphrodite indulged her in silence. Eurynome was heartbroken, and she deserved some lenience. "I returned her beauty. I gave her some sense of normalcy," Aphrodite calmly explained.

"You returned her beauty for your own enjoyment," Eurynome began.

Aphrodite lost her temper at that. "I returned her beauty because I couldn't stand what they'd done to her!" Breath heaving, she blinked rapidly. The pain she had been holding finally showed on her face.

"Mark these words, Eurynome. Even a God can be powerless."

And even a mortal can be unforgiving. Eurynome would not be moved by her sorrow. "A God can be whatever a God wants to be. *We* can only be what you allow." She began to walk away. "Take me to her."

Aphrodite laughed wearily. Vengeful. Arrogant. Eurynome would make quite a Goddess. She certainly made a wonderful mother. "First, there are some things we need to collect."

Alright, think! Where would Aphrodite have taken her?" Poseidon was growing tired of this cat and mouse game.

"Somewhere remote," Athena replied thoughtfully. "If she had taken her anywhere populated, I daresay we would've heard." Pacing, Athena tried to think strategically.

Poseidon's eyes flashed, and a knowing smile lit his face. "Her mother will know," he said.

Athena spared him an indulgent glance. "Her mother is dead," she scoffed.

Shaking his head, he rolled his eyes at her. The wise Athena could not handle any intelligent thought, unless it came from her head. "You know what I mean, Athena. Eurynome. Medusa will get word to her, I assure you."

"I doubt there has been enough time for that. She may not know. Even still, you will have to take care. Even if she *does* know, there's no guarantee she will tell you, especially depending on how much *word* Medusa was able to get to her."

Poseidon was furious. How dare Athena. Was he not a God? Was she suggesting that he tiptoe around a mere mortal? "What consequence is that to me?! The mortal will tell me all she knows. I will **make** her tell me all she knows."

Athena sighed, as a mother would to a pestering child. "Take care, Poseidon. With Zeus's strange mood, this all may still backfire. If Eurynome knows nothing, we do not want her alerting Father. Do not forget the favor she once found with him, the children she bore with him. Visit Eurynome, find out what she knows… discreetly."

Poseidon did not favor this approach. He was certain that if he squeezed the life out of her, she would quickly tell him all she knew. "And just how will *discretion* help us find out if she's gotten word from her yet."

Athena raised a haughty eyebrow. "Dear *Uncle*… if Eurynome knows what has happened to Medusa, I have no doubt it will show… the moment she sees your face."

My Lady, are you planning to take the entire room?" Eurynome inquired.

Aphrodite smiled and looked around. Eurynome wanted so badly to provoke her. "I just want her to be as comfortable as possible. I want her to have as much of home as she can."

Eurynome shot a curious glance at her.

A servant nervously entered. "The cart is ready, My Lady."

"Thank you, you may go," Eurynome said. The poor thing was

trembling and nearly weeping with fear.

"Very well. By the time I have returned, you should have the cart packed," Aphrodite said.

"Me?! What are you talking about? You are the one who wanted to haul all of this. I am tired of your games Aphrodite. Take me to Medusa now or…"

Her back slamming against the wall stalled any further words.

Aphrodite spoke very softly and very slowly. "Do not forget who you are, Eurynome … and ***never*** forget who I am." She raised an eyebrow at her.

Eurynome knew she had pushed the goddess too far. It was time she remembered her place. "Forgive me, My Lady," she rasped.

Aphrodite released her, and her feet hit the ground.

"I will pack the cart immediately," Eurynome added.

Aphrodite nodded. "Once you are done, come to the temple after nightfall." Then, she vanished.

Eurynome let out a relieved breath. When would she learn? She went in search for a servant. "Naida," she called.

"Hello Eurynome."

The familiar voice behind her brought the contents of her stomach up to her throat. Eurynome turned and immediately dropped into a bow. "My Lord," she said through the sickening rage. Keeping her eyes on the ground, she tried to tamp down her feelings to a manageable bubble.

Naida walked into the room. "Yes Mistress?" Upon viewing Poseidon, she gasped and dropped to her knees.

Rising, Eurynome could have kissed the girl for the needed distraction. She faced her, putting her back to Poseidon. "Help Stephen to finish loading the cart and take it over to the temple."

"Yes Mistress, right away," Naida said, and ran quickly from the room. *Was all of Olympus coming to this house?*

Steeling herself, Eurynome placed a mask of mild distaste on her face and willed herself to turn around. She narrowed her eyes. She didn't know why he was here, but she could guess. She would have to be very careful.

"My Lord. How long has it been? *Twelve* years?...since you brought your new plaything here to tell me I was no longer desired?"

Poseidon chuckled coolly. "You are still angry with me, I see."

Eurynome looked at him and felt the sting at the back of her eyes. She didn't know how long she could keep herself upright. Here she was standing in the same room as him, knowing what he'd done to Medusa. Every fiber wanted to reach out and take his life, yet she stood there, powerless, her only choice was to pretend she knew nothing. Turning away, she blinked away tears of frustration.

"Oh, my sweet Eurynome. I thought you, of all people, understood the way things are between Gods and mortals." Stepping to her, Poseidon grasped her shoulders.

Gasping, Eurynome recoiled sharply from him. "I am quite aware of *the way things* ***are*** between Gods and mortals!" she shouted. She moved a safe distance from him, and once she thought she was safe from betraying herself, she spoke calmly. "Is all well? My children?... Medusa?" Her heart nearly broke at the question.

"...All is well," he lied, smoothly.

Her heart *did* break, then. "So, My Lord, what brings you to my home, then?"

Poseidon, armed with his charming smile, leaned casually against the wall. "I was thinking of you. I've missed you."

Nearly overwhelmed with revulsion, Eurynome hitched her chin higher. "Oh? I find that quite impossible, with Aphrodisia in full swing." She crossed her arms with a challenging look.

"Same old Eurynome," he laughed. "I forgot what a delightful challenge you could be. Perhaps I shall visit you again… see if I can make myself as welcomed as I once was."

"You would have to undo the past, My Lord," she whispered.

Poseidon laughed out loud. Closing in on her, he stroked her cheek. "Eurynome, obviously you have forgotten exactly what I'm capable of." Saying that, he vanished.

Eurynome didn't know how long she stood there in shock but, all at once, reality came crashing down. Poseidon had been in her house, wooing her, touching her. She ran to a nearby vase and vomited. Sliding down to the floor, she screamed a sob of grief, a wounded cry of the helpless. "Naida!" she shouted.

"Oh Mistress! Are you alright?" Naida ran to her side and helped her up.

"Have Stephen ready a horse for me. I'm leaving, immediately." She handed her the vase. "And destroy this."

Glaucus was laughing hysterically by the time he neared the gate. With no sleep, hardly any food, and the pace he had been keeping, he was quite delirious. Dismounting, he took a look at himself, realizing for the first time that he was completely covered in dust. He could only imagine how he looked.

He could not meet Eurynome like this. It was bad enough he had lost her daughter, who had been left in **his** care, but now he was also coming to **her** for help in finding her, and in the dead of night no less. Sighing, he mounted his horse again. He would find an inn, clean himself up, and make himself more presentable.

Well, what did you find?" Athena asked. She had interrogated Peitho and, still, had gotten no answers. But, she refused to let Aphrodite beat her.

"Nothing. Eurynome was annoyed that I showed up after so long, but that was all." He smiled furtively. "I daresay I'd enjoy visiting her again later, to see if she's learned anything."

Athena rolled her eyes. "Well, Aphrodite has no choice but to return here at some point. She is probably holed up in some remote place, which is fine by me. I don't care where she **is.** I just want to be sure she is not where we do not **want** her to be. I will stay here and very near to my father. You watch Phorcys and Eurynome closely."

Poseidon was barely listening to her. "With pleasure."

BEAUTY LOST

Eurynome stumbled up the steps of the temple. Running inside, she spotted Aphrodite and rushed to her.

"Take me to her… Take me to her, now!" she demanded.

Aphrodite folded her arms and narrowed her eyes, when she noticed Eurynome's lower lip trembling. As she reached out to her, Eurynome lowered her head. "Eurynome… what happened?"

When she raised her head, she had a far off look. A ghost of a smile played across her lips. "Poseidon came to me. He…" She shook the memories from her head. "I was able to convince him nothing was amiss, but he will return. I have no doubt… he will return." Eurynome's heavy eyes connected with Aphrodite's. "… Please take me to her."

So many emotions crossed her face, and Aphrodite felt a new respect for Eurynome. Aphrodite knew what she had been through, and knew, she would do it again, anything to keep Medusa safe. She nodded, knowingly. "Once the cart arrives and we give them direction, we will go."

Glaucus awoke with a curse. He had sat back for just a moment after finishing his first meal in nearly two days, and he had fallen asleep. Chiding himself, he quickly dressed. He was very nervous about meeting Medusa's mother, but he had wasted enough time already. Looking at the dawn creeping through his window, he readied himself to leave.

As he made his way through the quiet streets, he let his mind wander. How long had it been since he'd seen her? How long would it be before he saw her again? He had so many questions. But there was one answer he was sure of. He would go to any length of distance and time. He would inhabit any realm, in this world and beyond, to find her.

Before long, the gates, once again, came into view. Dismounting, he approached the door and gave it a sharp, quick rap. His heart pounding, he waited for someone to answer. Finally, the door was opened by a tall, muscular servant, with a small, young lady peeking cautiously behind him. Glaucus realized what they must think, a young man, alone, calling at this hour.

"I nn-nn-need to speak with your mmm-mm-mistress, Eurynome. It is an urgent mmm-mm-matter."

Naida frowned slightly. Stepping forward, she studied the young man. He looked worn and weary, and he spoke with a faulty tongue. Still, with the activities of the night before, she could not be too cautious.

"My Mistress is not available at such an hour. May I have your name, and what this is regarding?"

"Mm-my name is Glaucus, son of Mm-mminos and P-p-pasiphaë. Is the Lady Mm-mm-medusa home? I nn-nn-need to fff-find her im-imm-mm-… I need your help."

Naida found the young man sincere, but still her loyalty was to her house, and she needed to be very careful.

"The Lady Medusa… is visiting on Olympus. She is not expected home for some time now…" She wondered how to proceed. "However, the Lord Poseidon did visit last night. I believe he would be returning, so he may be of more help."

Glaucus visibly deflated. It seemed the race for Medusa was on, and Glaucus felt horribly out of his depth. Taking a deep breath, he decided he would press on. It would not be safe for him to stay around here asking questions. Aphrodite **had** to return to Olympus soon.

"I apologize for the odd hour. I will go."

The poor man looked so distraught. Naida wanted to say more, but she must keep her Ladies safe. "I will tell my mistress you called."

Eurynome stood at the opening of the cave. Aphrodite stopped her as she tried to enter. "Remember what I have told you… prepare yourself."

Eurynome nodded and took a deep breath. They entered together, and Aphrodite called out to Medusa. Eurynome heard footsteps coming from deep inside the cave.

"Medusa?" she called impatiently. She was greeted with a sudden silence.

"…Mother?…" Medusa shyly stepped into the room.

Eurynome's hands went to her mouth. Her eyes filled, and she gasped silently. She reached out hesitantly and touched her face.

Medusa suddenly felt very self-conscious.

"Oh, my darling, thank the Gods you're alive!"

Eurynome enveloped her in a tight hug. She was oblivious to the serpents that tangled in her hair, and slithered along her cheeks. Her baby was safe. Everything else be damned.

Pulling away, she looked at Medusa fully. There were no tears, not a hint of a frown. This was a new Medusa, a harder Medusa. Eurynome sighed to herself. Poseidon had that effect on people. She was both saddened and relieved that a woman, tried and true, stood before her.

Eurynome smiled at her. "You really have your mother's eyes now."

Medusa's eyes lit up as she smiled. Aphrodite took in the scene and felt quite proud of herself. Hopefully, Eurynome would be able to keep Medusa company for a few days. She had already been gone from her festival for too long.

Fortunately, the threat to Crete was a plausible excuse. Still, she would have to go back to Mount Olympus soon and was not looking forward to telling Medusa that she would have to leave her.
In the meantime, she pasted a smile on her face. "We have some things from home on the way for you, my love."

"**μητέρα**... Why don't you take a look around and give us a moment alone?" Medusa said.

"I'll keep a watch out for the cart..." Eurynome excused herself.

Medusa threaded her fingers through Aphrodite's. "Thank you, My Lady."

"Medusa..." Aphrodite began.

"I know. You've neglected your duties far too long. It's time for you to go home." She smiled at her Goddess.

"If not for Aphrodisia, I would stay here with you…"

"Will you do something for me, my love?" Medusa asked.

"Of course… anything," she cautiously replied.

Medusa gave her hand a light squeeze. She looked at her for a long time. Aphrodite noticed that she seemed eerily calm, almost resolved. "When you return to Olympus… stay."

Aphrodite frowned. "I do not understand…"

"Yes, you do. I am asking you… do not return here." Medusa let her seriousness show.

Aphrodite backed away from her furiously. "I think you misunderstand who the goddess is here. You do not order me about. You are here for **my** pleasure, and you will do what **I** say!"

Medusa took her rage stoically. "Yes, My Lady," she said.

"Do not take that tone with me. You can not ask this of me!" Aphrodite shouted.

Medusa tried for a smile, then. "And *you* cannot spend every day in a cave with me. We both know how this will end. The visits will come less frequently, then not at all. Better it end while I can still survive it."

Aphrodite shook her head. "I can not, and I will not."

Medusa looked at her seriously, then. "The last time I lost you, it nearly killed me. Please…"

"Do you think you can survive against Poseidon and Athena *alone*?" she laughed. "Your mother certainly couldn't." She regretted the word as they left.

Medusa raised an eyebrow. "… What?"

Never one to back down, Aphrodite bravely trudged ahead. "Your mother… they destroyed her."

"You're lying."

"We are in her womb this very instant. It was the only way I could've returned your beauty."

Medusa was panting, deafened by the hisses surrounding her.

She decided to try a different tact. "You see? They will stop at nothing, and you cannot face them without me."

Medusa's jaw tightened. "I was ravaged, in body and soul. I was punished and tormented for crimes uncommitted. Oh, My Lady…I **have** faced them… without you. And now, I want you ***gone***."

"No! Not after all I've done! You are **mine!** You belong to **me!**" she shrieked. Her world was spiraling out of control.

"I *belong* to you?" Medusa asked calmly. "Very well, but for how long?"

Having Eurynome's words mirrored by Medusa gave Aphrodite pause. "All of this could not have been for nothing," she pleaded.

"No, all of this was supposed to be for love. Do you love me, Aphrodite?"

The goddess puffed herself up. "We will continue this discussion when I return. Agreed?"

Medusa gave her a formal bow. "Yes, My Lady."

BEAUTY GAINED

Eurynome made her way back inside. Not sure what to say, she quietly watched Medusa. Her daughter turned to her with a sad expression.

"Everything you've said about the Gods. The jealousy, the pettiness… They don't *really* care about us. You were right about everything." Her smile didn't quite reach her eyes. "You were right."

Eurynome took both of her hands. "So were you."

She sighed at Medusa's confused look. "We all were. When your mother gave you to me, she said you would be a queen among women. She was right."

Medusa smiled genuinely, then. She wished so much that she could've seen her mother, spoken with her.

"From the moment I first held you in my arms, I've done what I can to protect you… from everything. And from the very first moment you could form the words, you always assured me you would be fine. Do you remember? Every time. '*Eurynome, I'll be fine*'. '*Eurynome, do not worry so.*'"

Laughing, Medusa nodded.

"And you were right." Eurynome tilted her chin, so she met her eyes. "You are so much stronger than you know. I see your mother through your eyes, and feel her strength flowing through you. You can get through anything… and you will get through everything."

She turned to walk away, and Medusa's heart swelled with pride.

Stopping at the entrance, Eurynome turned back to her. "One thing I want you to remember, Medusa. We're all right about something, but none of us is right about everything. She does love you."

Medusa sighed at the feelings that statement provoked. Sitting on her bed, she laid back into the sweet fragrance left by her goddess.

Aphrodite strolled into the Great Hall. Looking around, and where she should feel relief and excitement, she felt only her temper rising. There was drinking and revelry. Scantily clad men and women danced provocatively. People ate and conversed gaily. It was as if she had never left. Had anyone even noticed she was gone?

Her festival was commencing without her. There was only one place in the world she wanted to be at this moment, and it was the one place she wasn't welcome. It stung beyond belief, though she would never admit it. Aphrodite had quite a conundrum. Should she give in to the wishes of a mere mortal, and deny her **own** desires? Could she allow herself to be ordered?

Over and over again, the same questions spun around in her mind.

"Do you love me, Aphrodite?"

She shook her head against Medusa's voice. All she'd ever done was think of her. The girl was making her weak. Her love was making her weak. So, the question remained. Did she love her? Mortals love like shooting stars, hot, bright and fast, knowing their life is short. Gods love with eternity in mind, guided by the knowledge of the ages. Loving so differently, can they **truly** love one another?

Grimacing she looked for a nearby servant. "Bring me wine. *Now.*"

Medusa and Eurynome sat on her bed, laughing. They had unpacked the cart, and the inside of the cave looked more and more like her room at home. *Home.*

Her home was no longer with Eurynome. Medusa bristled every time she thought about it. She hated not having the freedom to go anywhere she wanted, but she realized that she carried a great responsibility, and everyone would be safer if she stayed.

"I can stay with you, if you'd like." Eurynome jostled her out of her thoughts.

"No, Mother, you should get back on your way. I will be fine. Do not worry so." She laughed at the customary response Eurynome reminded her of earlier. When she looked at her, she could tell Eurynome was remembering as well. "I really will be fine. I promise."

"Well then, I suppose I should be on my way. I did leave abruptly, and I am sure I will be sorely missed."

Both sat in an awkward silence, neither wanting to make the first move towards a parting. Eurynome knew it was just a matter of time before Poseidon returned, and she did not want to arouse suspicion. Medusa knew she couldn't keep Eurynome there; could not substitute one crutch for another. She had to stand on her own two feet.

"Visit me again?" Medusa asked shyly.

Eurynome wrapped an arm around her shoulders. "Of course, my beauty. This is not goodbye. I will visit very soon."
With one last embrace, Eurynome quickly departed. Outside of the

cave, Eurynome ran her hand along the rock. "Mighty Ceto, I beg you, keep her safe."

Medusa looked around and realized that she was, for once, completely alone. She had never been completely alone before. She always had Eurynome, or Aphrodite… someone. Her steps echoed as she walked through her new home. Without the distraction of others, all of her thoughts came flooding to her.

She thought about the events of the last week. She'd found a love… lost a love. Actually, she threw love away. Sighing, she reminded herself it was the right decision. She'd been introduced to the intimacies between men and women… quite unpleasantly. She'd become exiled from her home, was cursed, and doomed to be alone forever.

Why exactly was sending everyone away a good idea? She laughed to herself. She sat alongside the pool that had become her favorite spot in her new home. Bending over the edge, she peered at her reflection. The serpents framing her face hissed at themselves curiously.

Eurynome is right you know… you are very strong, and you can get through everything. And **you** *are right as well… you really will be fine. There's no reason to worry.*

Leaning forward slightly, she kissed herself. After a daring smile, she plunged headfirst into the pool. She floated there under the water until the familiar peace washed over her. Shortly after, the faint humming she'd grown accustomed to began. Medusa began idly humming along as she rocked gently. Opening her eyes, she thought of something Aphrodite said.

Obviously, she had been wrong. She would never be truly alone.

Later, leaving the pool, Medusa stripped off her wet clothes and walked through her new home in a trancelike state, truly seeing it for the first time. It seemed to pulse with her every breath, vibrate with her heartbeat. She tenderly touched the walls as she moved through. Smiling, she nestled closer, pressing her ear against the side.

"Ceto…," she giggled deliriously. Closing her eyes, she began to slowly hum, her voice echoing through the caves. As she reached the entrance, she thought briefly of Aphrodite, her Goddess, her Love. Stepping out into the moonlight, she felt her there too, spreading slowly over her naked body. Her hair danced around the wind as she hummed softly, cradled by her mother, caressed by her lover.

Looking up at her silver deity, she stretched out her arms and began to sing the lullaby in her heart, the one she heard flowing through her blood.

Sleep, who takes the little ones come, take this one too.
Young - so young I gave it to you, grown-up bring it back to me.
Tall as a high mountain, straight as a cypress tree.
And its branches outstretched to the East and West.

She was never alone. She would **never** be alone.

Truly, for on this dark night with only the moon to guide him, a lone fisherman, who'd thought himself lost, was cowering in his boat. Looking over at land that had not before been there, he looked at the silhouette of a beautiful woman, a naked woman. She appeared to be worshipping the moon, singing, beckoning, luring him closer.

"O Poseidon… Deliver my soul… A Siren is upon me."

For once, Glaucus did not slink slowly into the great hall with his eyes lowered. He walked in boldly, actively scanning the crowd. He nearly shouted when he saw her.

He'd fully expected to have to wait for her, which he had been willing to do. He knew at some point, she'd have to return here.

Glaucus wasted no time as he made his way to Aphrodite. Dropping to a bow in front of her, he fought to keep his voice low and steady.

"Mm-mm-mmy Lady. I nnnneed to sp-speak with you."

When he raised his eyes to hers, he could see the Goddess of Love was quite intoxicated.

"You nn-nn-nneed to sp-sp-speak with me?" she mocked.

His jaw tightened as he pressed on. "Yes, mm-my Lady. It's v-v-vv… urgent."

Aphrodite rolled her eyes as she fondled the young man at her side. "Well, it will have to wait. I'm busy."

He grabbed her wrist, forcing her to look at him.

Eyes flaring, she reached for his throat. "How **dare** you!" *What was coming over these damned mortals? When would they learn their place?*

"P-p-please My Lady, I h-h-h-have to ffffind her!" Glaucus shouted in a strangled voice.

Aphrodite released him and he fell to the ground. He could see that she had sobered immensely.

"P-p-please…"

“Shut up!” she hissed.

“P-p-please just tell mm-mm-me where she is.”

Groaning loudly, Aphrodite grabbed him and vanished to her chambers. “Who sent you to me? And, what do you know?!”

Glaucus opened his eyes and fought the nausea that threatened to overtake him. He tried to focus on what Aphrodite was shouting at him. “I d-d-don’t know annn-nn-nything! That’s why I nn-nnneed you…,” he gasped.

With a flick of her wrist, he felt his chest constrict.

“What… do you know?” she asked again.

Panting, Glaucus felt like he was moments from death.

“I h-heard them sss-sssay she was cc-cc-cursed… all I know is ss-sshe disappeared. I’ve ss-sssearched everywhere!”

Slowly, Aphrodite let him breathe. “You are… Glaucus…?”

Glaucus couldn’t hide his shock. The Goddess Aphrodite *knew* him?

“But how did you *know* she disappeared?” she inquired, still suspicious of him.

“I w-w-was taking her h-home. She inss-ssisted on Athena’s ffff-forgiveness, b-b-but she nn-never returned.” He was still finding it difficult to breathe.

The poor boy was near tears and he, obviously, cared for Medusa. She wondered how much. “… You can never look upon her…”

“I mm-mm-mmust go to her!” Glaucus groaned, against the tightness in his chest.

"I said you can never look upon her… I never said you could not go to her." Aphrodite grabbed his face and looked into his eyes.

He loved her.

"With every step you take towards her, you will gain knowledge of the next. So long as you hold her with total faithfulness. Betray her, and you will lose all knowledge of her, and yourself. Do you still want it?"

"Yes," he answered.

No hesitation, no question. Smiling sadly, she breathed into his mouth. She turned towards her table to hide her rapidly filling eyes. Her tears spilled over as she looked at the pomegranate necklace.

"Th-th-thank you, My Lady."

She nodded. He need not thank her yet. The expedition to Medusa would be a long and trying one. She would make sure of it. She would make sure of **him**. With a final exhale, she released all hold she had on him. "Remember what I said. You must not look upon her."

"I will re-mm-mm-member." Glaucus went to leave, then paused, rubbing his chest. "Mm-my Lady?… What were you d-d-doing to mm-mm-me?"

"I was crushing your heart. You'll feel it again, if you ever lose her." He breathed deeply and nodded in understanding. "I felt like I was dying," he mumbled

Toying with the necklace, she didn't spare him a glance. "I know."

Just imagine if you were Immortal. Knowing you couldn't die… feeling like you were going to… and nearly wishing you had.

Glaucus crept towards the door. With each step, the next one fell in place, as if he knew exactly where he was going, although he could not tell you the destination.

"Wait…," she called out. "I have another task for you…"

BEAUTY DISCOVERED

The thing called to me… beckoning, her nude body silhouetted by the moon. She sang her spell song of doom!"

All around, eyes stared, unwavering, on the old man. For the first time in years, he felt the attention and devotion he had been missing since his beloved Melissa, his little Honey Bee, had died.

Every time he would come home, she would beg for stories of his journey. She would sit across from him as he ate his dinner, her brown eyes never leaving his, a warm smile on her face. Every now and then, she would let a wistful sigh escape, and say she wished she was there.

Oh, he embellished, of course. Nothing too exciting *ever* happened on his trips. Just work. She knew he embellished, and he knew that she knew. Somehow, that little shared truth made those times all the more special.

And now, here were all these eyes upon him. Each person riveted on what he had to say. Most nights he would sit and drink, with no one looking his way. Tonight, as he went careening in, shrieking about a siren, all of that changed.

People were bringing him drink after drink, wanting to hear more and more about what he encountered. With each word, the night in question grew darker, the moon fuller, the witch more beguiling, and her spell song more sinister. The only part that had no room to grow, was the slim miracle of faith, which allowed him to survive with his life… just barely.

"I prayed reverently to Mighty Poseidon. Again and again, my boat drifted to her jagged crags, but I fought! No matter how alluring her song was, I kept faith, and I escaped with my life… by a thread!"

All around, the women gasped, fanning themselves to stop their fluttering hearts, while the men took turns slapping him on the back, congratulating him on surviving such an obstacle, and living to tell the tale.

There was one group, however, that was not joining with the rest. A group of four young men, strong men, with a hunger for adventure.

"Do you think the old man speaks truth?" one asked.

"I think *he* believes he does," another chuckled.

The third, nodded thoughtfully. "I have no doubt he saw *something*. But still, it could very well be some old hag who's made her home there, singing lullabies to the snakes and rats. But still…"

"Yes still… with the recent attack still so fresh… it warrants at least some… consideration." The fourth, smiled mischievously.

While one man basked in the adoration of all those around him, four young men hatched a plan to save their piece of the world. They would find this witch, and they would destroy her. They would be the reason women and children could sleep at night. They would be the reason fishermen could make it home to their families.

They would be heroes.

Glaucus sniffed the air around him, the smell of meat making his stomach rumble. As much as he wanted to keep going, he knew he needed to eat, needed to keep up his strength. He had to make it to Medusa. He didn't know where she was, or how long it would take, but he had to make it.

Sitting down, he rubbed his eyes. If someone asked him how far he had walked, he couldn't say. A cup of wine clunked down in front of him. He glanced up into a pair of bright, silver eyes.

They were not merely gray. No, these eyes were the color of a sun-kissed snowflake, one instant before it melts. Almond shaped, and framed by long, raven lashes. She, shyly, kept averting her eyes, only to flash them again briefly.

"You look tired, my lord." She smiled sweetly at him.

He inhaled sharply and shook the fog from his brain. "I am t-t-tired… long j-j-journey."

She nodded, her eyes downcast, before slowly raising them. "Where does my lord go?" she asked quietly.

"To fffind something I lost. S-s-something very important."

Again, she nodded. "Well, I shall see you have some food in your belly… and, perhaps, a good night before continuing. If you need anything more, ask for Adara."

Glaucus inclined his head. He sipped his wine and felt a warmth rush through him. As she walked away, he couldn't help sparing a glance at her. She was truly magnificent. Her hair was black as the night, her smile, sweet and shy. Her body was ample and fertile and her manner was genuine, and unassuming. As he found himself watching the sway of her hips, he missed the grin that passed over her face.

The moon shone brightly on the water as the foursome rowed out towards the small island. Each heart pounded with the thrill of the hunt, the prospect of being a hero. Each mind played the battle scene, starring himself. Slaying the monster, saving his friends, each man saw his victory clearly under the billions of stars overhead.

Approaching the shore, they sat there in silence for several minutes, their eyes to the moon, hoping to catch a glimpse of the monster. The old man described her as nude, unearthly, with living hair. Well, they didn't see any nude woman, didn't hear any spell song.

"Alright men, if that witch is in here, she's as good as ours."

A round of smiles met each other.

"Alright, the three of us will go up together. Alexander, you stay here."

Angry confusion filled Alexander's face. "What?! I'm supposed to help. You said we would be heroes," he pouted.

"Alex, you know mother would kill me if you were ever in danger. Besides, we need someone to watch the boat."

Alexander rolled his eyes and shook his head. He was the youngest of their foursome, and was always left out of the most fun activities. Everything was always too dangerous, or would get him into too much trouble.

His brother looked at him fondly. Already, he could see him trying to blink away the moisture that was welling in his eyes. "We really do need you Alex."

"Yeah, to watch the boat…"

"No, truly. If there really is a witch up here, we will have our work cut out for us. We're going to have to get out of here pretty fast, so we'll need the boat in position, and for you to be ready to row like Poseidon himself." He spoke forcefully and deliberately and, before long, he saw the hopeful gleam in his brother's eye. "We'll need for you to help with our escape, so we'll live to tell this tale."

Alexander smiled brightly. "Alright. I'll be ready. You'll see! I'll have the boat in position, with both hands on the oars, ready at a moment's notice. I won't let you down, Jason."

"I know you won't."

Glaucus had a hard time keeping his eyes open. He squeezed them tightly before looking up and focusing on Adara's form swaying towards him.

Placing a plate in front of him, Adara's face softened, and she let her hand brush against his slightly. "Oh, my lord, you are dead where you sit. You need rest."

Glaucus sighed and pulled the plate closer to him. As he began to eat, Adara slid into the seat next to him. She, timidly, raised a hand to his shoulder and lightly stroked his arm.

"Tell me of your mission. What is it you seek?"

"A treasure… of s-s-sorts."

Her eyes lit up. "A journey for treasure… it sounds perilous."

Glaucus frowned. "I never considered. I s-s-suppose it may be." Glaucus expected his quest to be long, but he never considered the possibility that he would be in danger.

Adara gasped. "Oh, my lord. Are you certain you should continue?"

She slid slightly closer to him. "You are very kind, a good man. I would not want anything to happen to you."

Meeting her gaze, Glaucus smiled wearily. "Th-th-thank you, Adara. I shall be fine, I'm s-s-sure. I must press on."

She pouted very prettily and lowered her eyes. "Is your treasure so important, then?"

She spoke so low, Glaucus found himself leaning closer to hear her. She looked up so unexpectedly, he found it hard to breathe. Yet, there they were, only a breath apart. Vaguely, Glaucus remembered that she had spoken.

"Yes… v-very important."

"Well, you are in no condition to go for it tonight." She lowered her eyes again.

For reasons he couldn't explain, Glaucus wanted so badly for her to look at him again. Her eyes were so deep and enchanting.

"You need sleep, my lord. You need food, and a bath. I can arrange it…"

When her eyes weren't on him, his gaze couldn't help but fall to her full lips and, gradually, lower. They were well on their way when she lifted her eyes again.

"… let me take care of you."

On a shaky breath, Glaucus nodded. "I do need sleep. I s-ssuppose I can continue in the mm-mmorning."

Adara giggled and smiled excitedly. "I shall take care of everything… eat."

She rose slowly, gracing him with a sensuous smile. Glaucus, uneasily, smiled back. With a confused frown, he returned to his meal.

Three young men, bathed in moonlight, stood at the opening of the cave. Each heart pounded as they drew their swords and slowly entered.

Medusa was floating on her back, her belly full. She smiled to herself at what a good fisherman she was. It could not rival a banquet on Mount Olympus, but it was of her own doing. She had needed no one else to feed herself. It felt good to be free.

She was currently enjoying the little freedom she felt whenever she was surrounded by water. As always, she heard the faint humming, and began to hum along. Her voice reverberated off the cave walls and returned to her, creating a chorus, and making her feel like she wasn't so alone.

It also signaled the young men that they weren't alone. A faint voice reached their ears, though they couldn't tell where it originated. Voices seemed to come from every angle, humming a slow lullaby. With each note, the young men grew more nervous.

One, more than the others.

Jason suddenly felt they had made a mistake. He feared for their lives but, most of all, he feared for his brother.

"We should spread out. I can't tell where she is," one whispered.

"I can't tell how many there are. I think we should go," Jason responded.

"Hey, we made a plan, and we are going to stick to it. We're going to be heroes."

Two went forward, splitting off in different directions. Jason gave a glance to the opening, and moved forward very slowly. A voice sounded to the far right, and he swirled, clanging his sword against the wall.

Medusa sat up abruptly and looked around her. She eased herself out of the pool and walked naked in the direction of her bed chamber. With each step, she grew more uneasy.

"Hello?" she called out. As always, her own voice surrounded her. For once, however, she did not take comfort in the feeling of not being alone.

"Aphrodite?... Eurynome?"

Hearing the two names, the question of how many were in residence came back into the young men's minds. Perhaps, this was not such a good idea. They were all separated now. None could rightly abandon his brothers in arms, so, each boldly pressed on.

Medusa wrapped her arms around herself for protection, as well as modesty. She was fully convinced she was not alone. She wanted to call out again in the hopes that it was Eurynome, or Aphrodite, wanted to shout a warning, if it was not.

"Do not move, witch!"

A voice. A male voice. Medusa wished fervently that she could just disappear.

He suddenly noticed her bare backside. "Miss, what are you doing here? Do you live in this cave? Was that you singing?" The young man sheathed his sword.

"Leave! Take anyone with you and leave this place now!" Medusa shouted.

He laughed at the command in her sweet voice. "My Lady, we can help you. There is no need to fear me."

"You should fear *me*," she answered.

"Now, there's no need for that. I only want to help you." He began to walk closer.

Medusa felt his approach, and matched his steps, walking away from him. "No, you must leave. You are in great danger."

"Great danger from a beauty like you?" His stride was larger than hers, and he eventually began to catch up to her. He reached out to her and was met with vicious hissing. The light passed over her body and head.

The young man stopped dead in his tracks and unsheathed his sword again. "What ***are*** you?"

"Get out of here!" she shrieked, her voice bursting through the cavern. As the words bounced back from the walls, she broke into a run.

Medusa ran through her home, ducking, taking as many turns as she could, but the young man was never more than a few steps behind. Panting, her lungs burning, she tried to figure the best route while she was running. The path she was taking would lead her back to the pool, and by that way, she would try to get to the entrance.

In making her plan, she took a wrong turn. Upon seeing the dead end, she spun around, and looked right into the eyes of her pursuer.

Dropping his sword, the young man's scream died in his throat as it hardened into stone. The scream reached the ears of the other two young men and, down in the boat, Alexander looked up curiously.

"No… no no," Medusa whimpered. She gently touched the statue before her, tapping the young man's face, as if by her will alone, she could bring him back. Leaning forward, her forehead rested on his broad chest. She felt sick then, sliding down his granite form to her knees.

Picking up his sword, she rose, and cast one more look over him.

She walked slowly and quietly. She didn't know how many of them there were, but she didn't want to make the same mistake. She reached the point where she had made the wrong turn. She pressed her face against the wall and gritted her teeth against the wail that threatened to escape. Taking a deep breath, with all her might, she plunged the young man's sword into it.

An answering shudder rumbled throughout the caves. Medusa gasped and looked around confused. Finally, she slowly made her way back to the pool.

The vibrations nearly toppled the two remaining men. The winding caves were getting more and more confusing with every turn, and each one of them faced the fear that they may never find their way out, may not even have that choice.

One young man saw something up ahead and ran to it curiously. As he neared it, he realized it was a sword. Upon closer inspection, he realized it was his good friend's sword. Panic-stricken, he began frantically calling his name.

Medusa reached the pool and heard distant shouting. Gasping, she turned quickly. There **were** more of them. "I want you to leave. I want you all to leave!" she called out. "I have done nothing wrong. You have no right to be here. One of you has already paid for this offense. Now, I beg the rest of you to save yourselves." She tried not to think of how her voice wavered.

Jason, upon hearing the command, looked towards the way back to the entrance and, instinctively, took one step back.

The other, gripping the hilt of his friend's sword, growled, drew his own, and ran forward.

Medusa looked around, afraid to move, but also afraid to stay in plain sight. She hoped the path to her bed chamber was safe. She hoped the intruders would leave her be.

She took a tentative step forward and heard the sound of rushing footsteps. The serpents hissed in alarm.

"Die, witch!"

Medusa ran towards her bed chamber, before she was tackled from behind. Closing her eyes, she attempted to scramble away, kicking and clawing.

The young man attempted to wring her neck, and was struck repeatedly by the serpents. His cries of pain echoed against the walls.

Reaching an opening, Jason had a choice. His head turned, back and forth, between the path leading out and the path leading to his friend. As the sounds of struggle increased, he sent up a silent prayer for protection and ran towards the shouting.

"What did you do to my friend? Where is he?" the young man yelled.

Medusa cried out, nearly making it out of his grip. The ground beneath her began to rumble slightly, and she was able to kick away from him. She began to scurry to her knees, when he unsheathed his sword and pushed her down on her stomach.

Kneeling over her, he raised his sword with both hands.

Jason rounded the corner to see his friend atop a young woman, ready to strike.

Crying, Medusa turned around beneath him and opened her eyes. She suddenly felt the heavy weight pressing against her legs, and a young man saw his friend of flesh and blood, turn into stone before his eyes.

Panicking, Medusa pushed at the statue, screaming and scampering, afraid of being pinned beneath. She heard a nearby clang, as the last young man dropped his sword.

"Get out!" she screeched.

Jason stood there, dumbfounded. Closing her eyes once again she ran towards him, wailing like a banshee. Finding his wits again, he ran as if Hades himself was on his trail. As he ran through the winding caves, only one thought ran through his mind.

Alex... Alex

When, at last, he could find his voice, he began shouting his brother's name. "Alex! Get out of here... go!"

Alexander looked up from his position in the boat. Hearing the terror in his brother's voice, he decided he would not leave there until Jason was by his side. Alexander saw him then, looking down from above, waving frantically.

"Get out of here!" Jason shouted.

"Not without you!" he responded.

"No time! Get out of here!"

Alexander felt real fear then. His brother was the bravest person he knew. "Jump!... Jason, Jump!"

With a quick look to the opening of the cave, Jason knew he didn't have much choice. His brother wouldn't leave him, and he wanted him out of there and safe. With barely a deep breath, Jason jumped into the blackness, and blackness engulfed him.

Glaucus sat back and decided that was probably the best meal of his entire life. He was full, relaxed, and incredibly sleepy. As if on cue, Adara glided towards his table. He opened his mouth to thank her for her kindness, but she hushed him and reached for his hand.

"Come with me, my lord."

Rising, Glaucus allowed himself to be led. He walked through, each step feeling like a dream. He followed Adara to a private room. As he entered, nothing in the world looked better to him than that bed. His body ached and his mind could no longer keep him upright.

Coming around to face him, Adara began to undress him. Capturing her hands, he stepped back. "W-w-what are y-y-you d-d-doing?"

"Forgive me, but my lord is filthy." She gave him a charming smile. "I thought you might enjoy a bath." She pointed to a nearby tub filled with steaming water.

Suddenly, the bed was *second* best looking thing to him. He sighed wistfully. "I do want a b-b-bath very m-much. However, I am capable of und-d-dressing myself."

Adara giggled and continued her attempt. "Are you sure?" she flirted. "My lord can barely stand."

Glaucus caught her hands again. "True, but I'm s-s-sure. I can undress m-m-myself."

Adara arched an eyebrow, coyly, at him. "Alright, my lord. I will leave you to it then."

Nodding, he smiled at her. "Th-th-thank you, Adara."

She curtsied beautifully. "My lord."

Jason!" Alexander looked around frantically. He didn't take into consideration how high up Jason was when he told him to jump. He only knew he didn't want to leave without his brother, didn't want to be alone.

Finally, he saw him.

Rowing closer to him, Alexander lifted his head out of the water. A bruise was already starting to form. Above, he heard the most terrible screeching, the scream of a creature in pain… or enraged.

"Jason, please wake up… please. We have to go."

Alexander pulled and pulled at his brother, gaining an inch at a time. With all his strength, he was finally able to get him into the boat. Grabbing the oars, he began to row steadily, his arms throbbing, his chest aching from his panicked breaths. He never stopped talking to his brother, hoping Jason would wake soon, comforted by the rise and fall of his chest.

He tried to ignore the periodic wails he would hear coming from the island behind them. Alexander wasted no time putting distance between them and whatever had frightened his brother so. He rowed until his hands bled, then he rowed some more.

THE ROAD TO BEAUTY

Medusa didn't know how long she had sat there, afraid to move. But, for once, she had no trouble pinpointing what she was feeling. She had just destroyed two young men, maybe three. Something as simple as opening her eyes could cost someone their life. She was afraid, yes, but also something more. She was angry.

Rising, she began to look around. This was her home. She had been exiled here, against her wishes. This was not where she'd wanted to spend the rest of her life, but it was all she had left. They had no right to come in here. How did they even know she was here? She had tried… *tried* to warn them, to save them, yet they did nothing but attack her.

Served them right.

She walked towards the pool and glared at the still form of the young man, sword raised, ready to end her life. Growling, she ran towards it and pushed with all her might. It toppled, splitting in half. Panting, she shoved, scraping her fingers, as tears poured over her cheeks. Finally, one half plunged into the water, followed by the other. As they sank out of view, Medusa gritted her teeth.

It served them right.

This was her home. She would no longer be afraid. She did what she had to do, and she'd do it again. And anyone that came here would get the same thing.

Glaucus didn't know how long he had sat there. Judging by the temperature of the water, he'd say much longer than he should have. He must've fallen asleep. Rising, he stretched his aching muscles. A good night's sleep would do wonders for him. He pad, naked and wet, around the privacy screen to discover he was not alone.

Adara was there. In his bed. Naked.

He was so exhausted, it took him a moment to find his voice.

"Adara, w-w-what are you d-d-doing here?!"

"I'm ensuring you have a good night before your trip, my lord." Smiling sweetly, Adara sat up, letting the sheet fall to her waist.

Glaucus turned away quickly. He needed to think faster than he was capable of doing at that moment. "Adara, you m-m-must leave. I'm s-s-sorry."

"Do you not find me attractive, my lord?" she asked meekly.

"Y-y-you are v-very attractive, but,… I j-j-just c-can't."

She sniffled suddenly. "Then, my lord thinks me a whore…"

Glaucus turned and ran to her side. "Oh nn-no nn-no. D-don't cry. You are a g-g-good person…" He tenderly touched her shoulder.

Without preamble Adara launched herself at him, holding him to her naked body. "Love me, my lord. I promise I will make you happy."

"Adara, ss-ss-stop!" Grabbing her wrists, he lunged forward, pinning her to the bed. She instantly burst into tears.

"Why don't you want me?" she sadly whimpered.

Glaucus sighed wearily. "Adara, y-you are b-b-beautiful, and sweet. I… c-cannot. There is an-n-nother."

She nuzzled him gently. "She does not have to know."

"I w-would know. I c-c-cannot."

Her eyes softened, and she smiled. Glaucus slowly released her, on alert, if need be, for another attack. He also made a conscious effort not to look at her sublime body, not to be conscious of his own.

Darting up, he ran for his clothes. Once again, he missed the grin that passed over Adara's face. As soon as he was covered, Glaucus dropped into a nearby chair, feeling more at ease. Comfortable with her nudity, Adara sat cross-legged in the center of the bed.

"So, my lord. Tell me of this treasure you seek."

Instantly wary, Glaucus put his guard up. "It is just s-s-something that is imp-p-portant to me."

"Oh, my lord. You can trust me. I would never tell."

He felt deep in his soul that he could trust her. However, he would never risk it. He could never risk Poseidon or Athena finding his Honey.

Adara's eyes lit up. "Is it diamonds? Gold?" she prompted.

Glaucus got a far off look, and smiled faintly. He thought of Medusa then, her hair, her skin, and her eyes. "Yes. G-g-gold, and bronze. Emeralds. It is the mm-mmost v-v-valuable treasure on this earth."

"Where is it, my lord?"

His eyes turned sad. "F-f-far away. Mm-mm-much too ff-far away."

Adara's eyes filled and she looked away. Fixing a smile on her face, she nodded with a certain finality. "You may rest now. You've earned it."

She strode boldly to the door and, tossing a final smile over her shoulder, left the room.

Glaucus let out the breath he didn't realize he'd held. Mildly confused, he scuffed his way over to the bed and fell into it face first. Too tired to even pull the sheet over himself, he drifted off into his dreams on pillows that faintly smelled of pomegranates.

Outside his room, a flowing white gown covered a naked form, and fire red hair, replaced raven locks.

"I tell you, I barely made it out of there! If not for Alex… I would've been lost."

Jason, with a freshly bandaged head, sat down wearily next to his brother. Alexander beamed shyly at his praise, while their mother's face grew paler with each word.

With drinks all around, again, a group of listeners gathered to hear a daring tale of survival. The object of their attention was not an elderly fisherman, however. This time in the center of the melee was two young men.

"What was it like when you faced her?" someone called out.

"Sadly, I did not face her. I was concerned for my brother's safety, should I not return," Jason replied.

"And a good thing too!" his mother added. "Had he not gone to warn my little Alexi, he would've likely not returned!" Sniffling, she dabbed at her eyes while Alexander hugged her.

Sympathetic sounds came from all around. One by one, questions were shouted at them.

"Did you see her, at least?" someone asked.

Jason looked off into the distance. "I did…"

A hush descended over the room, as Jason seemed to relive the encounter. He shook his head slowly, frowning. "She was beautiful… naked…"

Gasps sounded all around.

"… There… There were snakes in her hair… all over. Peter drew to slay her… and…" He closed his eyes tightly to dispel the image. "He was frozen… like rock."

"Did she cast a spell on him?" someone asked.

Jason shook his head in confusion. "She spoke no words, she made no movement. One moment Peter was to be her demise, and the next… he was no more."

Voices raised from every direction. Some shouted in despair, others shouted in outrage. The crowd was divided into those that wanted to avenge their fallen young men, and those who lamented their fates, should the Gods not help them.

"We should gather an army and go and slay this siren!"

"We should pray for our lives to be spared!"

Jason rose to his feet. "Do what you will. I narrowly escaped death and have no desire to tempt the Fates again. I am alive, and will show my gratitude by remaining so." Reaching for his brother and mother, Jason gladly went home.

In the dark of night, a mother rocked in prayer, weeping. "Mighty Poseidon, I beg you, destroy her, this siren of the island. If she is of your doing, this serpent-haired witch, I beseech you, remove her." She began to sob, brokenly. "My son was an innocent… she had no right…"

He had found her. A smile broke over Poseidon's face. He had to inform Athena at once. She would be angry that she hadn't discovered Medusa's whereabouts first, which made this that much sweeter.

… Our men will find only death…

Poseidon prepared for his departure to Mount Olympus.

… Foul creature, luring with her naked body and spell songs…

In his underwater palace, he stood frozen. He began listening to the woman again. How could Medusa lure anyone with her body? She was hideous. He had seen it.

Mounting his chariot, he made his way to Crete.

In the city of Crete, a group of men gathered in secret. With much of the city living in fear, what they were planning to undertake would not be accepted by most of the population. Still, someone had to save them.

Someone had to avenge the young men they had lost.

The superstitious masses would rather rely on prayers and favor from the Gods to rid them of this creature. Well, they were of the mind that the Gods favored the strong. If they were to save themselves, and their families, they would have to go to the forbidden island, and slay the witch themselves.

BEAUTY PROTECTED

Glaucus awoke feeling well rested and ready to continue on his journey. Once his feet hit the ground, he groaned, cursing the walking he would have to do. But do it he would.

After enjoying his morning meal, he inquired after Adara, looking to thank her. The owner gave him a puzzled look, and replied that he didn't know any Adara. Confused, Glaucus took a deep breath and stepped out into the sunlight.

"Your horse, my lord." Glaucus looked at the fresh faced young boy that was handing the reigns to him.

"T-t-that is not my horse," Glaucus replied.

"Yes, my lord. A gift… to help you find your treasure."

Looking around him, Glaucus was grateful for the horse, but wondered how he would lead a horse to a location he was not aware of. But, thanking the boy, he mounted the horse. Once comfortably in the saddle, the horse began to walk.

"Well, at l-least one of us knows w-w-where we're going," he chuckled.

Medusa knew the exact moment the men arrived. She had been preparing for this since the moment of her last attack. She walked, unhurriedly, to the high vantage point she had picked out the day before.

Looking down, she chuckled to herself. It was certainly a change from before. Instead of four fresh faced young men, these six men were no doubt the pride of their village. They were seasoned, and strong… and loud.

Their war cries and boasts of victory echoed into the night. She rolled her eyes as she went back inside. Even the untrained boys had sensed the need for stealth.

As the cautioning hissing began, she stroked the serpents lovingly.

"Shh, my darlings. All will be well," she cooed.

As the men entered the cave, she heard one of them shush the others. This simple act, after their boisterous arrival thoroughly amused her. She chuckled dryly, her voice bouncing throughout the caves.

The men froze as the sound came to them from all angles. The next sound they heard was devoid of all humor.

"Turn back, or you will never leave," Medusa said.

The men looked at one another. Some didn't believe their ears, others were completely convinced. Still, none turned for the door.

"No?" she inquired. "Very well… come then. I am here."

Each of them looked around. None of them could tell where "here" was. They quietly tried to decide whether to travel en masse, to possibly be evaded, or to split up and cover more ground.

Once more, a menacing laugh surrounded them.

Medusa watched two men as they passed her. Hidden in the shadows, she quietly matched their steps. As expected, they felt her presence and, turning, their gasps faded away into silence. Two down. She went in search of the rest.

She moved effortlessly through the maze of caves, listening intently, knowing every move the men made. She found the second pair near her pool. That would not do. That was her place of peace. She did not want those men there.

She walked away from them and began humming her lullaby. Slowly, she was able to lure them towards her. As they neared, she wondered, briefly, if they hated her, blamed her for the young men that perished. Just a minor curiosity, though. She cared not how they felt about her. The only thing she truly wanted from any man was to heed her warning.

But not these men. She felt her heart harden. To her, these men were already dead.

Glaucus had never been so grateful as he was when the horse stopped. While riding, his feet sang with joy. But now, his thighs and buttocks wept with pain. He hoped he still retained most of his body by the time he made it to his Honey.

The horse stopped him near a river. He looked around. It was a fairly pleasant spot. He edged up to the river and took a drink of water. He went to sit, then thought better of it. Lying on his stomach, he heaved a sigh of relief, as his horse went in search of food.

Glaucus stretched, every muscle in his legs tightening. As his eyes closed, he thought of his treasure. He remembered sitting with her by the fountain, having her smile at him. Her warm smile, her sparkling eyes. Just thinking about her brought a smile to his face. His body could never ache enough. He could never be tired enough. No matter what it took, Glaucus would get to her.

Opening his eyes, Glaucus took another look around. His horse was nowhere to be seen. It looked as though getting to her would take some swimming. Rolling over, he allowed himself a frustrated whimper before closing his eyes again.

Medusa walked in a trance, strangely serene, barely conscious of anything but the feel of her gown swishing across her body. She reached out to caress each stone man she passed.

She looked at their faces, some etched in fear, others in anger. She felt no shame, and she felt no remorse. Like everything, they were given a chance.

She walked outside and breathed in the night air. Six men lost their lives tonight, and she knew this was only the beginning. More would come.

"Very well… come then. I am here."

Medusa stood and stretched. Glancing out of the cave's entrance, it looked to be a beautiful day. She would go for a swim, catch her breakfast and… "So, I find you at last, my beauty." Medusa would know that voice for all of eternity. "… and my beauty you are once again, I see."

Poseidon.

Against her will, Medusa began to tremble. Her breathing came in ragged gasps, drowned out by the hissing around her head.

"Ah, not able to restore your glorious locks, I see. No matter, the rest of you is just as delectable as ever," he purred.

Revulsion filled her very blood. She whipped around to face him, wishing with every fiber that he would be frozen where he stood.

Poseidon gasped quietly. "Oh yes, my love. I feel the power from your eyes… exhilarating." He began to walk towards her. "But, I am a God, and you cannot harm me." He gave her a smug smile.

Backing away from him, Medusa let the full weight of her hatred show. "And I am a mortal…" Grabbing a nearby dagger, she held it to her throat. "…and you, shall… not… touch… me," she said deliberately.

Poseidon moved in a flash. Taking her wrist, he spun her around, forcing the knife from her hand, and pinned her against the wall.

"You do not dictate the will of the Gods. We shall have what we want. ***I*** shall have what I want."

Hissing, her serpents struck out at him viciously, before falling, silently immobile.

"I don't believe we need your little friends for this next part." He gently kissed her shoulder.

Pressing her forehead against the wall, Medusa screamed in frustration. She began to feel very strange. She became dizzy as wave after wave of nausea hit her. She found it harder and harder to breathe, and found it impossible to go into her mind as she'd done before. As he began to raise the hem of her gown, she clawed at the wall.

"No… NO!" she cried.

The cave began to tremble beneath them, and the sound of faint roaring filled every nook. Medusa began to buck like a wild creature, shrieking and lashing out. She pushed back with the strength of 1,000 men.

Panting, she faced Poseidon with death in her eyes. They glowed even more unearthly than before. When she finally spoke, her voice was layered with hints of cruelty, and echoed inside his head.

"You… shall… not… touch… me!" She was visibly shaking.

Poseidon grew angry. "You dare deny me?!" The ground continued to rumble beneath his feet, but it was not his anger that caused it. Unsure of what else to do, he moved to strike her. "You ungrateful…"

Medusa reached out in defense and caught his hand. A surprised breath whooshed out of her. They stared at each other in shock and confusion. For once in their existence, Poseidon felt something he had never felt before, and Medusa saw something she had never seen before.

Fear.

Poseidon narrowed his eyes in unfulfilled rage. "You shall pay for this…"

"Perhaps, but not by **your** hand." Her every word dripped with a threat. Medusa did not know where the words were coming from, where that display of strength came from. She felt an overwhelming power pulsing through her. The power was the only thing holding her upright, so she took brave step forward. "Get out!" she shouted.

Poseidon growled impotently. "This is not over."

"Send whomever you like! Come back… if you dare. I shall not fear you. Do you hear me? You, and that **bitch,** can never harm me again!"

As he vanished, Medusa fell to her knees, weak and faint. The ground stilled as she lie on her side, hugging her knees to her chest. As she rocked, warmth filled the cave, along with the sound of faint humming.

BEAUTY UNLEASHED

Poseidon's roar could be heard throughout the hall. Mildly curious, Athena strolled to follow the sound. "Quite an entrance, Uncle."

Poseidon was locked in an agitated pace. "I want her dead, do you hear me? Dead!"

Indifferent to whatever he felt his latest plight was, Athena did her best to feign interest. "And who is it you want dead now?"

"Medusa!" he shouted.

She rolled her eyes. "Well, of course you do. So do I. Do not worry so, Uncle. We will find her..."

"I **have** found her!" he groaned.

She fixed him with a look of confused arrogance. "You have **found** her?" He still managed to look as though she were somehow slow.

"Found her and confronted her... do **try** and keep up, Athena!"

Annoyed at his flighty conversation, she folded her arms and glared at him. "Well, if you found her... why is she ... not... dead?" She ground out the last words to let her agitation show.

He stared off, frowning, for a brief moment. "... I couldn't."
Athena really rolled her eyes, then. "Don't tell me you had a change

of…"

"I'm telling you…," he growled, "… I **couldn't**."

Athena chuckled uneasily. "What do you mean you couldn't?"

"I couldn't even strike her," he whispered.

As he continued, Athena tuned him out. It was impossible. Medusa was mortal. How could he **not** strike her? Had Aphrodite given her powers? The whole thing was perplexing. Athena despised obstacles. She believed in victory, lived in victory. Defeat was not an option.

Medusa was becoming a vexation, unusual for such an unworthy adversary. But, like anything else that got in her path, Athena would crush her. She would've been satisfied with her slipping into obscurity, having been taught her lesson. But this show of defiance, this unwillingness to accept her station… she would have her head.

"Athena, are you listening to me?!"

She glanced at Poseidon as if she was surprised he was still there. "Start from the beginning, Uncle. And leave out nothing."

Poseidon tightened his jaw and took a deep breath. He now had to retell the story he had just finished.

Medusa walked regally, as if she were still in the halls of Olympus. These caves were her palace, these serpents were her crown. She was a queen among women. As she walked, she felt power pulse and flow through her. Stopping, she placed her hand against a wall, truly understanding for the first time.

She had known that she was living within her mother but, today, she discovered her mother now lived within her. "Mother… it is you. I feel you, holding me, protecting me."

As always, glowing warmth filled the cave; answering warmth. Smiling, Medusa slid down to the floor and leaned against the wall. What little remained of her mother was here, with her, strengthening her. She need not be afraid anymore. Poseidon could not harm her, and as for Athena… just let her try.

Try they would, though. Medusa was smart enough to know it wasn't over. They knew where she was, and they would come for her, one way or another. Oddly, this did not frighten her as it once had. Whatever fate had in store for her, one thing was certain; she would meet it standing on her own two feet, with her head held high.

She was Medusa, and she was a queen among women.

Poseidon finally finished his thorough, if edited, description of what happened. Athena remained amazingly stoic despite the anger bubbling inside her.

With a haughty sniff, she spoke very calmly and very slowly. "So, our little Medusa lives. And she lives… within Ceto. What are the odds?"

Poseidon frowned. "That shouldn't matter. Ceto is dead."

"Dead in body, perhaps," she tapped her chin, thoughtfully. "Her spirit will always live on. And, it appears it will live on through Medusa, or at least in her defense."

"Neither man nor God can escape the will of Fate." Poseidon's jaw tightened. "So it is hopeless, then."

"No, not hopeless, *Uncle*." Athena was ever shrewd, ever ruthless.

She would never accept defeat. If there was a winning strategy, she would find it. Poseidon rarely looked beyond what he wanted at the moment.

"But if she cannot ***die***...," Poseidon began.

Athena was disgusted with his ignorance. "She is a *mortal*, Uncle... she can **die**!" She rolled her eyes and tried to calm herself. Her eyes took on a thoughtful gleam. "...If not by our hands, then we shall just have to find out whose."

"Well, there is no shortage of hands at my disposal. I shall send all I have." With that, Poseidon stalked off.

Athena shook her head. Poseidon was the tide. He thought nothing of beating relentlessly against stone until it crumbled. She would take another tactic. It was time for her to do what she did best.

Glaucus stopped and tread water. He had almost made it halfway across the river, and somehow had to summon the strength to go the distance. His arms hurt, his legs were sore, and his chest was tight and constricted.

With his breaths coming in gasps, a decision had to be made. He had not passed the point of no return. He could turn back. The wind whipped and the water churned, the current pushing him towards his starting point. Discouraged, his body sank slightly. He could turn back.

He sighed quietly, and then with a large gasp, he turned his body and, kicking hard, launched himself into the oncoming waves. The water seemed to beat harder against him; the closer he got to the opposite shore. Yelling against the pressure, his progress was slowed, but he steadily inched his way closer to his goal.

Hours later, pummeled and battered, he heaved his body onto the bank, too exhausted to do anything but lie there, praying for his heartbeat to return to normal. He didn't have strength to move, barely had the will to breathe. Looking up, he stared into a pair of large, familiar eyes.

"H-h-h-how d-d-did you g-get ov-ver h-h-here, Hh-horse?" he rasped.

Two large brown eyes blinked nonchalantly and, despite the pain, Glaucus had no choice but to laugh.

Eurynome walked through her house, in a fog. She had barely slept or eaten since returning. Food was sour in her belly, and every time she closed her eyes, she was plagued with nightmares.

It was only a matter of time before Poseidon returned. The report of the strange man that came upon her departure did nothing to alleviate her fears. Poseidon would come back. He would either be bent on seduction, or bent on destruction. She wasn't sure which disturbed her more. She saw no way to protect herself from either.

When she heard the faint noise of hoof beats and commotion, her heart froze in her chest. Her reprieve was over. She tried to fight the urge to vomit as her head pounded. She stood there resolute, awaiting her fate.

A trio of voices reached her, frantically calling her name. She jumped slightly as the doors flew open, and her daughters came streaming in, peppering her with questions.

"Mother, where is Medusa? Is she here?"

"What has gone on?!"

"We can't get an answer from anyone!"

Eurynome's face wrinkled in confusion. She must be dreaming. So ready was she for either Poseidon's wrath, or his sickening touch, this onslaught of questions from her daughters, standing around her like three beautiful pillars of strength, seemed to come from a distant land.

Her vision suddenly cleared and, looking at their waiting expressions staring back at her, she realized they were really there. She wasn't alone.

Aglaea gently touched her shoulder. "Mother?…"

At the simple contact, Eurynome burst into tears.

"Mother, what's wrong?!" Thalia asked.

Eurynome reached out to them, one by one, touching them, assuring herself they were real. She gathered them to her tightly.

"Will you stay with me, please?!" she sobbed.

Euphrosyne wrapped her arms around her mother. "Of course we will. Please tell us what has happened."

Eurynome could not even form the words. She sat there and exorcised the past days from her heart. Her daughters sat around her, offering what comfort they could. They quietly looked at each other in alarm. Something was very wrong.

"Mother, you must talk to us. We've never seen you like that," Thalia said.

Eurynome wanted so badly to unburden herself. She felt so conflicted. She didn't know who she could trust and, what was worse;

she didn't know what position she would put her daughters in by confiding in them.

The only thing she was completely sure of was she was so relieved they were there.

"I've had the most horrible dreams. I fear something terrible has happened," she cautiously replied.

Euphrosyne frowned. "Do you think something happened to Medusa?"

Aglaea said nothing. She merely observed. Eurynome was hiding something from them. She had a feeling her mother knew where

Medusa was, and exactly what had happened. She was sure the only thing Eurynome **didn't** know, was whether or not to trust **them**. Not that she could blame her.

That night, boarding boats and mounting horses, soldiers from Delphi, Thebes, Corinth and Sparta, prepared for departure. One dozen soldiers each, they set out for an unknown island, to face an unknown adversary.

Each would do his duty, however. Despite the many unknowns, the men knew the only thing they must. This crusade was the will of the Gods.

BEAUTY HUNTED

For the first time in days, Eurynome was sleeping soundly. Very quietly, the Charities crept from her room. Once the door was closed, they collectively heaved a sigh. "Do you think she knows what happened?" Euphrosyne asked. "If she does, surely she would've told us," Thalia said. Once again, Aglaea was deep in thought. "She knows. And she is on her guard. We must get her to trust us."

As they spoke in private, Eurynome was beginning to open her eyes. She stretched, feeling more rested than she could remember being in a long time. What she wanted now was a nice long bath. Getting out of her bed, she stretched and began to lower her gown to her feet.

"I'd forgotten what a beautiful body you possess, Eurynome."

Eurynome let a yelp escape as she snatched the gown back up and whipped around. Seeing Poseidon again made her blood run cold, the only proof to her that this was really happening.

Poseidon leered at her. He enjoyed scaring her. This would not be the last. He suspected Eurynome knew more than she pretended, and he tired of waiting. He wanted answers.

"Do not cover up on my account," he chuckled. He slowly walked towards her. Eurynome reminded herself not to panic. She regarded him as coolly as possible, refusing to back down. "Mother, are you alri… Uncle Poseidon," Thalia furrowed her brow. Her sisters filed into the room behind her. "This is a surprise, Uncle," Euphrosyne chimed. All three girls hitched a brow in unison.

"My lovelies!" Poseidon laughed, "What are you doing here?"

Aglaea gave him a mirthless smile as she edged closer to her mother. "We were going to ask you the same thing Uncle."

Eurynome silently thanked Zeus for these three gifts.

Thalia took her mother's arm and led her to the bed. "Mother, you really do need your rest."

Euphrosyne linked her arm through Poseidon's. "Thank you for checking on her, Uncle. When we heard Medusa had gone missing from Olympus, we thought to check here as well."

Thalia shook her head as she helped Eurynome under the blankets. "As you can see, no news on this front. Mother has been sick with worry. Have you figured out anything?"

Aglaea's eyes never left Poseidon's face.

"Not as of yet. But believe me, I will." He looked pointedly at Eurynome.

Aglaea spoke, finally. "We will be staying here with Mother until we know anything." She looked pointedly at him. "On your return to Olympus, please keep your ears open, and inform us if there is any news."

Poseidon's jaw tightened at being thwarted yet again. He had just been dismissed, and could do nothing to Eurynome as long as the Charities were in residence. From the looks of it, he clearly got the message that they planned to visit for a prolonged period of time. He managed an indifferent mask and a faint smile before vanishing.

All four were silent for several moments. Thalia reached out and took Eurynome's hand.

"It's worse than we thought," Euphrosyne said.

Aglaea looked at Eurynome very seriously. "Mother, it's time you told us what is going on."

Glaucus yawned in the saddle. Soon it would be time to camp for the night. He shifted slightly, noticing he wasn't as sore as he had been… thankfully. Rounding a bend, he saw a figure up ahead. He rode nearer and saw it was an elderly woman trudging down the road, all hunched and hobbling.

"W-what are you d-doing all alone on the road?" he asked.

"Walking!" she sniffed.

That brought a smile to his face. He dismounted and came around to face her.

"C-can I offer you a ride m-my good lady?"

She eyed him warily. "And what will you be expecting in return, young man?"

Glaucus couldn't help but admire her spirit. "Just s-some good company until we part."

"Good!" she nodded brusquely. As she went to mount the horse, Glaucus attempted to help her up. His hand accidentally slipped to her backside and received a sound whack. "None of that! Good company's all you'll be getting from me today."

He laughed loudly at her rebuke. "So, w-where are you on your w-way to this day, m-my lady?"

"I am making my way to Crete."

Glaucus couldn't hide his concern. "Crete? That's a l-long voyage, especially alone. W-what is so important in C-crete?"

She sighed. "That is what I must find out. There is a man who wants to marry my daughter. I will see what sort of man he is before I allow it."

"Was there n-no one else who could make this trip f-for you?"

She gave him a haughty look of disapproval. "And who should make this trip? Someone younger? A man perhaps?" Rolling her eyes, she made a sound of disgust.

"I m-meant no d-disrespect. It just seems like an arduous t-task to take on alone."

She nodded. "That it is. But she is my treasure. The man who gets her love, must love her more than I. And only I can judge that."

Glaucus nodded in return. "W-well, Glaucus, s-son of Minos is at your s-service." He gave her an abbreviated bow.

"I am Sophie, young Glaucus." They shared a companionable smile. "So, where are *you* journeying to?" she asked him.

He contemplated that. It seemed hypocritical for him to question her pilgrimage, when the fact remained he did not know exactly where he was going. "…I too am on a quest of l-love," he cryptically answered.

Once Euphrosyne handed her a cup of wine, Eurynome sighed and sank against her pillows. She was grateful to have her daughters' protection, but she still worried over how much to disclose. She didn't want to put any of her children in danger. "Do you think Poseidon will find her?"

Euphrosyne shook her head slowly. "I don't know. We heard she was banished from Olympus. That's all we could find out."

Thalia looked concerned. "No one knows anything! Father's been sullen and will see no one. Athena and Uncle Poseidon are always holed up together, and Aphrodite is nowhere to be found."

"Mother, is Medusa alright?" Aglaea quietly asked. It was obvious to her that Eurynome knew where Medusa was.

"…y-yes." Eurynome wasn't sure how much she believed herself. It wasn't exactly true, yet it wasn't exactly a lie. She supposed for all intents and purposes that Medusa was alright.

Her daughters did not miss her hesitation. "Is there anything we can do?" Thalia inquired.

Eurynome frowned and shook her head. The Charities all nodded in acceptance. They came to sit around her.

"Then we shall speak no more on it," Aglaea declared. "We are here now, and we will take care of you. You take care of our cousin."

They all embraced each other tearfully.

Glaucus sat staring into the fire, thinking of his mission and its end. He and Sophie were camping for the night. He thought of her quest then, the noble task she would entrust to no one but herself. Glaucus was very glad he ran into her. He did not like the thought of her possibly camping out here by herself.

"Such deep thought for such a young mind…," Sophie interrupted.

Glaucus smiled at her. "You are right. I should be collecting my debt of good company. Tell me of this young man who has the daunting task of impressing you."

Sophie laughed, wagging her finger at him. "Oh no, I have told you much of my journey. Now, I would like to hear about yours. Tell me of this love. How is it she came to be so far away?"

His face saddened. "It is a very long story."

"Fair enough. Where did you come from?" Sophie was relentless.

"Mount Olympus," he chuckled.

At her incredulous look, he laughed harder. He began to tell her of his eventful trip, filled with curiosities and confusions.

Medusa lie out in the sun. For once, her hair lay completely still and silent, as the serpents basked in the warmth.

"Enjoying yourselves, darlings?"

She smiled and closed her eyes, listening to the soothing sounds of the sea. She had been unable to sleep last night, her mind jolted awake at the slightest sounds. Things had been quiet for a while and she felt herself, finally, able to relax.

Glaucus and Sophie chatted idly as they traveled along the road. He had to admit she was, actually, very good company. She was sharp and witty and very wise. He had told her as much that morning. They agreed to stay travel companions for as long as their paths went in the same direction.

"Alright, my lady, I have told you my story. It is your turn. Tell me of this young man. Have you met him?"

"... Briefly," she hesitated. "I have not spent enough time in his company to assess his worth."

She always made him smile with her tone. She spoke like royalty despite her station in life. "What have you been able to assess of him from your brief meeting."

"I know he seems to care for my darling," she conceded.

He raised his eyebrows. "Well, that's something, at least."

Sophie nodded. "Yes. However, very often, things are not as they seem."

A sudden chill awoke Medusa from her sleep. Disoriented, she looked around, realizing it was nearly nightfall. Her body ached from the hard ground, and she rubbed her arms against the cold. Standing, she looked out across the sea. There was a ship nearing, a small ship, but filled with men.

These were not adolescents, or angry commoners. These were soldiers, and they were ready for battle. Medusa backed slowly into her home. She could hear every beat of her heart. There were so many, and they would be here soon. She'd never had to fight anyone like this.

Medusa felt all the fear and insecurity of her age. Her whole body trembled and she wanted to run and hide. Run, she did. She found a sword and gripped it tightly, fighting the dizziness and nausea that threatened to consume her. Hands shaking, she dropped to her knees, her breath coming in short pants, tears escaping her eyes.

The ground beneath her began to move, and she felt her fear ebb away. She was not alone. A calming peace washed over her, and she closed her eyes to embrace the euphoria. Let them come. If she dies tonight, so be it. Her heart issued a command her mind did not fully believe. It swam through her blood and invaded her body.

Better to die with audacity than live with anxiety.

Athena waited in Zeus's chamber with trepidation. She didn't know why he requested an audience with her. Zeus had been very moody lately, his guilt over Ceto's death still gnawing at him, and his fights with Hera coming more frequently.

She and Poseidon both knew that, any day, their indiscretions could be revealed. Poseidon, of course, made himself scarce on Olympus, only returning if he needed to. She, on the other hand, was made to stay, reminded daily of her tremulous position.

The doors flew open, the hinges rattling from the force. Zeus strode in, distracted.

"Hello, daughter. I'm afraid I need your help. There seems to be a problem with my son."

His son? Despite her confusion, Athena allowed herself to relax. "Of course father, what do you need me to do?"

"Danae's suitor wishes to exile him, or worse. I need…"

Hera stormed into the room, eyes blazing. "I would have a word with you, Zeus!"

Zeus rolled his eyes, as thunder rumbled overhead. Athena placed a reassuring hand on his arm. "I will handle it, Father," she whispered. As she walked away, she smiled curiously.

BEAUTY'S FIGHT

The men were just outside her home. She could barely feel the fear anymore, it was pushed down so deep. It was a distant shiver from far away. With one swing, one fatal blow, any of those men could end her life. But with one flash of her eyes, she could end mankind. She need not fear them. "Get out of my home," she growled loudly.

She heard no response, sensed no retreat. So, she picked up her sword, and stood at the ready. There were no more than twenty. She was sure of it. Walking slowly, she let her sword drag across the ground. She was weary of games. She wanted them to come for her.

She heard the sound of footsteps shuffling towards her. Stepping into the shadow, she allowed them to pass. There were four of them, in tight formation, each looking in a separate direction. Very smart, but so many corners were hidden in darkness. If one's eyes were not accustomed, he could miss it.

Stepping cautiously, they began to fan away from each other. Medusa followed them and, banging her sword against the ground, drew their eyes to her own. The men were blessed with eternal expressions of surprise. A scrape behind her had her whipping around to meet the gaze of another young man. She stood to the side and observed his still form.

His mouth was open on a battle cry that never left his lips. His chest was spread with a breath he would never release. His arms were raised, sword in hand, ready to destroy an enemy he would never strike. She walked away with a mild sense of disappointment.

She grew bored with these men.

They could not defeat her. They could not even fight her. She heard more approaching. No doubt they had trained long and hard. And for what? Maybe, she would play with the next lot. What other joy does the cat get from the mouse?

Medusa traipsed deeper into the caves, humming seductively. She saw two soldiers rounding a corner and quietly stalked them. They were heading towards a dead end, which worked perfectly. Just as it was to be discovered, she gasped loudly and turned her back to them. Both men turned on her, swords drawn. Medusa dropped to her knees.

"Do not hurt me, please!" Dropping her sword away from her, her voice trembled. "…Please."

"You will die witch!" one man shouted.

"I am no witch, sir. Please do not strike this poor, cursed maiden!"

"Cursed?" the other curiously replied.

Smiling, Medusa rose leadenly. "Yes, let me show you, my lords." She innocently went to undo her clasp. "If you will but lower your swords, I will lower my gown."

Hearing the telltale clang of their swords, Medusa's lips curled in disgust. Head bowed, she pushed her gown down, and held it just below her waist.

"You see, I am, but a woman."

The two soldiers looked at the fine lines of her back and exchanged glances.

"We cannot be sure, lest you turn around," one sneered.

Medusa shifted her hips ever so slightly. "As you wish…"

She looked at their pleased faces and wished she could've prolonged their final moments. They repulsed her. She looked at their demeanor. Arms slack, swords dropped to their sides.

"Your fathers would be so proud," she purred.

The hissing at her ears alerted her she was no longer alone. She ducked in time to avoid the blade that was swung for her neck. Falling to the ground, she turned over and grabbed one of the soldier's swords and blocked another blow. She looked at her assailant, ending his life.

Catching her breath, she scurried from her position. After securing her gown in place, she went in search of the others. She walked through her halls confidently. There were still some left alive, and they were coming her way.

Four men walked together, uneasy, in the silence of the caves. There were no sounds of struggle, no sounds of battle. With each step, the apprehension grew. They looked all around them, careful to watch each other's backs.

Something in the distance caught the eye of one of them. Mesmerized, he drifted towards the sight, drawn to the foreign object, which was oddly familiar. As he neared, he realized it was a statue of some sort. Taking a closer look, his breath caught in his throat. He opened his mouth, but the words refused to come.

The three remaining men looked around, missing their forth comrade. A scream sounded behind them, and all three ran through the nearest arch, right into the path of their adversary. As their ears hardened and closed for all time, the last thing they heard was a hysterical cry.

"Stone! They're all stone!"

Medusa's eyes darted towards the sound. She broke out in a run, dashing through the weaving tunnels, until she could see the glow of the entrance ahead. The man, still screaming, scampered, nearly escaping. Medusa reached out for his arm, whipping him around to face her.

With a look of wonder in his eye, his body solidified. Medusa studied him, his mouth slightly opened, his free hand extended. In his last moment, he'd reached out to try and touch her face. It had been so long since anyone had looked at her like that.

Still clutching his arm, she rested her cheek against his open palm. It was cold and stiff, but she closed her eyes and allowed the illusion to cloak her. Standing there, the two of them were bathed in moonlight. To anyone looking, they could have easily been mistaken for lovers. But they were not. They were not even friends. He was her enemy, as they all were.

They had been sent to kill her, but they did not succeed. And their fates would be shared by anyone who came into her home. Releasing her hold, she tightened her jaw, raised her chin, and slowly returned to the darkness and shadow.

Athena stood on the shore of Seriphus, the night sea breeze rushing over her skin. The rich sand sank beneath her feet as the waves gently embraced. Closing her eyes, she inhaled deeply, savoring the taste of the Aegean salt.

Without thought, her mouth curved into a smile and her hands went to her hair, of their own accord. She removed her pins and began to unwind the braid that snaked around her hair. She sighed at the feel of its heavy weight on her back. As she began to loosen it, her hair was caught up in the draft and started to whirl wildly around her.

The strands brushed her cheeks and stroked her arms tenderly and, on the wind, ghostly voices from the past filled her ears.

"Have you never bathed naked, with your hair spread around you, floating on water like it was air?"

Her breaths shortened, and her hair caught on her wrists and wrapped loosely around her neck. She suddenly felt the sensation of hundreds of snakes curling themselves around her. She couldn't breathe. Athena's eyes flew open as she looked all around her. Her hair hung in a lifeless mass down her back. The sea was calm. There was no wind.

Blinking rapidly, Athena willed her breath to return, and her heart to slow. Still, in her ears, she could not ignore the soft spoken purr.

"You should wear your hair down more often, My Lady."

The memories of days past saddened her. She thought, then, of a golden haired beauty, with innocent, jade eyes, who had looked at her as if the sun rose beneath her feet. She wept silently for what she had done, and what she knew she would do. No fond memories could ever erase the vision of Medusa worshipping at the feet of her greatest rival.

The flow of her tears instantly ceased. To continue would show remorse and, as a Goddess, she could not know regret. Grabbing her hair tightly, she forced it into a neat bun and secured it with her pins. Then, with her head held high, she walked determinedly to the palace of Polydectes, while a storm mounted overhead.

Athena flashed into the king's private chambers in all her glory. A tempest raged against the windows, the lightning making her appearance more fearsome.

"Polydectes, you wish harm on the son of Zeus...," she

bellowed.

Polydectes fell to his knees before her. "No, My Lady! Never **harm**, My Lady. I desire his mother, Danae, but the boy thwarts my every advance! I only wish for his interference to cease." He bowed deeply, his face nearly touching the floor.

Athena stood and seemed to be pondering his request. She looked down her nose at him, first turning one way, and then another. Finally, she raised an eyebrow.

"Very well. Let no ill come to him. Send him away on a commission." She paused thoughtfully. "I was charged with cutting out your heart, for the threat to Zeus's son but, perhaps, you do not need to die." She fixed him with a very grave expression.

"Command that the boy bring you the head of the Gorgon, Medusa. While he is away, you shall be free to pursue his mother, and the threat to his life will be no more. He is to tell no one of his quest, and you are to tell no one of my leniency, or I shall be delivering **your** head."

Polydectes nodded fiercely. "Yes, My Lady. My eternal gratitude is yours!"

Without another word, Athena vanished from his chamber and the storm outside dissipated.

Arriving in the great hall on Olympus, Athena fell back against a large cushion. All around, the room echoed with her laughter. She would never tire of her own cleverness.

As he often did, Glaucus sat and stared off into space. Sophie grew accustomed to his long moments of silent brooding. He looked troubled, wistful with an air of impatience, and just a little bit afraid. He looked like a man in love.

"Thinking of your treasure, then?" she asked.

He blinked dazedly, and looked around. He'd forgotten she was with him.

"I'm sorry S-s-sophie. I've been extremely rude."

Sophie waved him off and shook her head. "Nonsense. I daresay you've done more for me than any one else around here would have. You are a good man, young Glaucus."

He smiled, sheepishly, at her.

"…Perhaps too good…" she continued.

Glaucus cocked his head curiously. "Too good? W-w-what do you m-m-mean?"

Sophie looked at him. There was a hint of sadness in her eyes… sadness, and something else he couldn't put his finger on. She patted his face fondly and smiled at him the way his mother used to.

"I just worry for you. You've already come so far, and you will go even farther. Can you be sure this girl is worth it?"

"Of course, she's worth it," he answered without hesitation.

Sophie shrugged nonchalantly. "I shall take your word for it. Still… even if you do find her…" At his upset glance, she thought better of her wording. "…*when* you do find her, what if she is not what you expect?"

He stared blankly at her. Sophie was skating on dangerous ground. "What d-do you mean?"

"Well… what if she is… taken? What if she already has another?"

Glaucus frowned. "None of that matters. There is no one else in this world for me. I love her, and will follow her beyond even death, for as long as she allows me to…" He liked Sophie, so he didn't like being upset with her. Before he could say anything out of anger, he stalked off.

BEAUTY'S BATTLE

Medusa awoke more tired than when she went to bed. She stretched and twisted, cataloguing all of her sore muscles. She staggered drowsily through the caves, squinting against the brightness streaming in. It was well past noon, and she'd slept longer than she wanted to.

She wanted nothing more than to relax her body in her pool, and then bake it in the sun. But, she needed to eat and prepare herself for another long night, for she had no doubt that once she looked out to the sea, there would be another ship, making its way to her.

With a heavy sigh, she stepped out into the blinding sunlight. Once her eyes adjusted, she stared off into the distance. She closed her eyes and let out a shaky breath. She had been wrong. There were **two** ships making their way towards her. They were different from each other, but seemed to be the same sized vessels as the one that brought last night's visitors. She would certainly be facing more than twenty tonight. The snakes slithered against her neck and face, a gesture she'd begun to find comforting.

"Come, loves. It is time for breakfast. And then, we shall prepare for our guests."

As she walked away, her companions hissed vehemently behind her.

Poseidon walked into the Great Hall quite pleased with himself. He'd formulated a plan, without the Mighty Athena's help, and he was very optimistic about the outcome. "Why Uncle, you're positively covered in canary feathers," Athena chuckled.

"Indeed, my dear. We will be rid of Medusa shortly."

Athena closed her eyes, enraptured. It was as if the statement itself was on her tongue, and she wanted to savor every word. "Indeed," she purred.

Poseidon looked at her skeptically. "What have you done, you dragon?"

"I am sending someone for our darling Medusa... Perseus, son of Zeus." Athena laughed giddily. "It could not be more perfect."

Poseidon did not look impressed. "You sent one mortal man after her?"

Athena rolled her eyes. She was in an unusually good mood, and Poseidon was ruining it. Why could he not simply concede to her victory, not to mention her wisdom, and go away? "Think of it, Uncle. The worst of it would be that he go to her and kill her. The best of it, would be if she kills *him.*"

At Poseidon's blank look, she groaned. "If Medusa kills the son of Zeus, he will no doubt be bent on revenge. Zeus would kill her, completely unchallenged, and it is unlikely that he will care one bit what mysterious tragedies had befallen her."

Poseidon gritted his teeth. She would use any opportunity to upstage him. "There may be nothing left for him. I've sent warriors from four lands to bring *me* her head."

"You sent a band of armored thugs with absolutely no direction after an extremely powerful monster?" Athena roared with laughter.

Poseidon turned on his heel. He didn't have to listen to her scoffing. It was *her* fault Medusa was so powerful.

Still laughing, Athena called after him. "You always did underestimate Medusa."

Poseidon whirled to face her. He hadn't actually looked at her before then. She was spread out on the cushions, her cheeks rosy from her laughter, her hair loose and flowing all around her. He smiled smugly at her. "That my dear, is a sin we've both committed." Satisfied with the flash of anger in her eyes, he took his leave.

Medusa ate woodenly. Food had no taste in her mouth. The sun had no warmth on her skin. Her every move was automatic, mechanical. All she wanted was to crawl back in bed, though she knew that wouldn't be possible.

She turned and checked on the progress of the ships. They should reach her just before nightfall. She still had time. She would have to be very focused tonight. She'd never faced so many at once. They would have to be killed quickly if she was to have any chance.

She felt like she'd spent her entire life fighting. She was tired and she was angry. She was filled with hate and disappointment. Life had not been the joy she'd thought it should've been, and she knew now it never would be. The disillusionment stung. There was infinite sadness over what could have been, yet she could summon no tears to purge it. All she could do was eat to conserve her strength. All she could do was what needed to be done to survive another day… so she could do it all again.

Sophie was laying out a light fare for them when Glaucus returned. Maybe she had gone too far, though that was the ultimate plan. She had to admit, he handled his anger very calmly. She looked up at him, cautiously, as he began to speak.

"My ap-p-pologies, Sophie." He spoke softly. He was still mildly upset, but he would not leave Sophie by herself with night approaching. She had disturbed him deeply, and forced him to think of things he hadn't up until this point.

What if Medusa had meant to leave without him? What if he had never crossed her mind? Worse, what if, after all this, she would never love him. They hadn't known each other for very long, but there was no doubt in his mind that she was the woman he was destined to spend the rest of his life with.

"My apologies as well, Glaucus." Sophie spoke hesitantly, as if she was unused to making amends. She invited him to sit with her and, as they ate, they silently forgave each other, reaching a comfortable truce.

Sophie broke the silence first. "You are such a nice young man, a good man, I think only of your happiness. You are the kind of man I would wish for my treasure."

Glaucus smiled shyly. "Really?"

Sophie nodded brightly. "Of course! You have dedication, good character, and a pleasant manner. And you must know you are a strong, strapping young man."

He was slightly embarrassed by her remarks. "We should get some sleep, Sophie. Tomorrow we acquire a boat, and get you to Crete."

Finishing his small meal, Glaucus blushed slightly and looked himself over. He'd never considered himself particularly handsome and certainly not strapping but, as he looked, he noticed a difference in himself. This long trek, filled with walking, swimming and riding horses had really made a difference in his body. His arms and legs were tightly corded with muscles. His stomach was rippled and firm.

Sophie broke into his thoughts. "You had quite a stutter, but even that's gotten better. In general, you are a fine young man." She nodded with finality.

How could he not have noticed that? She was right. He felt so comfortable talking with her. He no longer suffered the awful embarrassment that used to come every time he opened his mouth. He occasionally stumbled on a word or two, but nothing near the debilitating speech that caused him to isolate himself for so long.

As the sun set, a smirk of pride passed over his face. He'd been thinking all day about Sophie's question, thinking about what he would do if he found his Honey, and she was not what he was expecting. He'd never considered that *he* would have somehow changed. He may not be what *she's* expecting. Feeling good about himself, he folded his hands behind his head and lie under the rose tinted sky, waiting for the first star to show.

Medusa leaned casually against the cave entrance, staring up at the sky. One lone star shone brightly against the violet sky. It reminded her of a ripened pomegranate still clutching the tree, the sun glinting against a ruby curve. All around, faded pinpoints dotted the heavens, not able to show their true brilliance while the sun lingered. She backed up until she felt the security of her stone suitor at her back.

She found it strange that she was beholding so much beauty and tranquility, with the threat of death hovering mere minutes away. Well, Hades would have to wait. Life had rarely shown her charms of this sort. She would accept love in any form. With a small salute to the retreating daylight, she retreated from her warm feelings, and let the shadow consume her.

Medusa began to recognize the transformation that took place in her. Her heart thudded a dirge, and her hands fisted uncontrollably. She narrowed her eyes and tightened her jaw, a permanent scowl marring her beautiful face. Her skin felt cold to her own fingers, and she felt heavy and monstrous. It was as if she didn't know her own body.

A cracking in the distance caught her attention. So it began again. The vermin were crawling their way through the dirt and rock and, like all vermin, they needed to be exterminated.

They poured into her asylum, speaking in hushed tones. It seems as though the two small armies decided to band together. She had been hoping they would not do that. It seems the luck she's been having for the last few years was unrelenting. She would have to shake their confidence somehow.

She laughed evilly, knowing how the sound reverberated and merged. That never failed to set the men on edge.

"Come to me, my little rats. You will make a delicious snack for my pets." She knew how to make her voice raspy. She had no trouble turning her tone cold, and unfeeling. "Try not to scream too loudly, as they devour you."

Medusa could hear the frantic whispering, and smiled faintly. She'd nearly unhinged them. "Did you not see my lover at the entrance, his hand raised in entreaty? He begs you to leave this place, as he cannot… not anymore."

All whispers ceased. The poor frightened darlings. Not to be deterred, however, soon enough, the sound of shuffling feet and scraping armor reached her. Before long, Medusa stood, unwavering, at the end of a large cavernous room, watching as two dozen soldiers filed in to face her. Between them, the five young warriors she had met previously stood as a silent warning.

The men, paralyzed with fear, stood staring across at this beautifully formed maiden, half hidden in the gloom. Eyes downcast, she conveyed a final warning.

"These men were once like you. Leave with your life, or stay… for eternity. With one caress, you will belong to me."

Nervous glances were exchanged, and legs were poised for retreat. The two leaders, however, would never run away from a lone woman, no matter what powers she believed she possessed.

"Steady men! This demon shall not defeat us today!" one man shouted. They began to move slowly, en masse towards her position, tightly huddled.

"Bring me the demon's head! Do not let her touch you!" the other chimed.

The ground rumbled softly beneath their feet, and a deep hissing began to sound. Medusa let out an amused snort as she lifted her head and both arms, bearing swords. She would not have to ***touch*** them. She would, however, have to be very quick.

Not wanting to keep her fate waiting, she fearlessly ran forward, weapons raised. All she needed was a fraction of a second. With her swords, she blocked each advance, inevitably catching her assailant's eye. She dashed and wound her way around her five earthen swains, using her small stone army as shields. With each man she defeated, her ranks increased, while her foes diminished.

She never stayed in one spot for more than a moment, the dimness helping to keep her enemies confused. She dodged their blows, their rapt attention on her becoming their undoing. She kept rock to her back at all times. Her arms were full of scrapes and scuffs. Her hands ached, and pure survival was her only strength.

With each attack, she lifted those swords, though she swore it would be the last time she was capable. Again and again, she spun around her quarry of stone bodies, though she felt her legs could carry her no further. She screamed out her pain, her shrieks taking her the extra distance to win… to live. Slowly, the racket of war quieted.

Panting, she slumped against a solidified warrior, angry, saddened, and grateful to be alive. She was bleeding, her clothes in tatters, her skin scraped. None was so scarred as her heart. She hurt… and she hated.

A whimper caught her attention. On alert, she sought out the sound, dragging the swords at her sides. Accustomed to the dark, it did not take her long to find a huddled lump on the floor. She watched as he trembled, and felt nothing.

"…Look at me," she simply stated.

He shook his head quickly, his face pressed to the ground. His sword was abandoned long ago, along with any pride or bravado he once felt. Medusa turned her head this way and that, and still felt nothing. He seemed like a foreign object from far away, and she felt far removed from him. She briefly wondered if this was how the Gods saw mortals.

"Look at me!" she growled sternly.

He shook his head more slowly, trying to crawl backwards. "No… please. I'm not going to hurt you. I just want to leave."

She chuckled. "You **cannot** hurt me. And you cannot leave.

Now, look at me."

She stood before him. He sat back on his heels, with his head lowered. He slowly reached out and touched her feet.

"Please my lady, let me go." His voice wavered. "I beg you. I have a family."

"Look at me… look at me… look at me!" she repeated, her voice rising at ever turn. She kicked out at him, sending him reeling backwards. As he tried to crawl away, she struck him again and again, her eyes tearing with unforgiving rage. She cut off his escape, shutting her ears to his pleas.

He rose to his knees, breathing shakily. His shoulders slumped in defeat, but he still refused to meet her eyes. "Please… don't." Kneeling behind him, Medusa took his hair in her hands, and yanked his head backwards.

"…Forgive me," he whispered softly.

"No," she replied, and looked soullessly into his sad brown eyes. She didn't know how long she knelt there staring at him. Unsteadily, she got to her feet. She felt weary in every sense. There was no comforting warmth radiating off of the walls, there was no nurturing lullaby. That night, she was witch. That night, she was demon.

BEAUTY VISITED

Danae stood looking at her son. He looked as young to her now as he did the day they arrived on the island. This was her baby. They had never been separated, and now, who knows when she would see him next. Despite her best efforts, tears spilled over onto their joined hands. "Do not cry, Mother," Perseus soothed.

"How can I not?" she sniffled. "I have to watch you leave, not knowing where you will be, not knowing what dangers await you… this is a mother's nightmare!"

Smiling bravely, Perseus hugged his mother. Looking across, he saw Polydectes lurking a few yards away. The smile died on his face. He worried as much for his mother, as she did for him. The quicker he could dispatch this task, the better. Putting his smile back in place, he stood to face his mother.

"Mother, I will be safe, and I promise I will return to you. In the meantime… you take care of yourself. I love you." He kissed her gently on the cheek, and set out on his journey. He would go to the temple and make an offering to the Gods for protection… and guidance.

Medusa awoke, yet couldn't summon the strength to leave her bed. She did not want to see the sun that day. She did not want to see the sky. Her heart was heavy, making her chest ache and burn. Serpents coiled their way around her neck. She smiled at their attempts to comfort her. They sensed her feelings and fed from them. She, too, could differentiate their movements, even the tone of each hiss.

She laughed bitterly at the thought. This was just one more in a long line of strange relationships. She had never met her parents. The only mother she'd known for most of her life was the consort of a God who was kind enough to take her in. Her sisters, or 'cousins', she supposed, were children of another God, with same said woman.

She'd never had many friends growing up. Oh, everyone had known her, and everyone had liked her. She was always treated with warmth and respect, but she'd always felt like her life was rooted in isolation. Never one to complain, she'd always made the best of it.

Her first love was an Immortal - A beautiful Goddess who'd given her unparalleled experiences, but alas, a love with no future, at least not a real one. Her first true friend had turned on her, cast her aside… cursed her. It still pained her every time she thought of it. She'd loved Athena. She'd begged her for at least a moment to explain. Athena would not grant her even that.

Medusa thought of the night before. How she'd turned a deaf ear to the pleading of another. She reasoned with herself, told herself it wasn't the same. He hadn't been her friend and loyal servant.

He begged for his life.

So had she. She had begged for her life, and it had made no difference. Why should she show mercy, when none had ever found its way to her.

He begged for your forgiveness.

She had no cause to forgive him. Those men had come there to kill her. If she had let him go, he likely would've come back with more men the next night. He could not be trusted. He was just like all the other men. He was just like everyone else who had betrayed her, and left her for dead.

*And who are **you** like?*

That question gave her pause. She was strong, powerful, and fierce. She'd once thought to herself that she would trade all of her beauty, for a fraction of Athena's strength. It looked as though she had. She'd replaced what was taken from her. Her innocence had been taken, and in its place, was a wall of scorn. She was a fortress, a warrior. In the place of her beauty, she'd gained the armor of cynicism. She wore a helmet of self preservation, a mask of cruelty and, behind it, and the eyes of death itself.

The moment his foot touched the step, Perseus felt immediately at peace. The temple was small, but it was his favorite place on the whole island. He had never met his father face to face, but whenever he was here, he felt a deep, personal connection with him.

He stood looking at the statue of his father, when an uneasy feeling came over him. No sooner than it came did it pass, and he returned admiring Zeus's image.

"Perseus," a commanding voice rang out.

Spinning, Perseus came face to face with the Goddess Athena. Dropping to his knees, he fought to regain his composure. He had often been guided by the Gods, but never had one made their presence known.

"My Lady, I am honored at your presence. What do you wish of me?"

Athena chuckled warmly. "Rise, dear Perseus." Wrapping her hands around his arms, she helped him up. Smiling sweetly at him, she gave him a reassuring pat.

"You have come here for guidance, have you not? Your father would not allow you to face such a heady task without help," she tsked.

He heaved a sigh of relief, and thanked her. She strolled through the temple, leaving him to follow after her.

"The creature you are hunting is very dangerous, hideous in visage and grotesque in form. Her very gaze can turn you to stone." At his worried expression, Athena put her arm around him. "The journey is yours to make, Perseus. Usually, we are forbidden to interfere with mortals, but I promise you, I will help you all that I can, and give you the tools you need to be successful."

"I do not even know where to begin, My Lady…" Perseus felt very young at that moment. For once, he experienced a paralyzing fear. He'd never faced death before. He'd never left that island, or his mother's side. Not even his impressive lineage was able to give him comfort.

Athena smiled lovingly at him. "You will begin with the Graeae, the gray ones. They reside inside the Mountain of the Goddess, the birthplace of your father. Travel south to Crete. They can lead you to the Gorgon, and there you will find what you need to defeat her."

Perseus was more grateful than he could ever express. He bowed deeply, thanking and praising Athena for her wisdom and guidance. She affectionately stroked his head before vanishing from his sight. With a newfound courage, Perseus set out to rid the world of a monster.

Glaucus and Sophie packed up their camp quietly. Glaucus could only think that he wouldn't have her company much longer. He'd gotten very used to her stories, their long talks and jokes. It would be sad when he had to continue his quest alone, and a somber vibe overtook them both.

"Well Sophie, I must say, I'm quite jealous that soon you'll be in the company of another man," he laughed.

"I thought I'd abduct you, take you back to my treasure," she giggled. "Though, I suppose you are still determined to find your own treasure."

Glaucus nodded. "Yes. There is no power on earth, above or below, that could keep me from her. I will follow her wherever she goes." The serene smile he was wearing slowly faded into confusion. He had been struck, but his mind could not grasp the who, how, or why. He was concerned for Sophie's safety, but before he could utter her name, darkness closed on him.

Despite being half asleep, Medusa made her way through the labyrinth of caves effortlessly. Before long, she was standing at the side of her pool. Without preamble, she stripped off her clothes and dove in. Inhaling deeply, she sank beneath the water.

The tune she knew all to well danced around her. She opened her eyes to her aqua cradle. Blues and greens swirled around her, broken only by bright streams of light. She admired the beauty distantly. Arching her back, she propelled herself deeper, where the colors were richer, the light fainter.

She felt her chest tightening, deprived of air. Beyond that, there was a feeling of anxiety. No doubt, tonight would bring another battle, perhaps the fiercest one yet… perhaps her last. She must be at her best, always at her best. She was tired of constantly being on guard. She wanted to be able to sleep through the night. She wanted to be able to laugh the way she used to. She longed for the comfort she once allowed herself to feel.

Surfacing, she floated, trying to calm her mind. She weakly climbed out of the pool and wrapped a bath sheet around herself. Walking into the next chamber, she looked at her subjects, the Army of the Mountain as she'd named them. She strolled through their ranks, speaking to this one and that one.

They never answered her, never bowed in her honor, never smiled at her. But, they were the only company she had. She stood there, and had to chuckle to herself. She was Medusa, Queen of the Stone Court. Her chuckle turned into hysterical laughter that eventually faded into gasps of sadness; dizzying gasps, ending in a fit of self-deprecating giggles.

She was going mad. She'd been alone so long. Medusa came to realize that she'd ultimately killed the only people she'd come in contact with lately, and more would come.

Her life was death. Her home was a tomb for all who entered. Her future was haunted…

A sound outside stopped her cold.

BEAUTY REUNITED

Glaucus awoke with a splitting headache. The bright sun shining in his eyes was not helping matters any. He sat up quickly, looking around him. He was on the shore, though he did not know where. It seemed to be an island, but not one he'd ever been to. He decided to climb the rocks to a higher position, to get his bearing.

Pulling himself up, he found a spacious ledge to rest, and the opening of a cave. He entered it, grateful to be out of the sun, and for the chance to think. Once his eyes adjusted to the darkness, a figure startled him. He'd thought it was a man, but now saw it was a statue. He stared at it curiously, wondering how it came to be there.

He was a contradiction. He had the look of a soldier, but his face was softened with awe and a touch of sadness. One arm hung carelessly by his side. The other, reached out… to what, he did not know. He did know that someone had to have put this here.

"Hello," he called out, and was greeted with resonant laughter.

"Bold hunter, to stalk me in daylight. Have you come to join my stone court? Have you come to die, Hunter?"

Glaucus knotted his brow in confusion and slowly began to walk farther into the cave, looking around him. There was something familiar in the raspy whisper. The words were threatening, but the tone was ironic. It was as though someone was playing a game with him.

Medusa saw the lone shadow of his approach, and picked up her sword. "Oh yes, come to me. Will you chase me? Let me feel your rigid embrace… kiss your frozen lips?" She laughed again, a maniacal sound void of mirth. It was heart wrenching that she craved this interaction, these few minutes before they died.

Glaucus could only conclude some deranged woman lived in these caves. He called out again, louder this time.

"Hello?"

Medusa closed her eyes and savored the sound. "Ah, yes. Talk to me. But, speak slowly… very, very slowly."

Speak slowly… very, very slowly. Those words, reminiscent of past advice, and said so sweetly, gave him pause.

All of his breath rushed out, and his voice came on a sigh. "…Honey?"

The blood completely drained from Medusa's face. Only one person in the world called her Honey. Her eyes flew open and, inhaling sharply, she spun around.

"Glaucus, what are you doing here? You must get out. You must leave, now!" She turned and ran, trying to traverse the maze of tunnels with her head lowered. With every turn, she nearly wept with fear that she would come face to face with him.

"Honey, it's okay…" He had run after her and was catching up.

"No! Stay away from me…" Frantic, she screamed at him, her eyes closed tightly. She scampered over to the side, scraping her shoulder against a rock. She felt her way along the wall, losing her sense of direction in her panic.

"Honey?" He was just on the other side of the wall, searching for her.

"Stay where you are… please," she panted. "Just please… don't move."

Glaucus stood in place while his emotions ran throughout his body. He felt confusion, relief and, above all, indescribable joy.

Medusa's emotions were also in tumult. She felt confusion, happiness and, above all, fear that she had finally lost her senses. It couldn't be Glaucus. He hadn't looked like Glaucus, what little she had seen of him. She supposed he sounded like Glaucus, but where was his stutter?

It's not real. It cannot be real. Huddled in the corner, she hugged her legs to her chest and rested her head on her knees. Rocking, she tried to regain her composure.

"Honey, at least t-t-talk to me… please." He didn't know what to feel about her reaction to him, and her silence only made him more uneasy.

His unsure voice penetrated through all her doubts. It really was him. She didn't know how he'd found her, or why he'd come, nor did she care. Grabbing the edge of the bath sheet, she ripped a wide strip. Folding it, placed it over her eyes and tied it at the nape of her neck. She'd always prided herself on being able to navigate the caves with her eyes closed. It was time to test that theory.

Medusa rounded the corner slowly, not sure exactly where he was. "Glaucus?" She called out to him shyly. Sticking to the shadows, she heard him rustling. "Close your eyes," she said quickly. He couldn't see her like this, not yet. "Keep them closed," she warned. "No matter what."

Sensing her trepidation, the serpents began to hiss at Glaucus. She hushed them and continued further. Medusa could feel his presence, knew he was close. Reaching out, she touched heated flesh.

Gasping, she recoiled. How long had it been since she'd felt someone's skin? Her days were filled with the cold, rough scrape of stone. Suddenly, a warm, strong hand wrapped around hers. Her other hand went to his face, a searching brush across his eyes.

"Oh Honey!" He pulled her into his embrace. His arms wrapped around her waist, crushing her to him. Medusa instinctively bent backwards, trying to keep him away from her head. The serpents had other ideas, intently seeking him out, curious about the man allowed so close to their master. Medusa tried to push them back, using her other hand to hold Glaucus at bay.

"Wait, Glaucus," she pleaded.

He reluctantly released her, all but her hands, on which he placed two soft kisses. Medusa slipped her hands from his and went to stand behind him. Removing the cloth from her eyes, she placed it over his, and was sure to secure it tightly.

Stepping back, she looked at Glaucus thoroughly. She wasn't sure how long it had been since she'd last seen him, but it felt like a lifetime. He looked very different to her. Was he always that tall… that broad? She didn't recall him being very muscular. She watched his head turn, following her every move. He knew exactly where she was at all times. This was not the awkward, shy boy who sat at the fountain with her.

She frowned, unnerved by his presence. "How did you get here?"

He flashed her a crooked smile. "With great difficulty…"

She narrowed her eyes skeptically. "What happened to your stutter?"

"It is still there, though now, only when I am nervous."

"Are you not nervous now?" she challenged.

Glaucus now sported a full grin. He reached out and directly grabbed her hand. "Not anymore. I have found you, and you are alive." He released her and reached up to stroke her cheek. She caught his hand in hers and gave it a little squeeze.

For that moment, there was nothing and no one in the world but the two of them. She did not even notice the serpent poised to strike him. The attack was so fast; there was nothing to prevent it.

Glaucus snatched his hand back. "What was that?!"

Mortified, Medusa ran off. Glaucus removed his makeshift blindfold, and took off after her. Shortly, he reached the next room and stopped before the congregation of statues. He was confused by the scene before him. Where had *these* come from?

"They were like you once. Human… alive," Medusa began. Shutting her eyes, she stepped slowly into the light of the room. "One look from me, and you will become like them."

Glaucus looked at the sight before him. Her face held no shame, no fear, simply a calm acceptance of his judgment. Her brow was only faintly creased with worry. Standing there, her skin was no longer the deep bronze he remembered, but an antique gold, with an unearthly olive pallor. Around her head, countless serpents slithered and intertwined. They were also golden, striped with black, with pale, jade eyes. She looked like a pagan idol and, right or wrong, he worshipped her.

Glaucus walked through the ranks of his predecessors. "What happened to them?"

"**I** happened to them. I am a monster, and a murderer." For the first time, she felt a twinge of remorse for what she'd done. Glaucus had admired her once, and she felt so removed from the girl he'd said was more beautiful than any of the Goddesses. What would he think of her now? "They came here to kill the monster and, instead, created the murderer."

Medusa waited, trying to sense his reaction. She heard movement, but couldn't tell if it was away or towards her. Having him here was playing havoc with her usually sharp instincts. Suddenly, she felt him near. Before she could flinch, he placed a soft kiss on her lips. "I'm sorry Honey, so sorry for all you've endured."

Glaucus replaced his blindfold and leaned to kiss her again. This time Medusa managed to avoid it. She touched her fingers to his temple and, finding that he was once again blindfolded, she opened her eyes.

She looked at him, still expecting to awake from the strange dream she was obviously in. She was torn between the desire to send him away, and wanting desperately to be held by him, to feel like that girl on Mount Olympus. A war waged in her head, as well as above it. Sensing her conflicting emotions, the snakes were fighting amongst themselves, half in defense of Glaucus, the other mistrusting his intentions.

"You should not be here Glaucus. This place is cursed. I am cursed." Against her better judgment, she reached out to touch him. He stood perfectly still while her hand curved around his neck, gently brushed across his shoulder and down his chest. It took great control to regulate his breathing. Medusa slowly backed away from him, until the agonizing moment she pried her fingertips from his skin.

"You must go, Glaucus. And never return. This place is death, and I am a ghost to you."

Glaucus snatched her wrist before it was just out of reach. "My phantom, you have haunted me since I last laid my eyes on you. You have been an apparition in my dreams, and left a shrieking shadow on my heart. If this place is death, then consider my life forfeit, for it is now my home."

Had Glaucus been able to see her face, he would've considered her warning to run away, never to return. Instead, there he was, walking around, slowly. Reaching a far wall, he leaned casually against it.

"Are you hungry? If I recall, you still owe me a dinner." Glaucus gave her a cheeky grin.

Medusa looked at him in sheer panic. "Glaucus, you cannot **stay** here! Have you heard nothing I've said?"

He straightened, his head bowed, his brow furrowed. After an extended moment of silence, he lifted his head. "How does fish sound?"

BEAUTY INVADED

Athena plopped down dramatically and met a tolerant stare. She heaved a sigh and pouted. "I'm bored, Hermes."

"Tell me about it. Its been centuries since I've gotten into trouble," he groaned.

Hermes was tall and lean, which belied his strength. His shaggy hair was a deep auburn at the root, sparking into blonde tips. In a feat of agility, he bounced around Athena, falling over her at the last. She pushed him off with an annoyed snort.

"I find that hard to believe." She rolled her eyes at him, then, quickly felt her neck.

Hermes shrugged nonchalantly. "Cannot imagine why…" Chuckling, he began to twirl the necklace he had deftly lifted from her neck. His cherubic face made even his most diabolical grin look innocent.

Athena raised an eyebrow at him. "Impressive, I suppose. Although, a bit cliché in my opinion."

"Cliché? You did not feel a thing. Admit it."

She inclined her head. "True, but that is my point. You pilfered my necklace, yes. But, to do so, you had to distract me with physicality. And, essentially, I **did** notice."

Hermes tossed the necklace at her, frowning. "I am the best there is. There is nothing I can't get my hands on." At her skeptical look, he continued. "Name anything, and I will put it in your hands by Selene's waking moment," he boasted.

Athena pretended to give his challenge some thought. "How about Hades' helmet?" His sudden look of concern made her laugh.

"That's what I thought," she teased.

"I could do it; it would be all too easy." Even to his own ears, his words lacked conviction.

Athena placed a motherly hand on his leg. "I wouldn't dream of it, Hermes. It would be far too dangerous."

Thoroughly insulted, Hermes leapt to his feet. "I will get it Athena, and when I do, you will have to eat your words." He made it to the door before pausing. "**And**… I get your owl."

Athena thought about his offer. No doubt, he was attempting to forfeit with pride. She weighed the pros and cons of the wager, although she ultimately knew she would give up her precious pet to have this resolved. Never had any mortal given her so much trouble, but she had never lost a battle yet, and this would be no different.

She gave Hermes a conspiratorial grin. "Very well," she whispered.

Whooping triumphantly, he flew out the room, bound for the Underworld. Athena's grin widened as he departed. Humming lightly, she quickly crept to his chamber. It did not take her long to find what she was looking for. She sighed at the golden sandals in her hand. The feathery wings twitched at her touch.

"Hermes is sure to be angry with me for besting him once again, but so is the fate of all tricksters."

Poseidon paced irritably. Three of his four armies had not been heard from since their mission. He hated it when Athena was right. Thankfully, no one knew of his plot. He tired of all this intrigue. Zeus knew nothing, and Phorcys knew nothing, and it appeared as if it would stay that way.

If Medusa wanted to stay hidden, that was perfectly fine with him. He got what he wanted, and would be all too happy if she died on that island and never surfaced again. He was washing his hands of the whole situation.

Reclining, he realized just how much he'd missed just relaxing in his underwater palace. The only thing missing was a woman to fulfill his needs, especially the ones that were becoming increasingly pressing… against his leg to be exact. He wondered what Demeter was doing.

Medusa had never been so uncomfortable in her entire life.

The last few hours were absolute torture, and it appeared as though it would only get worse. Glaucus had excused himself and gone fishing. Before long, he was back, calling out to her so she could prepare to have him back. She was promptly exiled to her bedchamber while he prepared dinner. She spent that time pacing and feeling like she was losing her mind… yet again.

Hearing her name again, she slowly made her way to the side of her pool, where he was waiting for her, dutifully blindfolded, and surrounded by wonderfully prepared trout and heron, a plate of ripe olives, some bread, and various fruits.

"Where did you get all of this?" Her wariness and mistrust of him had deepened to a near panic state.

Turning towards her voice, he smiled sweetly at her. "I found my bag near where I woke up. I had a few things left from the journey." He asked her to sit then, which eventually, she did.

Now, here she was, sitting there staring at him suspiciously. She still couldn't believe he was there. She couldn't believe he had found her, and she especially couldn't believe that he refused to leave. If he could've seen her, the look of sheer incredulity on her face would've tickled him. But, as it stood, he was oblivious, eating happily while she continued to gawk at him.

Glaucus coughed, and then broke into a fit of laughter. "Honey, will you at least eat?"

"I am eating," she grumbled. She picked up a grape and popped it in her mouth to drive her point home.

He chuckled at her. "No… you are sitting there staring at me, and most certainly **not** eating."

She frowned at him. "And how would you know?" She waved her hand in front of his face. Smirking, he wiggled his fingers at her in return. "Oh Honey… I can feel every move you make. I don't think I've ever been more aware of another person in my entire life." He paused thoughtfully, then continued eating.

Medusa tried to eat as well, with each bite she swallowed threatening to return. She still had no idea how it came to be that she was sitting across from him, but one thing she was completely sure of… he **absolutely** had to leave!

Hermes closed the gate behind him, trying to avoid the inevitable squeak. As soon as it sounded, he heard the deep, rumbling growl above him. Pulling out his lyre, he grinned mischievously into three pairs of gleaming eyes.

"Hello Cerberus, my old friend. Would you like a song?" Slowly, he strummed the lyre, smiling continuously. "No one's been along to play with you, have they? That is a shame." He hummed faintly along with the music watching as the beast's lids grew heavier.

Cerberus sat back on his haunches, a soft whine sounding in his throat. Unable to help himself, he laid his head down on his massive paws, looking over at Hermes, whimpering.

Hermes placed an understanding hand on the bridge of his nose and stroked gently. "Not to worry, my friend, you will not get into trouble. No one will even know I was here. Sleep now."

With a final groan, Cerberus snored softly, and Hermes tiptoed around him.

Glaucus let out a satisfied sigh as he lay in repose. Medusa still sat in her place. Her back was ramrod stiff, her hands clenched into fists. She just couldn't seem to relax. Serpents cavorted around her head, amusing themselves, clearly more relaxed then she was.

Once more, Glaucus turned in her direction, seeming to look right at her. "What's on your mind, Honey?"

"I want you to leave," she said immediately.

"I'm afraid that will be impossible." She took offense to his matter of fact tone. This was her home, and if she hadn't let legions of soldiers invade it, this one man would not be the exception.

Medusa launched herself at him, only to be caught mid flight. Laughing, Glaucus held her up at arms length, trying to dodge the snakes that were nipping playfully at him. Sensing a scrimmage, they refused to be left out of the fun. Grabbing her waist, he rolled them both over and put his full weight on her.

"No…Get off me, get off me!" Being pinned against the ground brought the wrong type of memories to the forefront of Medusa's mind. Half crying, half screaming, she struggled against him like a cornered animal.

Swearing, Glaucus leapt to his feet, half dragging her up with him. "Honey, I'm so sorry. Did I hurt you?" He continued to apologize while trying to keep her from beating on him. Finally releasing her, she jumped at him.

"Get out of here! I want you to leave! I want you out of here now!" She clawed at his face, trying desperately to reach his eyes. "I swear I'll kill you."

"Honey, calm down…" Holding her at bay, he became painfully aware of how strong she could be.

"Don't you call me that…" Yanking her arms away, she ran a short distance away.

The telltale clang rang in his ears, and Glaucus knew that his sweet now had a weapon. He anticipated her first swing, and crouched in time for her to sweep clear over him. The swing threw her off balance, giving him the opportunity to grab her arm, forcing the sword to her side, and her other arm above her head.

With a few quick steps, he was able to back her up against a nearby wall. They were both panting and surging with emotion.

Even her little darlings were eerily silent, practically rendered immobile by the dynamics between the two of them.

Glaucus could feel her trembling. He loosened his grip on her, but refused to let her go until she calmed down. "I'm sorry, Honey," he whispered. "I would never hurt you." He allowed himself a small chuckle. "Obviously, you have a different set of rules for me."

Medusa was forced to laugh along with him. "I'm sorry, too," she mumbled. She dropped the sword, but he still held onto her. "Although, it didn't do me much good. She frowned slightly. "You couldn't see me. How did you do that?"

Letting her wrists go, he placed a loving hand on her hip. Leaning into her, he gave her a smile she found incredibly charming. "Would you like to learn?"

BEAUTY TRAINED

Medusa stood in the center of the room with her eyes closed. She heard the moment Glaucus entered, and her impatience worsened. Busy trying to get a handle on her feelings, she nearly jumped out of her skin when he brushed against her from behind. "Just me…" he said. She could hear the smile in his voice.

Glaucus got a slight thrill from how nervous he made her. He couldn't help but remember their first official meeting. He'd felt as though his very bones were rattling. He could barely speak, and ended up laughing like a fool every few seconds. Now, the tables had turned.

Removing the blindfold, he moved to place it over her eyes. Finally comfortable that he was a friend, the serpents curled around his hands in greeting. After securing the blindfold, Glaucus walked around to look at Medusa again.

Despite the obvious differences, she was still not the same girl he remembered. She was harder, more cynical. She was also more vulnerable, more afraid. There was a certain strength that came with being young and free, just as there was a certain weakness that came with wisdom and experience. Knowledge and ignorance were two sides of the same double-edged sword.

He moved closer to her, and Medusa could feel his presence nearly suffocating her. She wished he would back away, but she refused to show just how uneasy she was.

"Listen to me, and do as I say," he said seriously. "Trust me not to hurt you… but, most of all, trust in your own abilities."

Medusa nodded haltingly. Before she could even take a deep breath, Glaucus swept her up in his arms. She gasped and clung to his neck. He was walking and turning, and walking, and turning. The only thing she wanted was for him to put her down. If only she could get the words to leave her mouth. Again, she could feel him smiling. She wished that was all she could feel.

"You know these caves better than anyone else, but your knowledge of them is limited to your own control. Things will not always be in your control. You will have to learn to adjust."

She was trying to focus on what he was saying, and its meaning, but she couldn't help noticing that he was walking rather effortlessly despite her added weight. As soon as the thought crossed her mind, she felt him come to a stop.

"Being in control will not always keep you safe, and losing control will not always place you in danger."

Medusa did not like where this was headed. "Put me down, Glaucus," she commanded.

"I will, Honey, if you can tell me where you are."

She shrugged, for once, completely lost in her own home. Glaucus set her on her feet and, try as she might to gain her bearings, she had no clue where they were. They were still inside, she knew that much. But, with all the interweaving tunnels and caves, the possibilities were virtually endless.

"You were distracted. What were you thinking about?" he asked.

Medusa immediately felt defensive. She had been thinking of how it felt to be carried by him, then she berated herself for even thinking of him in that way. At some point, she may have vaguely wondered where he was taking her, but that had come at a distant second to her overwhelming desire for him to put her down.

"I was thinking nothing, only wondering how **any** of this was going to teach me to fight."

He walked around her, noticing she stayed completely still, facing straight ahead. Once he was beside her, he reached out to touch her arm. As he expected, she flinched. She took a deep breath to steady her nerves. Suddenly, she was uneasy in the dark. She wanted desperately to be able to see. She felt so out of control, and she did not like it.

"Listen to everything, focus on nothing. Follow my voice, turn towards me." He walked around, talking to her. "Don't let anything distract you. You should be able to tell me everything about where we are, including where I am and what I'm about to do."

She wouldn't wait around to find out what he was about to do. She backed up and turned to run… straight into a wall. Too much was going on, inside and out. Her heart was thumping against her ribs, and she felt like she couldn't breathe. She held her hands up and felt around frantically.

"I don't want to do this anymore; I don't like the darkness," she was gasping.

Glaucus held her shoulders and turned her, trying to calm her down. "You're fine. Trust me to keep you safe."

She scoffed at him. "Right."

"You have to **learn** your surroundings, not just know them. You have to sense things, and use all of your senses." He circled her, speaking softly. "I want you to hear me, I want you to anticipate me…" He was behind her now and leaned in close to her ear. "I want you to feel me." Before she could panic, he separated from her. "Do you know where we are, Honey?" He grabbed her hands and stroked her wrists with his thumbs.

"No, and I want to take this off." She tried to free her wrists.

"Calm down, Honey," he sighed. "You should know."

Frustrated, she whimpered. "I don't know…" She felt him smiling again, but this time, it felt sad.

"It's alright." He stroked her cheek. "You did very well, Honey. We will begin again tomorrow. Get some rest." Glaucus was silent for a short moment. "I left you for an hour, and never saw you again. For the first time ever, in all eternity, I had you in my arms. Where would I go?" He released her completely, leaving her feeling strangely isolated.

Medusa listened to his retreating footsteps, felt the absence of his presence. Her shoulders dropped and she let out a heavy sigh. She suddenly felt very tired. Tired and deeply confused. From the moment he'd lifted her, she'd wanted nothing more than for him to go away. Now that he had… She just didn't understand herself. Reaching up, she took off the blindfold, and attempted to ignore the shiver that traveled the length of her spine. Groaning, she flopped face first… onto her bed.

Glaucus let his own groan slip out as he walked through the empty caves. For her own good, she'd better stay in her room all night. The journey to get to her was not nearly as trying as forcing himself to leave her. But she needed to trust him. He needed her to trust him. Forever would be a long time without it.

Quickly disrobing, he dove into the large pool there and let the water cover him. He hoped to cool off, or at the very least exhaust himself. Anything that would get his mind off of his desire for Medusa would be welcome at this point. He swam, back and forth, at break neck speed, until he felt he could no longer move his arms or legs.

He hurled himself out of the pool, lying naked on his back on the side. He still couldn't believe he had found her. He had, obviously, proven himself worthy to be here. There was no doubt in his mind that it was, ultimately, Aphrodite that expedited his process to the island.

Suddenly, he remembered Sophie, and sent up a silent prayer that she had reached her destination safely. He couldn't believe he had not thought of her once. Medusa distracted him to no end. He hadn't even given her Aphrodite's message. Shaking his head, he grabbed his clothes and his bag and made his way to the entrance. He laid down a rough pallet and slumped down on it. That woman was going to turn his world upside down.

Athena tore through her room, in a searching frenzy. As of late, she took to loosening her hair in the privacy of her rooms. It now streamed behind her, every so often invading her sight. Finally, tucked away in a small corner, she found what she was looking for. Pushing her hair from her eyes, she took a good look at the sword in her lap.

Long and curved, it gleamed under the lamplight. She ran her fingers over the blade. Made from the strongest material, it would cut through anything, even a particularly difficult mortal. Grasping the hilt firmly, she disappeared from her room.

She appeared on Lemnos, climbing the path to the mouth of the volcano. By the time she reached the forge, her skin was flushed a rosy hue from the heat. Her gown clung to her moist body, and her hair cascaded down her back in damp tendrils.

Finally, she saw him, illuminated by firelight, hunched over his anvil. She took in the scene before her. Beneath the blacksmith apron, stretched bronzed arms corded with muscles. Hours upon hours of slaving over forge and flame had covered him with a slick sheen that was lightly sprinkled with soot. He really was a magnificent sight… from the waist up.

"Greetings Hephaestus," Athena called out. Smiling, she met a pair of charcoal eyes.

Hephaestus was momentarily speechless. It was rare that he was ever visited in his volcanic home. Usually, if the Gods required anything of him, they sent word through Hermes. Something very important must have gotten the Goddess of War to come down off of her mountain.

It had been a long time since he had seen Athena, but he had never seen her like this. Her hair was a wild riot around her face, her body damp and flushed. She looked like she had just left her lover's bed or, perhaps, was just on her way to it.

"Hello, Athena. What brings you here?"

As he rounded the anvil, all of her musings ended. She was reminded once again why he had once been banished from Mount Olympus. He limped towards her, dragging his lame leg behind him. She tried to keep her expression pleasant, even though his affliction disturbed her. Gods were perfect, and his imperfection was an abomination.

She held up the sword before he got too close to her. "I need this sword sharpened, rather quickly."

Hephaestus took the sword from her slowly. "It will be done," he quietly replied. He gazed at her before reaching out to grasp a lock of her hair. "You look… different." He stroked the side of her face.

Remembering herself, she backed away from him. How dare he touch her? No one touched her like that. In fact, no one had before Medusa; and no one since. "I shall return for it this evening." She spoke breathlessly, and a little too rapidly, and then disappeared in a flash. One could have easily mistaken her aversion for attraction. If she was honest with herself, she may have admitted she felt a little bit of both.

BEAUTY TAKEN

Medusa awoke, feeling like she never truly slept. She was plagued with strange dreams all night. They all started the same, with Glaucus. They were either training, or swimming, or doing some other seemingly ordinary activity. He was always too close, always touching her, making her… uncomfortable.

Inevitably, he kissed her, gently, sweetly. Sometimes she was stunned, other times she merely accepted it, but always, the kiss deepened. Before she knew it, they were wrapped in each other's arms, until the time when he would roll her beneath him.

The darkness would then fill around her, and she felt trapped and choked. She would look up, straight into the face of Poseidon, panting over her. She would hear Athena's shrieking in her ear, and see Aphrodite, above her, damning her.

Then, she would be lying in a bed of snakes, writhing around her, constricting her. She was helpless to do anything but watch as one massive one slithered towards her slowly. It crept up her legs, curling around her waist and chest. Finally it reared up, and with a vicious hiss, it struck, straight at her head.

Each time, she awoke, covered in sweat, unable to breathe. With a sigh, she would remember she was in her home, in her own bed, alone. This left her feeling immediately relieved, if not consequentially disappointed. It would've been nice to wake up next to someone, someone who would hold her, tell her all was well.

She shuffled out of her bedroom slowly. She called out to Glaucus, unsure if he had even stayed through the night. Medusa didn't know why her stomach clenched when he answered back. She found him sitting quietly, still at the edge of her pool, dutifully blindfolded. She couldn't help but smile at his back. She held the blindfold that he'd left her with last night, but it seemed he could always be counted on.

"Come, sit," he said.

She went to sit by him, although what she wanted more than anything was a bath, and some food and, perhaps, to crawl back into her bed again.

"Do you have your blindfold?" he asked.

She really didn't feel like training this day, and thought briefly about lying, though she had a feeling it would do her no good. She got comfortable next to him and put it on. She sighed and began to speak, when he stopped her.

"Shh… just listen."

Medusa sat there for a moment. Finally, she broke the silence. "Listen… to what?"

He laughed, and shook his head. "Listen to everything. Listen to the water, the wind. Listen to my breathing, my heart, if you can manage."

Medusa quieted everything in her mind and listened. She began to hear the wind, feel the direction it came from. She was sitting in front of the pool, so she knew the entrance to the caves was to their left, and the tunnels to the right led to her bedroom, and beyond.

She felt him move, and she could also hear breathing, and a booming heartbeat, but it didn't belong to Glaucus. He was close to her, directly behind her to be exact. He started with a hand at her shoulder, and then slowly trailed downward to capture her hand. Standing, he pulled her up with him. Walking backwards, he drew her to follow him, and follow him she did.

Medusa walked forward, backward, and sideways. She was spun around, but never once felt off balance. She always had his hand on her, guiding her every step. Medusa didn't know why, but she had the unwavering faith that as long as he was near, she would never be harmed. Before long, she found herself enjoying their semblance of a dance.

As he'd done before, Glaucus swept her up in his arms and walked around with her in tow. Once again, she wrapped her arms around his neck, though she had no overwhelming desire to be put down.

He stopped suddenly, then leaned in close to her ear.

"Did I succeed, my Honey?"

Her face dropped. "Succeed?"

"In distracting you…" He laughed a little too mischievously for her taste.

"Umm…"

"Can you tell me where we are?"

She attempted to listen, but all she could hear was a cacophony of emotions. This time, she decided on a hasty lie. She had no clue where they were, of course. She figured at the very worse, he'd taken her back to her bedroom which, in fact, is where she wanted to be all along. The fact that he would once again be in there with her was becoming less unfavorable by the moment.

"Of course I know where we are," she scoffed.

"And you approve of being here… with me?" he asked softly.

Unable to put her consent into words, she merely nodded.

Glaucus whispered against her ear. "Do I have your permission for what I do next?"

A shiver of anticipation worked its way through her body. She was afraid and, at the same time, excited. Whatever fears she had of being intimate with Glaucus were overshadowed by her trust of him. Again, she favored him with a shy nod.

Glaucus knew by her answers that she had absolutely no clue where he had taken her. He was torn between the satisfaction that he again served as a distraction to her senses, and the disappointment that her consent and surrender would be wasted on this innocent prank. "Very well," he answered. Then, holding her out, he dropped her.

Medusa's yelp ended in a splash as she plunged into her pool. She surfaced, sputtering, to the sound of Glaucus laughing raucously. Another splash sounded, along with a spray of water. Glaucus surfaced amid wild swings.

"Damn you, Glaucus!"

He caught her hands, apologies coming out in his laughter. "You said… you knew…" He could barely finish his statement. They both fell into fits of laughter, splashing and playing like children. Medusa couldn't remember the last time she'd had so much fun.

Before long, the laughter subsided and all that was left was a man and a woman who found joy just by being beside each other. For her part, Medusa felt more than joy. She felt hope for her future. She'd given up hope of ever again feeling a connection once she let Aphrodite go.

Glaucus felt a shift in Medusa, and wished he could read her mind. She seemed pensive but, about what, he couldn't be sure. "Let's get you dry, get you fed, and then, we can begin the hard part," he said. Grasping her waist, he lifted her onto the side.

As she braided her hair, Athena ran through her list of things to do. She had almost everything she needed. She was even already working on her contingency plan in case Hermes didn't come through for her. She could feel her personal triumph looming ever closer. She'd still never been bested. There was no contest where she would not emerge victorious.

She was, however, losing to her impatience. Waiting for Hermes' return was killing her. She decided to check with Hephaestus to see if the sword was complete. Lemnos was no less warm, despite it being closer to evening. Athena found Hephaestus exactly where she had left him. She had no doubt he'd been there the entire time of her absence.

This time, though, she didn't need to call out to him. He sensed her, and looked up immediately. He straightened, and made his arduous approach. "What happened to your hair?" he asked. He touched a hand to the nape of her neck and tugged at a braid until it fell. He began threading his thick fingers through her locks. "I liked it down. You should wear your hair down more often, My Lady."

Athena gasped at his statement and stumbled backwards. Hephaestus caught her, his eyes glittering with an unexplained hunger. Before she could speak, his mouth was on hers, his tongue penetrating. Athena was breathless. No man had ever touched her this way. No man ever dared. Hephaestus was doing more than daring.

Athena tried to push him away, but discovered all of his time spent at the forge had made him incredibly strong. He was nipping at her neck, his hands grasping at every bit of flesh he could reach. Her ears filled with whines and whimpers; noises she realized came from her own throat. Those wounded, helpless sounds were her own.

"Hephaestus… stop this!"

Her words ended as he took her mouth again. She scrambled backwards, trying to break the kiss, trying to break his embrace. His legs gave out, unable to keep her pace, and they fell to the floor. His clumsy infirmity disgusted her, and she fought him off as best as she could, to no avail.

For once in her life, the Goddess of War, the paragon of strength, was helpless. She struggled, near tears, as he pulled at her clothes. She was partially nude; her cries for help muffled by the roaring flames all around them.

Hephaestus felt they were both misunderstood creatures of immortality. He was bound for life to the most beautiful of Goddesses, but rejected by her constantly. Athena could not possibly want to be alone forever, with no man to love her. They were both lonely creatures, reaching out to each other. He knew she, like any virgin was fearful of her first time.

"Don't be afraid, my love. I do believe you'll find this to your liking," he breathed sincerely.

"No! Hephaestus, please?!"

Hephaestus held her tightly, to keep her from fighting. He loved how strong she was. He hadn't felt this alive in centuries. He finally let her go, to scratch at his back as he pried her legs open.

Athena could not think; she could barely breathe. It was appalling that this hobbling aberration could overpower her. She could not allow him to mate with her. How would she survive the humiliation? Her knees were currently astride his wide hips, and she could feel him pulsing against her thighs, hear him breathing heavily.

Hephaestus was so close to being inside her, if only he could get her to relax. He crooned soft love words in her ear, tried his best to soothe her, but she would not keep from squirming. Her endless writhing served no purpose other than to excite him further. Groaning, Hephaestus found his release before he was able to join with her.

Feeling the warm wetness on her thighs, Athena burst out in piercing screams. Hephaestus was lightly stroking her breasts and, in his post coital weakness, she was able to push him off. Scrambling away, she shakily made it to her feet and ran to the entrance, adjusting her clothes.

As she reached the sweet air outside, she tripped and fell to the ground. Wailing, she ripped a piece from the hem of her gown and cleaned herself off. With a grunt of repulsion, she threw the cloth to the ground and vanished.

She appeared in her room, so distracted; she failed to realize she was not alone. When the chuckle reached her ears, she jumped, visibly rattled.

"Well then, where have you been, coming back all sweaty and dazed? Not to mention…filthy!" Hermes threw up his hands. "Never mind! I do not want to know." Laughing, he drew the helmet from his bag and tossed it at her feet.

Athena tried to regain her poise, but failed miserably. She absently listened to his tale of danger and thievery, while she pondered her own dangerous adventure. She hoped above hope that she would hear no more of it.

"Athena, are you listening?!" Hermes was looking at her very curiously.

"Yes, yes! Well done, Hermes. Leave the helmet, take your prize and go," she said brusquely. "And leave the bag…" she added as an afterthought.

"Okay… are you alright?" Hermes had never seen Athena so out of sorts.

She looked at him blankly, before the question registered. "I'm perfectly fine Hermes. I'll take the helmet back to Hades. He'll never know it was missing."

Hermes smiled brightly. "I would appreciate that, Athena." I'm off to see what other mischief I can get into."

After he vanished, Athena let out a shaky breath. Collapsing to the floor, she drew her knees up to her chest, and wept for the first time in several lifetimes. She'd had enough mischief for one day.

BEAUTY GIVEN

Medusa found herself in the exact same spot as the day before, standing blind in the center of the room, with Glaucus circling her. This time, however, she knew every step he took. This time, when he reached out to touch her, she grabbed his hand. She'd never been more aware of another person in her entire life. "I think we're ready for the next level," he said.

Medusa waited in quiet acceptance. She had no doubt his explanation of *the next level*, was on its way. Glaucus did not disappoint. Kneeling at her feet, he took her hand and placed in it a very real, very sharp sword. Next level, indeed.

Removing his blindfold, Glaucus stood, sword in hand. He paced in front of her, giving instructions. She listened to his words but, also, began to notice the sounds surrounding them. She listened to his feet scrape the ground, his sword arcing through the air. And, when he took a swing at her, she'd already anticipated it, and brought her own sword up to meet his.

"Very good, Honey," he said proudly. "Let's begin."

Athena paced in her room, distractedly. Her mind could not reconcile what happened. How could someone so obviously beneath her, have nearly had his way with her? She remembered the day Zeus had given Aphrodite to Hephaestus. She'd thought it was the perfect justice: Beauty enslaved to the Beast.

She'd been to his forge many times. What had provoked that attack? And, why was she not able to stop it? Breathing heavily, Athena began to feel lightheaded, yet, she continued to trot, back and forth. She was agitated beyond measure and, quite literally, felt she was going out of her mind.

She couldn't get the image of him out of her head. She would never forget him kissing her, touching her. She needed to bathe immediately. Running out of her room, she nearly collided with Aphrodite.

"Watch it, Athena!" Aphrodite chided.

When no fitting retort came to mind, Athena simply let out a huff. Aphrodite cocked her head, and began to look very closely at her. After a moment, her scrutiny made Athena very uncomfortable.

"Are you planning to stare at me all day, or will you let me pass?"

Aphrodite noticed there was slightly less bile in her voice, and her words seemed to have lost their edge. Nodding, she stepped to one side while Athena pushed past her.

"Oh, Athena," she started sweetly, "in the future, I would like to remind you that I am **not** Hermes."

Athena rolled her eyes. "What are you talking about, now?"

Aphrodite approached her, smiling. She held out the adamantine sword. "My husband asked me to deliver this to you." She lightly fingered the blade. "He said you ran off so fast, you forgot it. Fortunately, I was on my way to Olympus. In the future, though, do not expect me to be your messenger."

Athena's eyes widened at the sight of the sword, and she felt physically ill. "I expect nothing from you…" Before she could betray herself, she snatched the sword from Aphrodite's hands and stomped down the hall.

Aphrodite looked after her curiously. Aphrodite had seen that look, the look of bewildered anger and self deprecation, on many a beautiful maiden's face. It's the same look she had seen on Medusa's face. *Could it be?*

The clang of swords, mixed with heavy pants and short grunts, made the music of the afternoon. Glaucus loved the way she moved. She followed his every step, blocked his every advance. Momentarily sidetracked by the sight of her, she was able to unarm him with a flick of her wrist. Laughing, he ducked her next swing and, catching her arm, pulled her against him.

All of her thoughts ceased when their lips met. She dropped the sword from her hand, and wrapped her free arm around him. She fell into the kiss, smiling against his mouth as their tongues tangled.

Medusa squealed when he tossed her over his shoulder. Each stride had a purpose, and she bounced happily, knowing exactly where they were going, and why. Reaching their destination, he set her down, and gently kissed her.

Glaucus slowly undressed her, thinking he'd never seen anything more beautiful. Every inch of skin he revealed, he immediately covered with kisses. His fingers explored the subtle curves of her shoulders, and the pronounced arch of her back.

Without her sight, Medusa felt with more intensity. Never ashamed of her nudity, she basked in the attention she was being paid. She felt the breeze caress her naked breasts, the strength of his fingertips, teasing her already sensitive points. His warm breath brushed her stomach as he knelt before her.

She was a goddess to him, and he worshipped her. He nibbled at her hips, placed tender kisses on her thighs, delighting in the small moans he could elicit. As he slowly worked his way back up her body, he couldn't help but notice her distinct lack of modesty.

"Have you ever been with a man, Honey?" he asked.

It took a moment for the question to penetrate the fog of ecstasy surrounding her. The full importance of it hit her like cold water. Would he still want her, after she'd been tarnished? Even if he did, how would she cope with the pain again?

"Umm… yes," she whispered. "And, it was… unsatisfactory."

Glaucus nodded, not sure exactly what that meant. As he undressed himself, so many questions entered his mind. But, he had his Honey, naked in front of him, and he wouldn't waste this opportunity with petty doubts. Grasping her waist, he fell backwards on her bed, pulling her on top of him.

"Well then, let us see if we can do better."

Medusa giggled, and was suddenly at a loss. She hadn't a clue what to do with a man, but she enjoyed feeling him. She stroked his chest and stomach, noting the differences. She had already known being with Glaucus would be different than Poseidon. It was even different than being with Aphrodite. Aphrodite was all soft curves where Glaucus was hard planes. Very hard.

Her hand closed around him, sliding up and down the length. She wished she could see him but, by his breathing, she could tell she was doing something right. She continued touching him, feathering light kisses over his body, until he finally took hold of her shoulders.

"Okay, that's enough," he chuckled. "If you continue, I'm afraid I'll be unsatisfying as well."

Medusa was slightly confused by that. She couldn't imagine he would hurt her for kissing and touching him. "What do I do, then?" she asked sincerely.

It was Glaucus' turn to be confused. For someone who had made love before, she seemed surprisingly ignorant. Whomever her lover was couldn't have been much of a man. He guided her into position astride him and gently pressed her hips down.

Medusa waited for the expected pain, but it didn't come. With her hands on his chest, he entered her, slowly, her body adjusting to hold him. He held still, waiting for her to move, feel her way. She lifted her hips slightly, testing the wonder of thrust and withdrawal. Eventually, she found her rhythm, one that he matched, drawing his name from her lips.

Glaucus hoped he could hold out as long as he needed to. Watching her bounce on top of him, hearing her moan promised to be his undoing. Once she began to tremble, he sat up, and wrapped his arms around her. She gasped loudly as he rocked into her. Winding her legs around his waist, she urged him deeper.

Her body began to pulsate around him a moment before he erupted. Holding onto each other, they weathered the storm of rapture, came together in delirium and crashed beaten and battered beside each other.

Warm and flushed, Medusa fought the dizziness. Her breath was coming too quickly, and she held her head to stop it from pounding. She could hear Glaucus having a similar problem, and couldn't help but giggle. Glaucus leaned across her, his head resting on her stomach. A final wave of euphoria passed over her and, as she stroked his head, she sighed in contentment.

He'd come all this way, just for her. She didn't know how, or why, but she had found love twice in one lifetime. She considered herself truly blessed. As though he read her mind, he kissed the curve of her hip.

"I love you, Honey," he whispered, before drifting to sleep.

She sent up a silent thanks to the Goddess of Love… then immediately felt ashamed. She still loved Aphrodite, yet, she'd been untrue. *Have I really?* she thought to herself. It hadn't felt wrong, giving herself to Glaucus. But, she had been wrong before, thinking she could love two, differently, but equally.

The sound of Glaucus snoring softly stopped her thoughts, and created a genuine smile on her face. Right or wrong, she loved him. The rest of the world be damned… she already was.

They spent the following days much in the same way, swimming and sparring, making love well into the twilight hours. It was bliss for both of them, waking beside each other, closeted in their own world. Medusa let go of her fears and doubts, and Glaucus gave thanks for every moment spent with the woman he loved.

BEAUTY'S FATE

Perseus stood at the gaping mouth of Mount Ida, an unexpected chill coming over him. Athena had told him to seek knowledge from the Graeae, The Gray Ones, three witches who have been in existence since the beginning of time. Daughters of Phorcys, they were rumored to be grotesque in appearance.

It was said that, in their own way, they were able to see a man's life, from beginning to end. It was also said, that they were the keepers of every man's fate. At the moment, his fate rested with the monster, Medusa, and the Graeae would tell him where to find it.

As he set foot inside the massive cave, the wind whipped all around him, carrying the voices of many souls. The laughter, screams, and tears of lifetimes past filled his ears and halted his steps. A very dim light shown up ahead, but Perseus hadn't the nerve to follow it.

A child's giggle had him searching the darkness around him.

"Hello there!" a girlish voice rang out to his left.

From his right, a surly boy sounded. "What are **you** doing here?"

A ghostly whisper from behind had Perseus whipping around in circles.

"*He* seeks The Gray Ones," a snide voice chimed.

"Well, he need seek no more. They will surely find **him**," another answered.

Adolescent murmurings surrounded him. His sword drawn, he called out, "Who's there?!" Turning once more, he saw the silhouette of a little girl, sitting cross-legged in the sliver of light.

"Do not pay them heed, sir," she said. She fussed over a little doll, while humming a sweet lullaby. Perseus slowly approached her, wondering how children came to be in this mountain, apparently alone.

"It has been a long time since anyone has visited," she began, not sparing him a glance. "I'm afraid they've quite forgotten their manners."

Perseus reached out to grab hold of her shoulder and, as his fingers passed through her like grains of sand, she looked up at him, with a face completely devoid of features. Perseus gasped, while mounds of dust passed over his feet, and thick gray smoke permeated the air.

Perseus choked as the wind picked up, watching the little girl blow away, right before his eyes. Tiny, sandy, fingers grasped him everywhere, and something grappled with his feet, until he was flat on his back, next to an abandoned doll. The last thing he heard before the darkness overtook him was a girl's angelic laughter.

"You shall meet The Gray Ones now…"

Perseus woke up some time later, on a gleaming black floor, face to face with his own disoriented reflection. He looked over the round, obsidian chamber. There were four entrances, and the room was composed of glassy, onyx bricks, tightly connected by thin threads spread throughout the walls and floor, ending at the center, where he sat. It looked as though he was trapped in a giant web. Peering closely at the floor, he noticed each brick contained a name. As he reached for one, a strong gust of wind blew throughout the room.

In one of the entrances, stood a female form. As it floated towards him, Perseus found himself petrified. Her skin looked like a fine, gray porcelain, smooth and flawless. He expected it would be cool to the touch. She had wispy, silver hair that reached the floor, covering her doll-like body. Like the children at the entrance, her face and body were blank slates, possessing no characteristics. He lent her gender to her soft curving.

The figure knelt before him, her lengthy hair brushing his tightened fists. Her head twisted, as if studying him. Then, a dimple appeared in the center of her face, expanding into a gaping chasm, from which a piercing shriek emerged.

Perseus covered his ears against the excruciating pain, until the sound ended abruptly. Two other entrances were occupied by identical figures. The first continued to study him. Her voice came out in a raspy sigh.

"Deino, Enyo… a man," she said.

The other two floated towards him, landing at his sides. One pressed her face to his, with an eerie gasp. "Smells of Zeus," she said. The other did the same, then gave a contemptuous snort. "Smells of mortal," she said. Both looked at the third expectantly. "Pemphredo?" they inquired in unison.

"The Eye," she responded.

The three of them rose and silently walked through their individual entrance. Perseus let out a shaky sigh at their retreat. He willed his legs to move, but he was weak from his encounter. He leaned back on his hands, and found the floor to be black sand. His hands began to merge with the floor. His feet, too, began to sink.

Perseus struggled for minutes upon minutes, only to find himself sinking more quickly in the end. His cries for help went unheard and unanswered. At last, he gave himself over to the abyss, and fell. He landed softly, in an enclosure of sand. He looked around him, realizing he was in the bottom of a large hourglass.

"You fought more than others," Pemphredo started.

"It is your father's blood," Deino continued.

"But you cannot fight fate, boy," Enyo finished.

Perseus located them, in the far corner of the room, standing around a large crystal, jutting from the cave floor. Atop the crystal, was a large rounded object. As one of them picked it up, he saw it was an eye… a Cyclops eye.

Enyo pressed the Eye to her face, and a socket materialized to accept it. She stared skyward and inhaled deeply as visions of Perseus' past came to her. "Loving," she huffed. "Protected his whole life… but, worthy." She removed the eye and passed it to her sister.

Deino repeated the process, and began to explore his present. "Defender, and his mother's pride." Then she tsked and shook her head. "Naïve, doubtful, but amenable." She seemed sad as she looked towards him. "Young," she sighed.

It appeared they all saw different things, and each only saw portions. They were collaborative in everything, in thought, word and deed. Perseus stared at them, fascinated.

Pemphredo took the Eye last. The moment she inserted it, it began to flutter rapidly. Suddenly, she emitted another piercing shriek that rattled the cave, and lightly cracked the glass of his prison.

Pemphredo threw herself against the hourglass and began clawing at it. "He seeks the path to our sister. He seeks to murder a daughter of Phorcys!"

Perseus stumbled backwards to the far wall as her sisters hauled her away, still screeching. Once they were out of earshot, he looked around for any escape. He fingered the crack caused by her wailing.

Repeatedly, with all his might, he began to beat against it.

Wake up. Honey, Wake up!"

Medusa was tossing and turning, muttering something unintelligible. She leapt up with a gasp, her eyes clenched, grasping the sheet.

"It's okay, Honey. You can open your eyes."

She looked around her, then to the man at her side. Panting, she let him soothe her, fighting the queasiness she felt. Her whole body was weak and listless.

Exhausted, she fell back on her pillow and groaned.

"Are you okay?" Glaucus asked, concerned.

"Yes, just a bad dream," she replied. She did not know what brought the reappearance of her nightmare, but she had a very uneasy feeling. Her eyes drifted shut again and she felt herself relax. Normally, her nightmare caused her to leave her bed but, today, she was just so tired.

Glaucus kissed her forehead and brushed her cheek. "Just relax here, and I'll get us some lunch." He left her side, and she, once again, counted herself fortunate to have him in her life. She had someone to kiss away her night terrors, and make her lunch, the latter becoming more and more unappealing by the second. *Lunch*, she thought to herself. She hadn't realized she'd slept so long.

The Graeae stood in the large ebony cave, engulfed in their web of lives. Deino and Enyo were motionless, while Pemphredo paced. "What did you see, sister?" they asked together. "I saw… deception. I saw remorse. I saw the head of the Gorgon, taken from the belly of the mother," she answered.

Deino and Enyo turned toward each other. Deino floated to a far wall, her fingers gliding over the bricks. She came to one and stopped, pulling it gently from the wall. Opening the brick, she removed a thread. She ran it through her fingers, analyzing it.

"Perseus," Deino whispered. "Strong cord, fine thread. A long, healthy life, a protected life… a good life"

Enyo scoffed and presented a pair of crude scissors. "Cut it…"

Deino waved her away. "Enyo, no. Bring Medusa to me."

Rolling her eyes, Enyo took flight and came to a stop high on another wall. She descended, holding another delicate brick. She opened it, and pulled out the thread inside. She concentrated over it, mumbling to herself. Her sisters joined her, each grasping a piece of the thread.

"How strange," Deino said.

BEAUTY'S GIFT

The smells wafting past her made Medusa's stomach lurch. She did not know what Glaucus was cooking, but it didn't seem to agree with her. She threw the sheet over her head and hoped she could return to sleep. She heard him calling her name, and swore emphatically.

As usual, she made her way to their favorite picnic spot by her pool. Glaucus sat, blindfolded and waiting, with everything he needed within arms length. She sat down, surprised that, even though their breakfast consisted of nothing different from their other meals, her stomach continued to churn.

"I was planning on taking one of the boats from the shore," he said.

"Mm-hmm," she answered absently.

Medusa grabbed a piece of bread and attempted to nibble, while he chattered. She tried to pay attention to what he was saying, but she just felt so warm and feverish.

"Are you alright, Honey? You've barely touched your food."

Terribly distracted, she threw a piece of bread in her mouth and mumbled a quick "Fine."

Glaucus babbled nervously, continuing straight through her monosyllabic answers. Finally, he paused thoughtfully. "Honey, I have to l-l-leave you… for a little while."

Medusa was breathing deeply between waves of sickness. The smell of fish seemed to be choking her. *Oh Gods… no*, she thought to herself. She began to calculate in her head. When his statement finally reached her, she frowned. "Leave me?"

Glaucus heard the worry in her voice and laughed affectionately. "I will return, Honey. It will just be for a little while. I need to give word to my family that I'm alright. And, besides, there are a couple of things I want to get for you."

She smiled warmly. "You don't have to give me anything, Glaucus."

"It's too late, my mind's made up." He reached out his hands to her. She rose, ignoring the dizziness and went to his side. "D-don't for one second d-doubt my return," he warned. He wrapped his arms around her and kissed her soundly on the lips. "And trying to run away again will do you no good," he chided. "I will follow you anywhere."

With a quick kiss, he made his goodbyes brief. Medusa hadn't missed the return of his stutter but, admittedly, was grateful for his hasty retreat. He was barely on his way before she vomited.

Glaucus prepared the boat for his trip. He checked to make sure he had everything he needed. He looked back up to at the only place in the world he called home. He really had wanted to say more, wanted to have a proper farewell, but she seemed so distracted, and he admitted to himself that he was nervous.

He hoped he would be more courageous when he had the time came to ask her to be his wife. Glaucus breathed deeply and, with a renewed sense of life, he began to row towards Lemnos.

Medusa puffed, splashing water on her face. It had not completely registered that Glaucus was gone, and she didn't know where, or for how long. All she knew was that her time was short. She needed to think, needed to figure out what she was going to do. Only one solution came to mind, and she immediately knelt in fervent prayer to Aphrodite.

Soon, she felt a warm glow around her, followed by the familiar scent of pomegranates. Long lost lovers looked at each other across a short distance. Both sorely missed the love of past times. Each had much to say to the other. Neither knew where to begin.

Medusa wanted to tell Aphrodite how she cherished their days together, and that she would always hold a special place in her heart. She wanted to beg her forgiveness for loving another. She wanted to sit and laugh as they used to, wrapped in each other's arms, when the world was perfect.

Aphrodite wanted to tell her how beautiful she still found her, would always find her. She wanted to tell her that, although she wished to keep her for her own always, she wished for Medusa to find trust, and love and, above all, happiness.

Seeing Medusa again reawakened Aphrodite's seething hatred of Athena and Poseidon. Somehow, she would exact her revenge on them both. A content smile passed over her face. She concentrated on Medusa's face. She didn't seem pleased. She seemed… almost afraid.

"My Lady… My Love," Medusa whispered.

"Still?" Aphrodite answered.

"Always…"

Aphrodite's heart soared at the response. She knew it was selfish of her, but she did not care. It was nice knowing she would not be replaced. "Have you found love, my darling?"

Medusa cast her eyes down in shame. "Forgive me, Aphrodite."

"Oh no, my love. You commit no crime," she said gently. "I told you a love like ours was not meant to last. I sent young Glaucus to you in the hopes that he would please you."

So many questions dashed through Medusa's mind. What had she meant, that she'd *sent* Glaucus to her?

"He does, please you… doesn't he?" Aphrodite asked.

Medusa came out of her reverie and attempted to focus on the matter at hand. All the fears and insecurities that she had tucked away came to the forefront. She felt every one of her meager years, and wanted nothing more than to be back in her perfect world. Aphrodite saw the tears rolling down her face, and ran to embrace her.

As she approached, Medusa grabbed her hands, and placed them on her belly. Aphrodite gasped and looked at her delightedly.

"What is it?" Medusa asked seriously.

"It's a baby!" Aphrodite squealed, and leapt in jubilation.

"No, Aphrodite. What **is** it?" she clarified.

Aphrodite looked momentarily confused, until the question became clear. "A son. You're going to give birth to a beautiful boy, who will hopefully get his father's hair, and his mother's speech," she tittered.

Medusa sank to her knees, hyperventilating, while Aphrodite giggled about how handsome he would be, and favored by the gods. She looked over to see Medusa trembling on the ground. "My darling, what is wrong?" she asked.

Medusa held complete desolation in her eyes. "I am having a son." At Aphrodite's blank look, she continued. "A son, Aphrodite… a male."

Understanding dawned on the goddess's face, and her heart ached for her precious Medusa. "Oh my pet." Kneeling, she clasped her hands. "I'm so sorry."

Medusa got to her feet and shuffled sadly to her bedroom. Aphrodite followed after her, lamenting the cruel jokes the Fates always seemed to play on her. Medusa crawled under the covers and curled up into a ball. Aphrodite lay down next to her, stroking her arm.

Glaucus made his way to the forge. Too excited over his plans, he barely noticed the oppressive heat surrounding him. He searched around until, finally, he located the master. Bowing low, Glaucus addressed him breathlessly.

"My Lord Hephaestus, I beg for a moment of your time."

Hephaestus looked up from his latest project at the prostrate figure before him. It was rare that anyone ever disturbed him. But, it seemed, these days, he was getting more company than he could stand. He straightened slightly, and looked inquisitively at the young man.

"I am Glaucus, son of Minos. My Lady, Aphrodite, told me you could help me."

"Are you one of her lovers?" Hephaestus asked.

Glaucus held out the necklace he had been keeping since he last saw Aphrodite. "No, My Lord. I belong to the Lady Medusa, and it is **this** love that drives me to ask for your assistance," he answered.

Glaucus had effectively piqued his interest. Hephaestus took the necklace from his hand and waited for him to continue.

Sensing his cue, Glaucus began talking rapidly. "She thought you could use its contents to fashion a ring for my love, that I might take her for my wife."

Hephaestus nodded. He removed the chain and placed the pendant back in Glaucus' hand. He was rather curious why his wife had taken so much interest in this man's love, and he would find out.

"Come, young Glaucus. Tell me of your lady."

BEAUTY'S FUTURE

Medusa was rocking silently, thinking of the irony of how lifetimes repeated. She would no more be able to keep her child, than her mother was able to keep her. She would not even be able to get a first, or last, glance at her son.

Her son. She let the thought sink in; a physical extension of herself. A living, breathing expression of the love she and Glaucus shared. She thought of Glaucus. How could she tell him? At his age, he already found himself saddled with a monster. Now, she was adding a child; a child he would be solely responsible for. She ran into the comfort of Aphrodite's arms. She wanted to die. She wanted to cry.

She wanted her mother.

"All will be well, my love. Is there anything I can do?"

"Will you bring Eurynome to me?" she whispered.

Each day, Eurynome began to relax a little bit more. She'd seen no sign of Poseidon, and started to believe that everything would, one day, be alright. She was finally able to enjoy having her daughters around her. They never asked for any details about all that happened, a fact she was grateful for. Still, the truth hung heavily in the air between them.

The bright light of Aphrodite's arrival made her heart sink. No good news had ever been delivered by the goddess. She waited expectantly for the latest lamentation. Aphrodite, unsure how to effectively explain the situation, simply extended a hand to Eurynome.

"Come with me, quickly."

The moment they arrived, Eurynome took off, yelling Medusa's name. She found her in the bedroom, and immediately descended on her, in a flurry of motherly affection.

"Oh, my little Medusa. You must tell me how you've been! Is anything wrong? You look wonderful. What have you been doing?"

As always, Medusa waited for the tornado of questions to subside. Aphrodite leaned casually against the entrance. Eurynome looked from one to the other, waiting for whatever news was so important. Medusa and Aphrodite shared a glance, but remained silent. Each had much to say… and neither knew where to begin.

Perseus was in the midst of hurling himself against the glass, when the three sisters returned. Pemphredo lifted a hand, and the glass shattered, spilling the sand, and sending Perseus tumbling at their feet.

"Ask your questions, boy," Enyo hissed.

"I… I seek the Gorgon, Medusa… and a way to defeat her," Perseus replied.

Deino inhaled deeply. "The Gorgon lives in the body of the mother, the island of the sea beast, embraced by the Aegean.

"The Gorgon is strong, and fierce, and your life will cease if she sets her eyes on you," Pemphredo added.

"Then, how am I to defeat her?" Perseus asked.

Enyo scoffed. "Oh, you have your share of protectors. You shall have your prize, boy. The Gorgon's head will be yours."

Athena stood at the entrance of Mount Ida, less enthusiastic than she'd hoped. It was almost over. This vendetta seemed almost irrelevant by now, but she would see it through to the end. She unceremoniously dropped her items on the ground. She placed the winged shoes and helmet in the bag, and made of display of them with the sword and her shield.

It would all be over soon.

Eurynome sat, stunned, on the bed. Her stoic appearance was a mask for a riot of emotions coursing through her body. Her baby, her little Medusa, was going to be a mother. She was no longer very little at all. She was a woman, a woman in love. Her eyes watered with a mixture of pride, excitement, and sadness.

"Mother, please say something," Medusa pleaded.

Eurynome looked at her, and immediately recognized the parallel. Medusa never could hide her feelings. She was always so expressive, always so open and giving of herself. It hurt Eurynome's heart that life could take someone so giving, and leave them with nothing.

"I will stay with you," Eurynome said. "And, when the time comes, I will take him."

Medusa grasped her hands and squeezed. "Thank you, Mother." The two of them sat there for a long time in companionable silence.

"Besides," Eurynome sighed, "perhaps it will give me an opportunity to meet this young man of yours."

Medusa's laugh rang in Aphrodite's ears, and she discovered what a truly wonderful woman Eurynome was. It pleased her that Medusa was so very loved. "I shall go to Eileithyia and bring her back immediately. Your baby will be truly blessed, darling. You have my word."

Hephaestus listened to the young man at his side, and smiled at the enthusiasm of youth. Glaucus was obviously smitten with his lovely Medusa, and had no designs on his wife. He told Glaucus he would craft a ring, and another piece to give his love as a wedding present. Glaucus had to agreed to stay and help at the forge until the pieces were completed.

They had just begun to work when Hermes came bursting in, covered in feathers. "That blasted beast!" he shouted.

"Hermes, what has happened to you?" Hephaestus chuckled.

"I won Athena's owl in a wager, and the creature keeps escaping. I need a cage, Hephaestus, one that will keep the thing contained," he grumbled.

Mention of Athena's name made his knees weak. Hephaestus swore to himself he would gain her favor somehow. "Why not just give it back, Hermes?" he asked.

"Give it back?" Hermes scoffed. "She mocked my skills, and lost fair and square. I shall never give it back. Now make me a cage."

"It will have to wait. I am working on something else," Hephaestus teased.

"Oh, please Hephaestus. I shall pay any price you ask. This thing is driving me mad!" He emphasized his plight by pulling feathers from his hair.

"Alright, Hermes. I shall make your cage, and you shall owe me whatever I ask."

Hermes cheered loudly. "Agreed!"

Glaucus looked between the two Gods and anxiously returned to his work. He shot a quick glance at Hephaestus, who returned his concern with a reassuring wink.

Perseus exited the mountain, more unsure, and more afraid than when he went in. He was assured victory in a task that would, inevitably, deem him a hero. So, why did it feel like something was terribly wrong? Why did he desire, above all, to forget this quest, and return to his mother's side?

He paused outside, and noticed the cache of supplies. He reached for the bag, and removed the winged sandals and the helmet. He placed the helmet on his head, and angled the shield to check his reflection. He was shaken when nothing stared back at him. Gasping, he removed the helmet, and saw his form appear.

He tested the helmet a few more times, chuckling at its novelty. Placing it back on his head, he grabbed the hilt of the sword and swung it through the air, watching as it seemed to move on its own.

As often happens in youth, his troubles and doubts were momentarily forgotten in the wake of a new toy.

Aphrodite stood in the center of the black room, and waited for her presence to be acknowledged. She hadn't really wanted to come here, but she had to speak with Eileithyia at once. Aphrodite looked around anxiously. She hoped to intercept Eileithyia without running into the Graeae. Those witches made her skin crawl.

"My Lady Aphrodite, what brings you here?" a sweet voice asked.

Handmaiden to the Graeae, Eileithyia was the goddess of fertility and childbirth. Every thread of life in this chamber began with her. With her chestnut skin and sumptuous curves, she was the epitome of motherhood. She had a warm beauty that drew every eye. Eileithyia held out her hands to Aphrodite, and kissed both of her cheeks.

"Dearest Eileithyia, I'm in need of your help. Will you come with me?" Aphrodite asked.

Eileithyia looked around cautiously. "I cannot be gone long. What is it you need?"

"I am not entirely sure," Aphrodite answered. "It is not for me, but for my darling Medusa."

Eileithyia raised an eyebrow. "Medusa? That name has been the topic of *much* discussion today."

"Has it?" Aphrodite asked.

Medusa and Eurynome were drifting asleep, having run through several choices of baby names. A persistent scraping penetrated Medusa's mind. She knew that sound anywhere. She leapt from the bed, jolting Eurynome awake.

"What is it?" she whispered.

Medusa had almost forgotten about Eurynome's presence. She had thought the attacks were at an end, but it appeared she was wrong. Now, not only did she have her mother to worry about, but the little life inside her.

She stood there, seething, the serpents hissing at her ears. The ground beneath her feet began to shake. Walking around the bed, she retrieved two swords. Placing one in front of Eurynome she commanded her to stay there and moved to leave.

"Medusa, what are you doing?! You cant go out there!"

"Quiet mother! I need you to stay here, and keep quiet."

Eurynome clutched the sword with both hands. Her heart was pounding at the thought of Medusa going to face whatever was out there, alone. She'd never seen that look in her eyes before. It was like she was another person, one full of anger and hate.

The soldiers had been watching the island. The mysterious man had left, and had still not returned. They came to reason he would not return before the morning, which meant the monster was left unguarded. They had sent inquiries, when they had seen other soldiers on their way to this same island. Reports stated those other men had never been heard from again.

After keeping vigilant watch, they'd seen no one come or go from that island but that one man. They did not know what awaited them inside, but they were on a mission to carry out the will of the Gods, and they would do their duty. Those other men may have failed, but those other men were not Spartans. As they reached the entrance of the caves, the ground began to shudder.

"Leave my home, or join your predecessors." The unearthly growl halted them momentarily. The leader lifted his head to try to ascertain the source of the sound. "Show yourself, witch! One of our lives will be forfeit today!" A chorus of cheers rang out behind him, as they stormed inside.

"So be it," Medusa whispered.

She ran out to meet them, the avenging angel of her unborn child. Screaming, she swung with all her might at the first man in her path, the leader. When her sword connected with the flesh of his neck, his life became forfeit, and his severed head became stone.

Eurynome heard a ruckus, and could no longer sit idle, while her daughter was in danger. Clenching the sword, she slowly made her way towards the commotion. What she saw, was inexplicable. There was a battle ensuing, and in the middle, was Medusa. But, this was not her Medusa.

This was a raging lioness, protecting all she held dear. Eurynome stood speechless as she watched the carnage. One by one, the men stood as stone for all time. There were only three left. Medusa was fighting two, when the third lunged at her with his sword. She spun, but not before he cut her deeply on her arm.

Bellowing, Eurynome ran forward, blade drawn. As the man raised his arms for another strike, she plunged her sword through him.

When his body dropped, she looked up to see the other two men, their faces frozen in horror forever. Eurynome stood trembling at all she had witnessed. She glanced down at Medusa, her arm bleeding, and ran to her.

"Here, let me see," she said. Medusa looked up at her, and she resembled her baby once more. "Come, lets fix you up."

BEAUTY'S DECISION

Hephaestus held up the cage for inspection. Hermes examined it carefully and an exultant smile lit his face. "This will be perfect. I'd like to see that monster break free of this one." He placed it in his bag and looked at Hephaestus. "Now then, what is my price for this fine item."

Hephaestus smiled diabolically. "When I decide upon one, I shall let you know."

"I hardly think that is fair, Hephaestus," Hermes disagreed.

"What do you have to worry about, Hermes? Whatever you do not have, do you not simply take anyway?" he countered.

Hermes shared his smile. "True. Very well, then. I shall owe you one." He turned to leave. "And, **only** one."

After he left, Hephaestus turned to Glaucus. "Now, my boy, for you." Hephaestus held up a delicate gold ring.

Glaucus took the ring from him and examined it. Two beautiful golden snakes, twined around each other in an endless circle. Hephaestus pressed them together in the center, and they separated, becoming two.

"If you two must ever be apart, you can take one with you," he whispered.

Glaucus was taken by surprise. He had not expected such sensitivity from Hephaestus. He bowed appreciatively. "My Lord, it is perfect. I thank you with everything I am." Finally seeing the ring in his hands, Glaucus wanted nothing more than to marry his Honey.

Hephaestus recognized the impatience in him. He was sure he'd displayed that same look a few times in his existence. He liked having young Glaucus around. He was a good man, and it was nice not being alone all the time.

"Give me the pendant," he said. When Glaucus handed it to him, he smiled. "If you vow your service in my forge for a month, you may go and get your bride. I will begin the second piece in your absence."

Panting, Glaucus grinned excitedly. "You have my word, My Lord."

As Eurynome tended to her, Medusa's mind spun. With a hand to her belly, she couldn't stop the thoughts that were running rampant. She was in danger. She would always be in danger, and anyone around her would always be in danger. Not only had she **not** protected her mother, but she herself, not to mention her child, would be dead, if not for Eurynome.

She had to get them away from her.

"What is on your mind, my darling?" Eurynome intruded on her thoughts.

"You saved my life. You saved my son," she answered sadly.

Eurynome held her chin. "My love, we all need to be saved sometime. You cannot battle the world on your own." She sniffled at the memory of what occurred. "I'm astonished you've survived alone all this time."

But she wasn't alone. Not anymore. She could no longer think of herself only. She smelled pomegranates and turned her head.

"By Zeus! What has happened?" Aphrodite shouted. She pushed Eurynome out of the way and healed Medusa's arm. She began fussing over her, looking for more injuries.

"We were attacked, Ditie. It's alright. They're… gone."

"And, rightly so!" Aphrodite huffed.

Medusa was looking past her to the beautiful woman watching them. Aphrodite introduced Eileithyia and explained that she was going to bestow a blessing, protecting Medusa's son. Medusa burst into tears of joy. She turned to Eurynome.

"Mother, when you said you would take him, did you mean it?" she asked.

"Of course I meant it, darling!" Eurynome replied.

"Good, then take him now," she said emphatically.

Eurynome stared at her. She saw sadness, and pain, but above all, resolve.

"Mother, he cannot stay here. This is no place for him, even now."

Eileithyia sat down in front of Medusa, and gazed into her eyes. Slowly, she pressed her hands to Medusa's belly and chanted. She stopped and, all at once, Medusa felt empty. She then placed her hands on Eurynome, and did the same.

"Is it done?" Medusa asked.

"It is," Eileithyia answered.

"Aphrodite, take Eurynome away from here."

"Darling, someone is coming for you. I must protect you," Aphrodite protested.

"Someone is always coming for me!" she shouted. Sighing, she held Aphrodite's hands. "Save my child. Please."

"Come, Eurynome."

Eurynome thought of arguing, but knew it would do no good. There was no use fighting against fate. She walked towards Aphrodite, pausing to hug and kiss her daughter. Medusa placed a kiss on her belly and told her son that she would always love him.

"What shall I call him?" Eurynome asked.

"Bellerophon," Medusa whispered.

"Do not worry. Your child will be blessed, and favored by the Gods," Eileithyia promised.

"I am eternally grateful to you," Medusa said to the group as a whole.

Eurynome and Eileithyia headed towards the exit, while Aphrodite lagged behind. "Do not give up. I beg you."

Medusa took her face in her hands, and kissed her tenderly. "The one thing unavoidable by man and God alike, is fate."

Hearing her own words from Medusa's lips made Aphrodite shiver. She grabbed Medusa's shoulders and shook her. "No! We can beat them. I swear we can still have our revenge."

Medusa shook her head. "My Lady, My Love, the best revenge, is not needing revenge." She smiled sadly at her. "They cannot hurt me anymore." Tears spilled over her cheeks, and she bravely tried to blink them away.

"I will take Eurynome home, and take care of a few things, but I will return here… at least until your Glaucus comes back. Wait for me… promise me," Aphrodite pleaded.

"I will see you soon," Medusa replied.

Once they'd left, Medusa crawled into her bed once again. Curling herself into a ball, she felt more utterly alone than ever. She did not even have the company of her child to soothe her. Medusa wrapped her arms around her stomach, hoping to feel some remnant of what used to be, but all she felt was fractured and incomplete.

She realized she had been fooling herself. She had not been allowed to truly live these past days. Those that loved her had not been living either. She had a man she could never lay eyes on; a son she would never hold. She was tired of being hunted, tired of hiding. Crying, she pulled out parchment and ink, and began a letter.

Aphrodite burst into Poseidon's private chamber, startling the young beauty that was straddling him. She grabbed the young lady's arm, and tossed her off the bed. She climbed on top of a shocked Poseidon, and grasped his throat tightly.

I curse you, and your seed
From this day, no woman will ever desire you
Your appetites will be quenched by feint or by force
Your offspring will suffer at their own hand
This I swear by the Goddess Styx

Poseidon pushed her off. "Stop your ranting, woman!" he shouted.

Aphrodite stood and pointed a damning finger at him. "You mark my words, Poseidon."

The young lady, who had been cowering on the floor, rose dazedly.

She looked at Poseidon, and cringed. With one last disgusted look, she ran for the door.

Aphrodite notched her chin higher and stared daggers into him. "Pray you never cross me again, Poseidon. I will find a way to kill you." As she left, she felt a sense of pride and accomplishment. Medusa may not have needed revenge, but she had.

BEAUTY'S DEATH

Perseus found the entrance to the cave rather easily. The winged sandals helped his ascension a great deal. Placing the helmet on his head, he took the sword and shield in his hands, and cautiously entered. He examined the statue at the entrance, and took the warning to heart.

He tread very quietly, using his shield for sight. He traveled down the tunnel into a larger room, filled with statues. He began to fear for his life, until he remembered the prediction of the Graeae. He would come out victorious. He would succeed where others had failed. He traveled down another tunnel, until the faint sound of crying reached his ears.

Medusa finished her letter to Glaucus, and rose to have one last swim in her pool. This was no place for her anymore. There **was** no place for her anymore. She wanted peace, she wanted deliverance. Silently, she prayed for death. The loss of her child was more than she could bear.

She'd committed no crime, done wrong to no one, yet, The Fates were determined to see her suffer, and leave her with nothing. She could fight them no longer. On this night, she would leave the safety of her mother's womb, and give herself to the sea for eternity.

She knelt at the edge of her pool. "Forgive me, mother," she breathed. Closing her eyes, she began to hum her lullaby. Then, she heard a nearby crunch. She spun her head around in all directions, but saw no one.

Perseus was on the floor, his back to a wall. He extended his shield to look into the room inside. He saw a large pool in the distance. Sitting by the water was a woman. She seemed sad, and completely alone. He wondered if she was being held prisoner by the monster. He stood up slowly, and as quietly as possible.

Still using his shield, he saw her looking all around. She sensed him, but couldn't see him. She stood, closing her eyes, and became very still. "I know you are there," she said. "Who are you? What do you want?"

"I am Perseus," he called, "son of Zeus. I have come to rescue you."

Medusa laughed softly. "No, young Perseus. You have come to kill me."

"Oh no, my lady. I come to kill the Gorgon monster, and **free** you!" he said, triumphantly.

A flash of metal caught her attention and, as she turned, she saw a shield. She smiled sadly. "You **can** free me, Perseus." She walked towards him, becoming clearer as she neared.

Perseus watched her reflection intently. At once, he noticed the unholy glow of her eyes, the snakes writhing around her head, and he wanted to run, but his legs would not carry him.

"I am the monster you seek, and you are the angel I prayed for. So, carry out your task." She closed her eyes and awaited her fate.

Perseus rounded the corner, sword in hand, ready to strike. His hands trembled, and his knees knocked. This was not how it was supposed to be. He was here to fell a beast, not a helpless woman.

"Do it… Kill me, or I shall kill you. One look from me, and you will join so many others. Make your choice!" Medusa shouted desperately. Still, Perseus hesitated.

Medusa fell to her knees and sobbed. "You must… Athena will never stop."

Perseus dropped the sword at her side. "What?"

Medusa reached for him. She placed the sword back in his hand, and placed a kiss on his wrist. "I am tired, Perseus. I cannot be with the man I love. I cannot bear him sons. I cannot leave this place and I am hunted relentlessly." The agony in her voice broke his heart.

Perseus raised the sword once again, his jaw clenched, tears in his eyes. He felt like such a fool, but this was his destiny, his fate. He could not escape it, no matter how badly he wanted to. Breathing heavily, he tried to find the will to strike.

Medusa clutched her letter to Glaucus in her hands and looked straight ahead; a peaceful smile coming over her face.

"My hero," she whispered.

"Forgive me…" With a cry, Perseus swung down with all his strength.

She fell silently… gracefully. Perseus dropped his sword and went to her body. He straightened her, placing her arms beside her. He lightly touched the letter in her hand and felt unworthy of reading it.

He heard a quiet gasp, and spun around. Recognizing the Goddess Aphrodite, he bowed quickly. She let out a piercing wail and pounced on him.

"What have you done?!" she screamed. She threw him to the ground and looked at her darling Medusa's still form. She touched her lightly, crying silently. There was nothing she could do.

She struck Perseus across his face, hard. In talking to Eileithyia, she already knew who Perseus was, so her hands were tied, much like the Graeae. She could not kill Zeus' son. "Take what you came for, and go," she growled.

He crawled over to Medusa's head and placed it in the bag he carried, careful not to look at it. As he lifted it, two drops of blood fell to the ground. The cave began to tremble, and the ground sizzled and hissed, causing him to expedite his exit.

The smoke cleared, and Aphrodite saw two forms lying next to Medusa's body. The first was a baby; a very large baby. The second was a tiny, white, winged horse. Sniffling, Aphrodite stood at Medusa's feet. "I am sorry, My Love. I tried to protect you as best I could. No one can harm you now."

She took the letter from her hand, and read it tearfully. With a raise of her hands, Aphrodite made Medusa's clothes disappear. Exhaling softly, she brought thin layers of dust to cover her body, and hardened them into rock, determined that Medusa's beauty would last forever. She placed the letter beside her, and gathered the two children in her arms. "Come Chrysaor, come Pegasus."

EPILOGUE

Seeing home was bittersweet for Perseus. He was, once again, grateful to the winged sandals for shortening his journey. He could not bring himself to face the King, or his mother just yet. He went straight to the temple, to his father's statue.

"Father, forgive me. I fear I have done something horrible."

Glaucus gave the ring one last squeeze before entering the cave. "Honey!" he called loudly. He walked through cautiously, eyes downcast, and continued to call her. He figured she must be swimming. He made his way to the next room.

Glaucus stopped cold. He looked at the form on the ground, and forced himself to breathe. "Honey?" He ran to her, falling over her body. He scratched at the stone, until his fingers bled, pleading with the Gods to bring her back. Weakly, he lay beside her, weeping.

He closed his eyes as he embraced the cold rock. *She can't be gone,* he thought. He stayed there, unmoving for several moments. Finally, he sat up, accepting that she was lost to him. The letter caught his eye, and he reached for it.

My Dearest Love,
I thank you for the love you brought into my life. Please, always know it is returned tenfold. It is because of that love, that I must leave you. There is no life to be had at my side. It pains me that I can never see you, can never look into your eyes, or have you see your devotion, reflected in mine. I am sorry that my intense love for you will cause you sadness, but I have gone where you cannot follow. Forgive me for running away again. I do so in the hopes that you will find happiness, and a true life someday.

All My Love
Forever
Your Honey

Glaucus crushed the letter in his hands and roared. He lifted her granite form and began to drag it towards the entrance. He leaned her against a wall tucked into a far corner. Separating the rings, he placed one in her slightly curled palm.

Standing on the edge of the cliff, he stared at the water below. Glaucus was of a mind to make it his permanent home. He edged closer, feeling his stomach clench, his pulse race. Smoothing out the letter, he took a final look at it, so that the last voice in his head would be hers.

She'd felt there was no life to be had at her side. She was wrong. She'd wanted him to find happiness. Well, there was no happiness to be found without her. She was wrong. Angry, he ripped up the letter, tossing its pieces into the sea.

He walked back into the cave, furious. Approaching her still body, he reached into her hand, retrieved the ring, and placed a farewell kiss on her hand, before storming out. She was wrong.

There was nowhere she could go, that he would not follow.

Zeus had been elated to hear his son's voice, until he heard what he had to say. He'd gone to his son, then he'd gone to see the Graeae. It had been a long time since Zeus had visited their solemn chambers in the mountain's belly.

They had told him of the arrival of his son, of his perilous mission. They told him also, of the arrival of Aphrodite, and of her desperate need of their handmaiden, Eileithyia, not to mention, her return, with two unexplained bundles.

Now, Zeus paced before his throne, a storm rumbling overhead.

It seemed as though much went on without his knowledge, unacceptable for a God King. He had yet to put all of the pieces together, but he knew of three who could give him some insight. He did notice that those very pieces were missing from Mount Olympus. There was one piece he would deal with first, however.

"Hermes!" His thunderous voice shouted.

Hermes flew in quickly, frightened beyond words. "Yes, My Lord?"

Zeus sat on his throne, silent and imposing for a short moment. Then, he looked at Hermes very seriously.

"Summon my brother to me."

Athena sat in her room, melancholy and despondent. She had not slept, for whenever she did, she saw the face of Hephaestus, heard his heavy panting. Even in her waking hours, she felt as though her thigh burned from his seed. She was disturbed by how powerless she'd felt. He had been deaf to her pleas, and no one had come to her aide.

She'd fought him with all her strength, yet she knew, she could not have stopped him from penetrating her, had it come to that. Sometimes in her mind, she heard her own cries for help, for mercy. More often than not, her voice blended with that of Medusa. Together, they rang in her ears, swirling around her mind until she felt she'd go mad.

Her door burst open, halting her thoughts. Aphrodite stood in the entrance to her chamber, sporting an inscrutable expression.

"You have succeeded, Athena. Perseus has taken the head of Medusa… his mission is over," she said plainly.

Athena glared at her haughtily. "So, I have won, and it is over. You may leave now." Athena had more pressing matters on her mind than Medusa's death, or Aphrodite's rage.

Aphrodite came and sat opposite Athena, shaking her head sadly. "I said you've *succeeded*, not won. Someone like you cannot truly win, of that you can be sure."

Athena growled over her cryptic messages. "Aphrodite, give it up! As always, in time, we will forget all about this mess. And, **you** will keep your mouth *shut*." She drew out a dagger to punctuate the threat.

Aphrodite thought of her return to the Graeae, and of what she'd leaned there. Taking one look at the knife, she burst into a fit of laughter. Rising, she was nearly cackling by the time she reached the door. "Do not worry, darling Athena. I swear, on the Goddess Styx, I will not utter a word!"

"Very wise, Ditie. Let us all move on. As you've said, it is over,"

Athena said.

“Again, you’ve misheard me. It is **far** from over.” She blew Athena a kiss and bounced out of the room, her departure leaving a chill creeping up Athena’s spine.

An Excerpt From 2nd Book Of The Series

Set In Stone: Afterlife

by

R.C. BERRY

AVAILABLE NOW

HELL'S FURY

Hades' bellows sounded throughout the entire underworld. He paced in frustration, muttering to himself in ancient languages. The nerve of his brother, thinking he could command him. They had argued well into the night, sometimes, becoming so heated, the walls shook. By the time Hades stormed out, without being dismissed, he had still not agreed to Zeus' request. The underworld was his dominion, and no one, not even the King of Olympus, was going to tell him how to run it. His chest heaved as he bristled. He did not even sense his wife's presence.

"My husband is angry. The king must have offended," Persephone said, with a smile in her voice.

A frown creasing his brow, Hades did not even turn around. He didn't like for Persephone to see his face twisted in rage. "It is the king's right, his privilege, and likely his favorite pastime," he sighed.

Her sweet laugh filled his ears and, her tiny hands wrapping around his waist, warmed his heart. When she pressed her cheek against his back, all trace of anger left his face, and his shoulders were no longer tensed.

"Tell me about your meeting," she whispered, placing a kiss on his back.

He chuckled at her own brand of white magic, in his world filled with death. Turning, he took her in his arms and kissed her gently. "It was lengthy, and unnecessary. The king has commanded, and I must obey…" he paused.

Persephone smiled at the mischievous twinkle in his eye. "But…" she began.

"I shall obey, but in my own time, and on my own terms." He took her chin in his hands and smiled into her eyes. "We are all kings and queens of something, my love. There are things even Zeus has no dominion over."

Persephone squeezed her husband tighter. He was always sullen after meeting with his brothers, especially if he was ever summoned. But, he was truly special. He could always find a silver lining, even in the darkness of the underworld. Placing her head on his chest, she sighed, as he stroked her hair.

A sudden flash caught his attention. Looking up, he saw a cloaked figure, and a bare hand, clutching a helmet… his helmet. The form was gone before he could identify who it was.

Feeling the tension return, Persephone looked up into her husband's face, curiously.

Hades pasted a weary smile on his face. "I fear my meeting has left me tired, my dear. I have a few things to attend to, but I will join you for the evening meal, I promise."

Placated, she smiled and gave him a final kiss before releasing him.

Hades followed the path of the mysterious figure. It was a curiosity, a minor annoyance only. Whoever it was, had to have gotten past Cerberus, so it was narrowed down to a God, or a Goddess. He came to a room that held many of his weapons and prized possessions. Peeking in, he saw the figure again. He leaned against the door frame, and it creaked, causing the someone to turn quickly.

Athena, he thought to himself.

She looked around, as though she was looking for something specific. Finally, she carefully, and quietly, placed the helmet in the place it always rested. She pulled the cloak closer around her and made a hasty exit.

Watching her depart, Hades stood deeply intrigued. Athena descended from on high, and risked his wrath by stealing his things. That, along with his meeting with Zeus, gave him a slight pause. He did not know what all was occurring on Mount Olympus but, somehow, he'd been placed in the middle of it.

Walking back to his throne room, he bit his lip thoughtfully.

"Charon!" he called out. "Yes, My Lord?" a deep voice immediately answered. "Go to the shores of Acheron…"

Medusa stood on the shore, looking out across the murky waters and, for once, felt total peace. She looked around at the others on the shores. Many cast curious glances her way but no one screamed in fear, no one threatened her. A young man walked by and looked right at her. She could've wept from glee as he kept walking. She couldn't hurt anyone here, and no one could hurt her. They were all beyond harm.

She reached out her arms and took a closer look at herself. Her skin was translucent and fathomless. Leaning over, she caught her reflection in the river. She glowed with a faint aura, her hair, the wavy locks she remembered from her youth. Yet, it pulsed and snaked around her head, as though still alive.

There were others that looked like her, others without bodies to be ferried. What really interested her, was her eyes. Everyone she'd seen had bereft eyes, holding sadness or despair, but mostly, confusion. Her eyes were the eyes of the living. They were alert and bright, and flashed from the abyss of her soul with the pale green light of vitality.

So, this is what my soul looks like, she thought. She was beautiful and, in all honesty, unsettling. She turned away from her reflection and found a far corner to be alone. This would be her home for the next century. She had no coin to pay the ferryman, so she must wander the shores for one hundred years, along with everyone else on the shores.

The newcomers wailed and cried constantly, bemoaning their fate. Medusa curled up on a flat rock and leaned back, a serene smile on her face. Glaucus was safe, her baby was safe, and Athena could never get her. To her, their raised voices were the music of freedom.

Sudden clamoring brought her mind to the present. Medusa looked over and saw a boat approaching the shore. She decided to ignore it and, once again, closed her eyes.

"Medusa, you are called!" a deep voice called.

Gasping, Medusa shrank back, hoping not to be noticed. The ferryman departed the boat, and was immediately set upon by the dead. He continued calling her name, as they beseeched him.

"I am the Medusa you seek," one woman replied.

"You are not, madam," he answered simply.

Oh no, he must know me. How can he know me? she wondered. Rising, she tried to weave through and blend into the crowd.

Charon made his way straight to her, cutting off her escape. Grabbing her wrist gently, he tugged her along. "You are to come with me," he said.

Whimpering, Medusa dug her heels in, trying to slip his grasp, unsuccessfully. All around her, more and more of the deceased pressed in close to them, begging to be taken off the shore. Nearing the boat, Medusa panicked and fought harder against Charon.

Suddenly, the crowd began to riot.

"She does not want to go, take me instead!" one called out.

"I have been here longer, I deserve to go!" another yelled.

Men and women alike, clawed to separate the two. At once, Medusa was released from Charon's grip and tossed to the ground, where she immediately began to be trampled. She crawled, trying to make her way to safety, but more and more waves of people came, resolved to board the boat.

Charon jumped into the boat and, reaching down, pulled out his oar. He held it up, where it glinted in the light. Charon's oar was six feet in length, and made of steel, forged in the fires of Lemnos, by Hephaestus himself. The edges were razor sharp, and its sting was not soon forgotten. Those who had been on the shores the longest, wisely halted. A few of the newer ones, foolishly pressed forward, and were met with a warning lash.

Moving through the crowd a little easier, he found Medusa huddled on the ground, curled to protect herself. Bending, he scooped her up with one arm. Lifting her off the ground, he cradled her to him. She was trembling against him, and he shushed her.

"I have you. Do no fear," he whispered.

He jumped in the boat and deposited her gently on the seat, before casting away from the shore. Even as they moved away, people still pursued the boat, though less enthusiastically than before.

It took a few moments for Medusa to calm herself enough to speak. "Where are you taking me?" she asked. He was silent, and she thought he might not answer.

"...Domos Aidaou..." Charon said simply.

The domain of Hades? she thought. *This is all the domain of Hades.*

"I have no coin to pay you," she said quickly. Maybe he would take her back.

"No coin. You are summoned," he answered.

"Summoned?" she asked. "By whom?"

"By the Lord Hades."

Printed in Great Britain
by Amazon

66041581R00180